Works by Amanda Marie

To Rule the Universe

Torii
Raevon

Etched in History

Amanda Marie

Printed in the United States of America
Edited by: K.R. Morrison
Cover Design: Linkville Graphics

Linkville Press
linkvillepress.com
linkvillepress@gmail.com

ISBN-10: 1-947794-00-0
ISBN-13: 978-1-947794-00-9

A portion of all proceeds goes to Villalobos Rescue Center.
vrcpitbull.com

For my boys....
...may you always follow your dreams...
...and don't let anyone tell you
it's impossible.

To my dear friend Keith...
...who inspired the story on these pages.

To my family...
...and all my friends...
...thank you for always being there.

Here's to your dreams coming true next.

Written in memory of my
great-grandmother,
Madaline Francis Newnham.
You're always in my heart.

Prologue

A Promise

*V*irginia clutched the small, cold, wrinkled hand in hers. She ignored the tears streaming down her face. This was the end. The end she feared coming for several years. Her grandmother had no more life in her. She lay still now, shivering under the flannel blanket Virginia had made for her.

She leaned down and kissed the cold, liver-spotted forehead. In Virginia's other hand she clutched the picture of the white woman and black man. She knew who the woman was; she was Nana's great-grandmother, but the man?

Nana opened her eyes, a tear sliding down her wrinkled cheek. Virginia wiped it away gently, setting the picture down. Nana gave her hand a weak squeeze and a small smile. Virginia tapped the picture. "Please don't go. I want to know the story, Nana!"

Her hands signed the words she wanted to speak: *I love you. You will know someday.* Nana closed her eyes, and took her last breath.

Virginia kissed the cold lifeless hand and laid it

down on the still stomach. "I love you, too." She slid the picture underneath Nana's small hands, then headed to the phone and dialed the number for Hospice. They would take care of her Nana as she was transported to the funeral home.

She went to sleep that night with one regret; that she hadn't learned everything she could about her Nana's great-grandparents. Now she was determined to find it, but where to begin? She would wait until after the funeral. Then her search would begin.

For three long months Virginia searched. She had always looked up at the grand mansion at the top of the hill, but had never gone in. Living in a historical town had never drawn her interest until the moment she set foot behind its doors to take the tour.

It was a magical mansion, fit for a king, and that was precisely what they had called him: The Copper King. He was so named because of his fortune, which he had laid into his grand mansion. When it was built in the mid-1880s it was valued at a half-million dollars. This seemed like a fortune now, and it was then, but this was only a half-day's income to Butte, Montana's Copper King. Today, Mr. Clark certainly seemed to hold the key to finding the answers she so desperately wanted, and needed.

As the tour was led into the kitchen, Virginia laid her eyes on a picture of one of the cooks. There was no story with the picture, but she would not forget that face, or those curls. She herself had those same long black tresses; the only one in her family to have gotten them. There was something else, however. Her eyes were exactly like Virginia's beloved grandmother's. The longer she looked at the picture, the more she was certain it was her.

"Excuse me...?"

She didn't want to interrupt the tour guide, but her heart leapt at the thought of being so close to an answer. The tour guide looked up, waiting to learn what the interruption was about. "I'm sorry, but the woman in this picture. Do you know who she is?"

The tour guide crossed the room, sliding her fingers across the top of the old icebox, to look at the photograph. The woman in the picture was wearing an apron, and held a book in her hand.

"Oh, her name is...um...give me a moment." She stood looking at the photograph carefully. "I believe her name was Hope something-or-other. She was only here for a short time."

A man who had been watching the small TV in the room looked up. "That's right. Hope was a temporary replacement for Mr. Clark after his first cook left. I believe he paid her nearly three hundred dollars for the week she was here."

Virginia felt the tears threatening to come. "Where was she from?"

"Oregon, a place called Linkville, if I remember right."

One of the other tourists spoke up then. "Wasn't Hope Bryant the recipient of the first corrective eye surgery? She was from Oregon."

The tears flowed freely then. This was her. Virginia had finally found the first piece of information that would bring her to the final telling of her family history. "Yes. She was."

The man studied Virginia then. Coming closer, he took her hand in his. "What's this? Tears? Is there more to your questions than just simple questions?"

Virginia nodded. "My nana just passed away. I

never asked her about our family, though it meant the world to her. Hope was her great-grandmother."

Virginia spent the rest of the week searching for Linkville, Oregon, in Butte's historical archive, but the moment she got close to something it somehow fell away. Finally, she decided to go to Oregon. She would start at the top and work her way south.

For six more months she searched, and still she found nothing. She had been to Portland, Oregon City, Bend, Florence, Reedsport, Ashland, and many other cities and towns, and still had found nothing. Now she found herself staring up at a four-story brick building in a small town in Southern Oregon. It had been an old hotel, and she had been drawn to it like nothing else before.

An hour ago she hadn't even planned to go inside. There was a highway a few feet in front of her, and the sounds of trucks driving by didn't even faze her. She turned and sat on the old wood steps next to the building, still not really wanting to go inside, yet something was drawing her there.

She stared towards the other side of the street. There was a park across the way, and it surrounded a small lake. She shook her head at the amount of ducks swimming around, waiting to be fed by the people rollerblading and skateboarding. Halfway across the lake, the sound of a jet boat cut through the other sounds, and the glare of the sun on the water nearly blinded her. Her nose searched the park for the smell of charcoal and meat. There was a family with a portable bar-b-que, and it looked as though they were having a party.

Sighing, she looked up at the old building again. For nearly a year she had been searching, and she had come up with nothing. The only hint she had was the name of a town, and the name didn't seem to exist anymore. Finally, after careful consideration, she stood up and walked to the old front doors.

The name "Baldwin Hotel" glistened back at her. The smell of wood and dust hit her nose as she opened the door. A young girl in a Victorian costume greeted her with a smile.

Virginia, tired, smiled back. "I'd like to take a tour. Are they available?"

"Yes, it will be $10 for the full tour."

After a couple of minutes spent paying for the tour and signing the guest book, Virginia followed the tour guide through the building. Most of it she didn't care about, so it went in one ear and out the other. She was only interested in finding one thing.

She looked on, slightly bored, as they passed room after room of old clothes and toys, pewter toothbrushes and mirrors, potbellied stoves and dirty, musty old sinks. Only when they entered the bridal suite on the second floor did she finally start paying attention.

The dress; she'd seen it before. There were others on the tour asking about the toilet (an original, manually-filled water-closet), but Virginia's gaze was on the dress, and the suit right next to it. They were dirty and faded, but she had never seen anything more beautiful. The orange-blossom bouquet next to the dress could only belong to one person. Moving closer, she spotted it, just as the tour guide brought the group out of the bathroom.

"I see you've spotted the photo of Miss Hope and

Joshua."

Virginia wiped a salty, hot tear from her green eyes. She pulled her curly black hair behind her shoulder. "What was the name of this town?"

"Originally it was called Linkville."

More tears came down her cheeks then. "Almost a year I've been trying to find my family history. This dress belonged to my great-great-great grandmother."

The tour guide smiled. "Miss Hope was a strong influence here. We've had the dress and a journal for quite some time."

The tour guide finished the tour for the other guests. Once they were back in the lobby an hour later, Virginia sat down with the other tour guides. For the first time, she would hear the story, from the museum curator, that her grandmother could never tell her.

He sat down, a smile on his face, and shook her hand. "It's good to finally meet some more of the family. I met your grandmother, Hailey, one time when we had a memorial celebration of Miss Hope's anniversary, right here in fact. Miss Hailey brought the wedding dress and suit to us. We've had it here ever since. Along with this journal, but we've never opened it."

He slid a leather-bound book across the table. Virginia wiped her face dry and slowly opened it.

The handwriting was elegant and smooth; ruler-straight and small. The first page read 'Hope in Love by Hope Virginia Bryant Tandra with writings by Elijah and Mia Bryant, Thomas and Georgia Bryant, Joseph and Esther May Tandra, and Joshua Joseph Tandra.'

"Virginia. I was named for her. I never knew that."

"You've never been told any of this before, have you?"

She shook her head.

6

"Your grandmother never spoke to anyone while she was here. We never knew why."

Virginia shook her head again. "She couldn't speak. She lost her vocal chords in an automobile accident. She was in her twenties then."

"And she was the last one to know the story?"

"Yes. My father didn't know either. He regrets never asking her."

The curator set a warm hand on hers. "Please. The museums are closed for the day, and I have nowhere to be right now. We would like to hear the story with you."

Another tear slid down her face. She took a long, deep breath, and turned the first musty, yellowed page and began to read...

Chapter 1

A New Beginning

Hope

When in the Course of human events, it becomes necessary for one people to dissolve the political bonds which have connected them with another, and to assume among the powers of the earth, the separate and equal station to which the Laws of Nature and of Nature's God entitle them, a decent respect to the opinions of mankind requires that they should declare the causes which impel them to the separation.

We hold these truths to be self-evident, that all men are created equal, that they are endowed by their Creator with certain unalienable Rights, that among

Men, deriving their just powers from the consent of the governed, [...]
That whenever any Form of Government becomes destructive of these ends, it is the Right of the People to alter or abolish it, and to institute new Government, laying its foundation on such principles and organizing its powers in such form, as to them shall seem likely to effect their Safety and Happiness.

Were these the words that brought cause to the greatest war in American history? Even decades later, and possibly into the future, the cause of the Civil War is still questioned. Was it about slavery or some other issue? If there had been no slavery, would there have been a war? What was interesting is that, although slavery was the main issue of the time, most Americans had very little interest in it. The majority of the Southern states were made up of small farmers who couldn't afford slaves, and most of the North had never even seen one.

Still, the issue divided the land. If the South lost their slaves, they feared their entire economic system would collapse. The North was both for and against slavery. Even then the Southern politicians found a way to convince most of those in the South that their neighbors to the North threatened their way of life.

The numbers were great. Three million people fought and six hundred thousand lost their lives. John Brown's raid at Harpers Ferry in 1859 began a war that would become the only war fought by Americans on American soil. The first battle fell upon Fort Sumter on April 12, and by the spring of 1861, the Union headed for Richmond, therefore beginning the Civil War.

For four years the Northern soldiers tried to get to Richmond. For four years their attempts failed. The war was mostly fought in a small strip of Virginia territory. It was the Confederates against the Union, and the Union became victorious on June 23, 1865 when the last Confederate army surrendered.

Every person who fought in the Civil War had a reason and a story. My pa believed that the slaves would remain as such. He felt that colored folk shouldn't be allowed to make their own way in life—that was the white man's place; and besides, why disrupt something that worked so well?

Pa was a tough man, born to a hard-working farmer and a school teacher. He was tall and slim, and his arms could kill with very little effort, but that would not have been his choice. As a boy, the school children learned quickly to leave him alone. When it was time for him to leave school and make his own way in life, Pa left Rolla, Missouri for a "soul-seeking" holiday. Everyone was shocked when the tough man returned from his holiday with her on his arm.

Ma was a kind-hearted woman—warm and caring. I remember her blonde curls as if they had been photographed in my memory, and I'll never forget her rosy cheeks. Her green eyes were warm and inviting, and most folks fell in love with her the moment they saw her. She had been raised by very young parents, who had been married at fifteen and raised under the theory that love conquered all. There was only one time when I thought my parents' love might fail, but it never did, and they were buried together some years ago.

A year after the beginning of the war, and then months following General Sigel's takeover of Rolla, Pa told his family that he felt drawn to the war and would follow the other men to fight. At least that was his excuse. Now, knowing what happened to him there, I'm not so sure that's what his real reasons were.

He took Ma first on a short holiday, and then they returned home. He prepared the fields and hired a farm hand to help with the rest. Rolla was in Union hands, and heavily guarded by Colonel Wyman and the 13th Illinois Regiment. Pa felt his family was safe.

As he boarded the train to leave for war, Ma hugged him and told him she was pregnant.

"Really?" His voice hiccoughed as he tried not to cry.

She simply nodded as the train pulled away.

My brother was born on January 15, 1863. He was two when Pa returned home at the end of the war in 1865, so for him the adjustment to suddenly having Pa around was quick and easy. Pa's usual toughness seemed to diminish when he was around Elijah, but otherwise he was still the same hard-working and tough farmer that he had been before the war.

A rare set of blizzards hit Rolla during the winter of 1865-66 and nearly destroyed farms. Ma worried every time Pa sat up and stared out the dark windows, wondering if the fields would make it through.

By the spring, the school was in need of a teacher. Those who filled these positions were usually single women during that time, but when there was no one else, married women were allowed. Pa had been trying for weeks to save what was left of his fields, and Elijah was put in the care of our neighbor while Ma went to teach. When the summer of 1866 arrived, the fields were ready, but there was not enough money coming in from the teaching. Pa took a job in town, making deliveries for the mercantile.

This continued for quite some time. In the meantime, Ma and Pa were excited to learn I was on the way.

I was born on November 20, 1866. A new teacher had been found by that time, and Pa was preparing the fields for winter. For seven years we lived on that land, and the mercantile deliveries sustained our family. My brother and I were always told we were bright and cheerful. My brother's blonde hair turned a fine black to match my own hair color. I was always excited when he came home with stories of Indians from the books he borrowed from our teacher, and I basked in these stories with curiosity and intrigue.

Everything seemed to be going our way until a storm hit Missouri in late 1873. This is when my story really starts.

Farms all over the territory had been destroyed, and Pa came in late that night, tears on his face. My brother and I watched worriedly from the kitchen table as he talked in hushed whispers to Ma. I looked at Elijah quickly when Ma's face fell. What was going on?

"What are you saying, Thomas?" The whispering was over.

Pa pulled out the travel bags, slipping the money he was counting into his pocket. "As soon as the store is open tomorrow, I'm going to town to buy a couple of oxen and supplies. Have the children ready. The wagon train leaves at nine in the morning."

We knew it was one of the hardest decisions of his life, and scary for us, but staying was no longer an option. We headed out in the spring of 1874 and joined a wagon train heading west. I didn't know where we were going, but the adventure was exciting.

"Pa, when are we going to get there?" It was a cool late-spring night, and the trees were illuminated by the orange glow of the campfires. Our wagon sat in the middle of the others, and all the other children had already gone to bed. I was leaning against Pa's chest, watching the orange embers fly into the sky and then pop away. I looked up at him as I asked my questions, and he smiled back at me.

"If all goes well, we will be able to spend your eighth birthday at our new home." Pa took a drink from his water cup.

The idea of being in a new place for my birthday both excited and frightened me. What if they didn't like us? What if Pa made us move again? Where were we going? I realized then that he'd never told us. We seemed to be just travelling aimlessly. "Where are we going?"

He smiled again. "To a place called Oregon."

"Is it near the ocean?"

Pa shrugged. "I think we'll be close, but still very far away."

"Will I get to see it someday?" I had seen the ocean in a picture book once, and it was described that the water was always moving, but I couldn't see how. The thought of seeing that mysterious blue excited me. The closer we were, the better!

"Perhaps someday. Now, you and Elijah go get into bed. It's getting late and we need to get an early start in the morning."

"Yes, Pa." I looked over at Elijah, and he reached out for my hand. I took it and we stood up. Elijah pulled me into the wagon and I turned around, watching my parents move closer together. Pa wrapped his arms around Ma and looked her in the eyes.

"Those are some mighty fine children you have

there, ma'am." He grinned at her and she smiled, her green eyes sparkling in the firelight.

"I couldn't have done it without my mean, nasty husband." Pa's eyes narrowed at her, and she laughed. "Come on, let's get to bed, too."

I yawned, rolled up into my blanket, and was asleep fast, grateful for the chance for slumber that came rarely. Trouble was, on the trail the nights seemed short, and each one was cold and sometimes sleepless. Like the others, Ma and Pa always worried about Indians and wild animals, adding extra stress to the families in the wagon train.

It was September before the train came to the state of Nevada. It was new to all of us, and we stopped just outside the town of Virginia City for the night. It was a town of saloons, gambling, and silver miners, and an almost sleepless place because of all the noise.

The sights of the city entranced me. I had never been close to any city, and took in as much of it as I could before Pa caught me looking in the saloons. I was fascinated by the behavior of the men. I didn't understand why they were acting so crazy and why they were hitting each other, breaking tables and windows, and sucking on giant brown sticks that had smoke coming off the end of them. Pa had never done any of those things for what seemed like fun to those men doing them.

One of the things that intrigued me most was the women dressed in fancy dresses. I loved their long, full-skirted gowns with bright colors and hats to match. The women's hair was done up, sometimes in buns, sometimes in flowing spiral curls a lot like mine. Each of them wore white gloves and had pretty, embroidered umbrellas.

Ma didn't like the noise of the city, and she was anxious to leave this place. Elijah, like me, was curious as well, and continued to ask Pa about different things, and we still hadn't seen any Indians! That night, even though I was only seven, I made a promise to myself that I would come back to Virginia City someday, and drifted off to sleep to the sounds of music and shattering glass.

By the first of November, I was very aware that my birthday was drawing nearer, and I refused to let Pa forget it. "Pa, are we there yet? It's almost my birthday. You said we could spend my birthday in our new home." I gave him the biggest puppy-dog look I could give him. He wouldn't deny me the answer I wanted.

"I think we're very close. We still have a few days, so just try to be patient, like your brother." Pa slapped the reins on the horses to tell them to go faster.

Most of the wagons had left the trail, deciding on settling in nice places we had seen on the way. Pa's worries became more prominent as the wagon count fell to three wagons, but being in the lead meant that he could make the decisions. He promised me he would find a place to settle before my birthday, and I could tell he was determined to keep it.

"Pa?"

"Yes, Elijah?"

"Will we get to see Indians where we're going?" Elijah shifted in the wagon so he could get closer to the front where Pa was sitting. Elijah wanted to learn whatever he could about Indians and would be happy to see one in person. I was anxious to see one, too, but so far we hadn't seen any.

Pa laughed a little. "Yes, son, unfortunately we probably will."

The word confused me. I pulled on Elijah's sleeve and he fell back beside me in the wagon. "What's 'unfortunately'?"

"'Unfortunately' is when something happens and you don't really want it to."

"Why would you not want to see them, Pa?"

Pa glanced over at Ma. She nodded and turned back to look at us. "There are a lot of bad people, Hope, and sometimes Indians are very mean. They like to attack people like us, and sometimes those people get killed."

"But if they're so mean, why did God make them?"

Pa smiled. "That's just one of God's mysteries, child." Ma smiled and laid her head on his shoulder. Ahead of us still lay several hundred miles, a few more cold, short nights, and long, grueling days, but we were ready for it.

Chapter 2

First Encounter

Joshua

Slavery was a cruel evil. I'd know; I was born on the run in an abandon ol' shack. My ma and pa told me we liked to die that night. It were Christmas Day 1858 when I was born, and Ma was already weak from the bad treatment on the plantation and not eatin' no more than a few frozen berries and whatever else Pa managed to catch, but we survived.

We was caught and taken back to the plantation, and they took Pa away as he was owned by someone else.

"Owned." What a horrible word. No human bein' should have to endure that. Ma was beaten and I not fed for a day, as if I were being punish for existing.

After that, Ma was only allowed to see me for ten minutes a day. I spent the firs' five years of my life in the care of Gram, who was too old to do most of the work. Soon as I could walk I was put to work cleanin' floors and gathrin' chicken eggs and any other task a one-year ol' could endure. When I was five, Gram woke me in the middle of the night. "You mus' get up boy. An' hush." I rubbed my sleepy eyes and stretched. My ribs poked out from my shirt an' my stomach growled. She stood beside my bedroll with a travel pack in one hand an' a small black box in the other. "Get up, boy!"

I obeyed, sliding my feet into the boots too big for me. "What's wrong?"

I couldn't miss the tear on her cheek. "Yer Pa be comin' fer you an' yer ma, so you be quick."

My heart ached. Leave Gram behind? It hurt. "What 'bout you?"

"I'm-a too old to be runnin'!" She pulle' an ol' holey coat over me and shoved the pack in my arms. "Dis box be yours to keep in yer pocket. Don't be givin' it to no one. You understan' what it for when you growed. Promise me!"

I let a tear fall. "Yes'm. I promise."

She shoved the box in my pocket and hugged me. I knowed it was the last time we be together. I could tell by how she didn't look me in the eyes.

Ma was waitin' for us outside. She hug Gram and tooked my hand.

"Keep dat boy safe, Esther."

Ma said no words as we walk across the field. When we was a good distance away she knelt in front of me. "I know you don't know him, but your Pa be a good man. He be keepin' us safe."

I nodded; my heart ached from leaving Gram. I wanted her to come with us, but understood why she wasn't comin'. We would have one shot at this. If we don' get away they be killin' us. I seen it. There was only one thing to say. "I trust you, Mamma." We continued on, and I met Pa for the first time.

Pa was a tall man, and he carried his thumbs under his suspenders. As I was led up to him, he knelt down. It was too dark to really see his face, but I had instant trust in him. I hug him, and then we ran.

It was a long time for the dogs to stop huntin', but we was free. We stayed in an ol' abandon cabin on a river. It was my first night with my parents, and they told me family stories.

Ma's grandparents, Ida an' Harry, was purchase' an' brought to the Carolinas to work on the cotton plantation. Their daughter, my Gram, Rosa, was born there. She, too, try to run away with a freed slave. They found a hidin' place for almost a year, and that be where my Ma was born, but hidin' a baby was too hard, and Gram was forced back to the plantation. When Ma turn' fifteen, her owner die, and Gram found Gramps again. Before long a new owner came, and Gram and Ma was force' back to work. Gramps followed and come to work so he could be with Gram.

Pa was also from a slave family in the Carolinas, but had escaped and he marry Ma when she was seventeen. They, too, was in hidin' for near a year, but I made it impossible to stay in hidin' and dey was separated.

As the stories die' out I remember the box Gram shoved in my pocket. I pulled it out and open it. Inside was a small ring with a blueberry-colored stone.

"What you gots there?"

I handed it to Pa. "Gram gave it to me."

He smiled, looking it over. "Aw, that be a fine stone. It come from Africa. It took many a summer to get enough heat to bring dat color. Only seen one other. Miss Ida mus'a had it first."

"Gram said I would know what it for when I growed."

He smiled and put it in my pocket. "She means you to give it to a lady when you ol' enough."

I was confused. "Why would I do that?"

Pa laughed. "All in time, son."

The next mornin' we travel on.

It was several months before Ma an' Pa was relaxed enough to settle down. We came to a place call Linkville in the Oregon Territory. It was a small town, but a high-class one. It was like no other town we been to. There was several large homes and great lands for farms. We passed big elm trees, that was tall and proud of the town they was shadin'. There was two large lakes and a river, the Klamath River. A small lake was nestled in the town and a small river, the Link River. Dis river, I found out, had many fish and was visited by fishermen often. A small waterfall was in the middle of the Link River, and the older children was callin' it the "love falls."

There was two tribes of Injuns who come to town sometimes. They come to town to trade furs for goods. Some brought gifts for the childrin of Linkville. There was also some who come ridin' in on horses, paint on their faces and carryin' weapons. They watched the white men like they was wantin' to fight them, but most folks was tryin' to get everyone to live together, and most of us did. Many animals was in the area. The Injuns traded beaver skin and deer and elk meat. I loved my new home, and never wanted to leave.

Linkville was hos' to sevcral differin' kinds of businesses, several name' after the large flock of pelicans on the lakes. The George Nurse schoolhouse stood at the end of town, and the church was a bit down the road. The Pelican Hotel was a place for new folks to stay while they waited for new homes to be built. Across the road was a pos' office and a doctor. There was a restrant too, and the Nurse Mercantile was one of the first buildings in town. Ma, Pa, and me made our home on the other end of town, above our bak'ry.

Tandra Bakery was found by the smell of fresh-baked bread. The tables was line' with checkered tablecloths and candles. The chairs was made of pine, an' the hardwood floors had hardly any marks at all. The counter was full of baked bread, pastries, cake, and other treats. Ma loved to bake, an' her store not only provided for us but used her talents to share with the residents an' visitors of Linkville. We settled in fast, an' one of my uncles was the only one who knew where we was. We was free.

There was no work for childrin in Linkville, except of course my books and chores. Still, I loved it there. I was known as 'Jay', an' loved to work with Pa. As the years passed, I learned to love farmin' and wanted to farm the biggest land in town. Ma said I was to finish school first, an' that's what I was about to do, just before my sixteenth birthday.

"Mornin', Ma."

I grabbed a plate an' a pancake, excited. "Me an' Pa is gonna work on the house today. We's tryna finish before the next storm hits."

Ma looked at me, a frown on her brown face. I stopped eatin', lookin' back at her. "I wish you wasn't leavin' so soon."

I sighed; she was doin' it again... "Ma, I'm just goin' to the other side of town."

"I know, bu…"

"No, 'buts,' Ma. There's no land for me to work in town. I want to be farmin', I want animals, an' I want dirt on my face, and sweat under my arms." She nodded. "I'm gonna leave eventually, an' I'm not leavin' the area."

Pa came out of their room. "You ready to go, son?" He picked up a dry pancake an' shove' it in his mouth. "Ah-um."

"Don't be no pig, Joseph."

He smiled at Ma an' kiss' her cheek. She slapped at his shoulder with her dish rag. "Go get dem horses saddled. Let da boy finish his breakfast."

"I be there in a minute, Pa."

He nodded, puttin' on his coat an' hat an' headin' outside.

Joseph

Da air was crisp for November mornin', an' da sun shone brightly, reflectin' off da wet groun'. Da town was quiet and liked to be deserted, as it usually be on Saturday mornin'. Dat mornin' marked a new beginnin'. For ten years we been livin' as free folk. Sure we still had troubles like most colored folk, but we was still free. I was nowhere near ready to see my son leave home, but he had a right to leave if he wanted to. He would make his own path.

I was preparin' da horses we kep' house' at da town liv'ry when da Revrin Hunt pull up to da church in his buggy. He look my way just as I come outside.

"Mornin', Joseph." He wave' with a big smile on his face.

"Mornin'. How you be, Revrin?"

"I'm good." He paused. "Say, Joe, I got a telegram last week telling me that there's a new family coming to town. They've been on the trail with a wagon train and someone down the line told them about us. They're due in sometime today or tomorrow. Would Esther May or Joshua, or you for that matter, mind showing them their way around?"

Somehow this didn' seem like a good idea, but I would make an attempt. "Well, Revrin, I reckon we could, but it would have to be after church t'morra. Me and Jay be goin' to work on da house. That's where we headed now."

He grin. "Well, that would be just fine. God bless you." He turn and walk inside da church.

I looked around for a sign of da newcomers, but there was no noise. Esther May and Joshua came outside and met me in da middle of the street. I kisse' her forehead as she handed us some sacks. "There be sandwiches. If it shows any signs of rain or snow, you come straight home, ya hear?"

Joshua rolled his eyes. "Yes, Ma."

I punch his arm. "Don't be rollin' your eyes at your mother." I hande' him da black reins to da mare and climbed on da brown thoroughbred. "There be a new family come today. Da Revrin aks us to show dem aroun' t'morra."

Esther May sighed. "Joe, you know new folk don' take too kin'ly to us. They don't all be used to seein' folk like us makin' our own livin'."

"What you be wantin' me to do? Turn da Revrin' down?" She shook her head. Joshua pointed down da road. "Look, Pa. That could be them."

A dusty covered wagon was comin' 'round da corner 'cross da Link River Bridge.

"Could be."

Hope

"Wake up, we're almost to town." Ma's voice woke us up and I stretched, yawning. As soon as I realized what she had said, Elijah and I jumped up.

"Really?" Elijah nearly knocked me over in his excitement.

"Hey!"

He stuck his tongue out. I pushed my way up so I could look out.

We passed several large hills and a few farms before coming to a lake with a river flowing into it. I was growing more and more excited, looking forward to all the fish I was going to catch in the river. When I mentioned it, Elijah shook his head. "Lakes are better for swimming."

We crossed a bridge over the river, and I spotted the first buildings of Linkville. There were some people standing not too far off. As we got closer I saw their dark skin, and my stomach sank. Pa wasn't going to be happy. I looked up at him.

In that moment I didn't think he was going to settle us there, not the way he looked at them. His eyes were cold, and I was actually scared of the look in his eyes. I had never been scared of him before.

"What do you make of that?" He slowed the wagon down.

"Thomas, you promised you'd try to be more open-minded." Ma looked at him with pleading in her eyes. He sighed and nodded, stopping a few feet from them to let her talk.

"Good morning."

"Mornin', Ma'am." The older man on the horse smiled and tipped his hat. "You be da new folk or be just passin' through?"

He looked like a tall man, and very out of place on the brown thoroughbred he was perched on. His pants were faded and coming apart at the knees, his shirt sleeves rolled up and fraying on the ends. His hat looked like it had been through a lot of dirt and sun, but his eyes were bright and welcoming. I didn't see what was so bad about him.

"We're the new folk. Would you mind telling us where the hotel is?"

The woman spoke up. "Of course. I be Esther May." She turned to the two men on the horses. "This here be my husban' Joseph an' he be our son, Joshua." Joshua tipped his hat.

"Pleased to meet you. I'm Georgia." Ma started to extend her hand, but Pa stopped her. She looked at him, disappointed.

"You come fin' us come da end of Sunday service t'morra an' we be showin' ya aroun'."

Pa released the wagon brake roughly, making me jump. He obviously thought we had stayed there long enough. "We can get along, so if you'll just point us in the right direction we'll be on our way."

Esther May's smile slowly faded and she lowered her eyes to the ground. Joseph moved his horse to the side a bit and glared at Pa. "Up da road, on da right."

Pa started the team without a "thank-you." Ma

27

glared at him.

"Don't look at me that way. The best way to learn your way around town is to find it yourself."

Ma looked ahead without saying a word.

Chapter 3

First Encounter

That night, I had a surprisingly easy time sleeping in that strange bed in that new town. The bed was soft, though lumpy, but I had way more room than in the cramped-up wagon. I was excited to go to Sunday school and learn about the other kids.

There were a lot more people in town on Sunday. We learned very quickly just how many people lived in the area. Many drove into town late on Sundays and spent the night in the hotel. When the hotel was full, which happened a lot, they would stay with families in town, in their barns or on the floors of their houses. Linkville was like a whole new place. The only thing that separated it from a city was the lack of saloons.

There was a big red barn just outside of town that served as the church when the in-town church wouldn't hold everyone. This, however, was news that hadn't reached us yet.

On our first morning in Linkville, we were sitting on the front steps of the church, fighting the cold. Elijah and I were huddled in Ma's arms, wishing we could go back to the warmth of our hotel room.

"It is Sunday, isn't it?" Ma pulled us closer, trying to keep us, and her, warm.

Pa looked up and down the street. It was deserted except for a wagon with the colored family from yesterday. I was old enough to know Pa wasn't happy about seeing them headed our way. He shook his head. "Lazy niggers. They could easily walk here. What do they need a wagon for?" Ma gave him a nudge, warning him to be nice, as the wagon stopped in front of us.

"Mornin'. You be Thomas, yes?" Esther May gave us a warm smile from atop the wagon.

Pa was not so warm and inviting. "It's Mr. Bryant."

Esther May's smile turned down, hurt. "Mr. Bryant," she took her husband's arm and looked away, "Sunday service be in da red barn out of town. Since you bein' cold to me, I'm-a be cold back. I be only tellin' ya so da childrin don't be freezin' their pale arses off."

Joseph didn't wait for Pa to respond before urging the horses on; they headed out of town.

Pa growled and turned to face us. "Back to the hotel, children. We'll be missing Sunday service this week." He didn't wait for us, but headed down the street towards the hotel.

Ma waited until he was inside before she urged us to our feet. "Come, let's get inside and warm up. We'll prepare your gloves and clothes for school tomorrow." Shivering, I got up behind Elijah, and we followed Ma into the hotel.

She asked us to return to our room, and watched us go up the stairs. We lingered out of her sight to listen as she turned on Pa.

"I'm disappointed in you, Thomas."

He merely chuckled and stared into the fireplace. I could see the anger on her face as she shook her head at him. She turned and came up the stairs in silence. We hurried into our room before she could see us listening. Innocent as lambs, we did what she told us to do, as she helped us prepare for our first day of school.

November was cold, but remarkably warmer than what we were used to in Missouri. I was excited, yet nervous, as we walked to our new schoolhouse. Looking ahead, I could see children rushing inside, the winter coats bundled up around them. I shivered beneath mine, clutching at my knitted gloves.

Just as we reached the steps to go inside, a small snowflake fluttered down. It was snowing!

I grinned, turning around to watch the white frozen powder float down from the puffy clouds. It started to stick to the dirt below, falling faster and faster. By lunch time there would be snow to play in. I was sticking out my tongue to catch a cold flake, when there was a tap on my shoulder.

"Class is starting, best get a move on inside."

I turned around, my cheeks warming, to face my new teacher. I was sure my cheeks and ears were flaming red from embarrassment as I met her gaze.

Miss Strong was a stunning woman. Her dress was simple, yet elegant, to match her hair's tightly-wound, perfect bun. The freckles on her face were dark against her pale complexion, and her blue eyes sparkled as she smiled down on me.

"Sorry. I love snow."

Her grin broadened and she held her hand out for me. I took it and she led me inside. "Yes, I too, love snow, but I love school even more."

Inside, the seats were already full. All the kids turned to look, curious. I felt my face flush again as they stared, and I shuffled my feet, nervous. Miss Strong pulled me to the front of the classroom and waved for Elijah to follow. He joined me at my side and we turned to face the kids. "Class, we have two new students today. They've joined us all the way from Rolla, Missouri. This is Elijah and Hope."

There was some clapping, and Elijah returned to his seat. I could tell he was just as embarrassed as I was. I scanned the room, looking for a place to sit, but everywhere was full. In the back, there was one seat open.

My heart sank. Joshua looked at me from next to the open seat. With a heavy heart, I made my way to the empty seat and slid in next to him.

He smiled down at me with his chocolate-brown eyes and I swallowed. What was I supposed to do? I knew Pa wouldn't like me sitting here, but there was nowhere else to go.

"Hello, Miss Hope. How are you enjoyin' Linkville?"

I smiled shyly up at him and quickly looked down at the desk in front of us. "It's alright. We haven't been here long enough to decide, though."

I looked up to the front, trying to focus on what Miss Strong was saying, but I couldn't. He was so close I could smell him. He'd obviously used his Pa's cologne. It made my head spin, and I glanced up at him. He was staring at me.

"Forgive me, Miss Hope. I'd a never met someone with such pretty green eyes as yours."

For what seemed like the millionth time that day, my face flushed, and I again studied the grainy desk. I cleared my throat. "I've never met a colored person before."

Joshua chuckled lightly so as not to interrupt the class. "I kinda figured the way you was staring at me when you first got here."

Neither one of us spoke again for a while, and I focused on the lessons. I liked our new teacher, and was learning fast. When she released us for the day, I smiled up at Joshua.

"See you t'morra." He slid out of the seat and went to collect his things.

Elijah stood nearby, horror spread on his face. "Hope, what are you doing?"

I shrugged, feeling slightly annoyed at him. Why was Joshua so bad anyway? He seemed very nice. "Nothin'."

Elijah scooted me out the door, with our homework in his lunch pail, and ushered me down the street. "You know you can't be friends with the likes of him. Pa would skin your hide."

"Why does Pa have so much against him anyway? Joshua was very nice."

Elijah shook his head, appalled. "Doesn't matter. He's a nigger."

I fought back a tear, but didn't respond to him. I couldn't. I didn't care what anyone said. He was a very nice boy, and I could talk to who I wanted.

It was December, and outside the snow was coming down very quickly. It was hard to believe we had been in this new place for over a month. I had made some friends, and enjoyed, though I shouldn't have admitted it, the company of Joshua Tandra. Nobody really wanted to talk to him much, but I found him funny and entertaining. Though, some of the other kids did talk to him. Still, I think some of them could have been nicer.

It was December 10, 1874, and the schoolhouse was packed with some of the parents. Joshua was graduating today. He would be sixteen in a couple of weeks, and most folks were preparing for Christmas. Joshua was preparing for his move to his own house.

He stood in front of us all and smiled.

"I remember the first time I stepped into this school house. My parents an' I was the first colore' folk here, and y'all made me...made us...feel so welcome. My only wish an' hope for the future is that everyone will learn what it means to love, because the way I see it, any person who would be mean just because the skin was the wrong color, they haven't learned what true love is." He stopped and looked nervously at our teacher, Miss Strong. "Well, I...I guess that's it."

Miss Strong smiled and everyone in the room clapped. When the applause died away, she handed a rolled-up piece of paper to Joshua and shook his hand. "Those were marvelous words, Jay. We're sure going to miss you around here."

He smiled. "Thank you, ma'am." Everyone clapped for him again as he and his parents left the schoolhouse. Joshua clutched the certificate in his hand as he left. I could tell he was proud, as he was the first Tandra to ever receive one.

The rest of that evening, he enjoyed the company of his parents. That night would be the last night he slept in his childhood room.

I would miss seeing him in school. He and I had gotten to know each other a little during school, but every time Pa came around and saw us talking he would yell at me. It was those actions that made Joshua want to know what had turned Pa so sour. Most of the folks in Linkville found they were able to forget their prejudices. My Pa was definitely not one of them.

Christmas morning in Oregon was cold and wet. Linkville could almost pass as a ghost town. Nobody ventured to town in the cold unless they had to, and the only thing open was the hotel, with its hot, swirling chimney smoke. What made the cold worse was the nearly-cloudless sky. The trees seemed to shiver with every drop of rain that hit their grey-brown branches. The sun had not yet broken over the valley's snow-capped mountains, but there was still movement in the cold, deserted street.

At the far end of the street near the Link River Bridge, a small group of Indians stood, talking in frantic whispers. Reverend Hunt came out of the church house then, followed by Joseph Tandra. Upon reaching the bridge, the reverend shook hands with the three natives.

"Won't you please come inside? It's awfully cold and wet." Reverend Hunt spoke to the English-speaking Indian as if he were an old friend.

The Indian turned to the others and passed along the invitation. All of them nodded. "Yes, we go." Reverend Hunt smiled and led them down the road to the hotel.

Inside, an orange glow from the fire greeted them, and Reverend Hunt led them in. Ma and Pa had been huddled on the floor in front of the fire. Pa jumped up when he saw who, or what, rather, had come in.

"Ah, Mr. Bryant, I'm glad you're here." Pa gave the Indians his usual cold stare as they sat down on the floor around the fire. He stepped in front of Ma as though she were in danger. "Please, return to your seat, Mr. Bryant. Our friends have come for urgent assistance. Go on."

He turned to the strangers. "Oh, could we have your names?"

Reverend Hunt handed the English-speaking one blankets. He took them, wrapped himself, and passed on the others before he spoke. "Me Makya, this Dyami and Kuruk. We come for help. We have one missing. She is daughter of chief."

Reverend Hunt looked at the troubled Indians sitting before him, his face full of concern. It was very cold outside. "I see. How long has she been missing?"

Makya turned to the others and asked in their language. The one called Dyami, or Eagle, let out a sigh. "?onaa naat ?a Geet maans wac hihas Gaskana. Lobiitdal' geena y' ayn' a."

Makya turned back to Reverend Hunt. "Dyami say we ride horses all day yesterday. We got to east mountain to the top. We did not find her."

"I'm more than happy to help." Reverend Hunt turned to Joseph. "We will need riders, of course. Esther May, I'm sure, will feed us well." He sighed and turned to Pa, who had been sitting uneasily, protecting Ma. "I know that you have your prejudices, Mr. Bryant, but I hope you can find it in your Christian heart to help look for this missing child."

Pa opened his mouth to protest, but the commotion had finally aroused me and Elijah, and brought us downstairs. Elijah stopped mid-step, me crashing into him, and stared at the three Indians on the floor. "Indians!" He raced forward, but Pa jumped up to stop him. "Aw, Pa. I want to see them!"

Pa looked down at us sternly. "Go back upstairs, children."

"But, Pa…"

"Now!" We knew better than to fight him when he was like that. Elijah dropped his head and we headed upstairs long enough for him to think we were in the room, then we snuck back to the stairs to listen.

Pa turned back to the reverend. "Of course I'll help."

The men of Linkville headed out into the Christmas cold to search for the young Indian girl. Hours went by, and they still found no trace of her. Thankfully, it had not yet begun to snow and the rain had stopped.

Pa had just come off of the mountain a few miles north of town. He and his horse took a drink from the run-off on the side of the hill and turned to look out across the frozen lake. It was the first time he had really been to that side of town. The sky was blue and clear and the sun shown off of the blue lake.

Pa shivered, a reminder of how cold it was, and returned to his horse's back. He had passed the Indian reservation a couple of hours ago. They were all huddled around a fire. Many of the women were crying, and as much as he hated to admit it, he couldn't help feeling sorry for them.

Pa made his way towards the schoolhouse and decided to look inside. He tied the horse to the steps' rail and went in. It was quiet and at first seemed empty. He was about to leave when he spotted her. Sitting on top of Miss Strong's desk was a small Indian girl with her nose buried in a book.

"There you are!"

The girl dropped the book and jumped off of the desk in surprise. She stood staring at Pa for several minutes, and then she spoke. "Hello."

"You speak English?" Pa was surprised when the girl nodded. "I see, and, what is your name? Why are you here?" Though he was trying to stay calm, he was definitely showing some anger.

She pointed at the book on the floor, bent over, and picked it up. She set it back on the desk and faced him again. "My name is Miakoda. We don't have books, not like these. I come to read."

He nodded, and sat down in one of the small chairs. He invited Miakoda to sit down with him, something he normally wouldn't have done. "I see, and how did you learn to read and speak English?"

"I sneak into town and sit outside and listen to the teacher." Miakoda looked up at him with soft, warm, adoring eyes. She was a pretty girl, but she certainly didn't belong in town, according to Pa. If he had had his way, no one other than his own white men would be allowed in town.

"There are a lot of people out looking for you." He suddenly realized how he had ended up there, and it angered him. "Why did you make them worry? Are you stupid, child?"

Miakoda never budged, and she didn't answer. He sighed and took her by the arm. He led her aggressively out of the schoolhouse, and walked her and his horse down the icy street.

The Indians were resting inside the hotel. Pa didn't like this at all. He put the girl on the cold, wet steps of the hotel and tied his horse to the rail. "Don't you move, girl, or I'll have your hide."

He marched inside, and we all jumped when he came in the door. We had been listening to a story one of the Indians was telling. Ma always said of that moment...if looks could kill.

"What on EARTH is going on here?!"

Ma jumped up and came to his side. "Now, Thomas, don't be irrational."

"Irrational?!" His face turned a slight shade of purple. "What have I told you," he turned to me and Elijah; we were hiding behind Ma, "all of you?!"

A small tear fell from Elijah's cheek. "Did you find her, Pa?"

Pa looked down at him. Elijah's face was suddenly full of tears, nearly petrified. I saw a funny look cross Pa's face at that moment, almost as if he was disciplining himself. He hugged Elijah and turned to the Indians, who were all watching with interest. "The child is outside."

Chapter 4

Mia

*W*inter in Linkville had gone, spring was quickly arriving, and we were looking forward to the spring break, even if we did have to help with the planting. The winter had been cold and wet, and the snow was starting to diminish, leaving a big muddy mess. Pa was excited, saying that the ground was perfect for a great crop that would surely thrive. Ma was enjoying the good weather, perfect for getting out of the house. Birds were migrating slowly back to Linkville, and the Tandra Bakery was as busy as ever.

The trees were still brown and bare, but the grasses were starting to shoot higher after each rain. The sun shone down on the lakes and sent bright reflections all around. It wouldn't be long before the flowers started their ascent through the ground. Buds were forming, and soon the wildflowers would be abundant.

Miakoda, the Indian girl, continued to come into town during school, but now she was allowed to sit with the rest of us. The other Indian children were given the option of coming to school, but Mia—as she liked to be called—was the only one who did.

Though Pa had forbidden him, Elijah was becoming good friends with her. She enjoyed having someone to talk to who treated her as a normal girl and not the Indian that she was.

Elijah had learned that her birthday was two days after his, on January 17, and he had given her two cookies for her birthday present. They were both twelve, and both of them were feeling more than they probably realized. Children in the 1800s weren't expected to wait until they were eighteen to be an adult. This meant that most of the children were having their first relationships at eleven or twelve. Some were even married at fifteen or sixteen. Elijah, however, was too scared of Pa to admit he felt anything for Mia, and so far their relationship was secret from everyone except me.

I was always told I was an active child, but I was able to make friends quickly. I loved playing base ball with the boys and hardly ever played any of the games the girls liked. I wore my hair in curly pigtails. That way it would be out of my face for base ball. The boys at school treated me like one of them most of the time.

On March 1, 1875, we were in the middle of one particular game when Elijah and Mia decided they wanted to play. They stood in between me and the pitcher, and I glared at Mia. "Get out of the way, Elijah! We're winning!"

He shook his head. "Let us play and we'll move."

I glared then at my brother. "You can't play; it's the end of the game. One more ace and we win!" I was a stubborn eight-year-old and held my ground. "Move!"

Mia walked up and stood in front of me. "Let us play."

"No!"

Mia bent to the ground and put her fingers in a mud puddle from that morning's snowmelt. She wiped it on her face like war paint and stood back up. "We want to play."

I dropped the bat and looked up into her eyes. We were nearly the same height despite our four-year age difference, so she did not intimidate me. "You're interrupting our game! Now move!" I know I probably shouldn't have let her get to me that way, but I was very competitive.

Mia lunged at me, and we found ourselves in a brawl. We weren't fighting like girls, but like the boys that now surrounded us, clapping and cheering us on. It went on for two minutes before strong hands finally came and pulled us apart.

Out of breath, I turned my red face up and found Joshua Tandra's big brown eyes glaring at us.

"What is goin' on here?"

"She started it," we both said together, pointing at each other.

Joshua sighed and, loosening his grip on my arm a little, led us back into the schoolhouse. Miss Strong was inside, grading some papers. She looked up, startled, and looked between Joshua and us. "Sorry to interrupt, ma'am. I jus' pulled these two out of a figh' outside."

"Hope? Mia?" Miss Strong got up and stood before us. "Is this true?"

I felt the heat rise to my cheeks and I dropped my eyes to the ground. What was Pa going to say? "Yes'm," we both said.

Joshua released us. "Have a g'day, Miss Strong."

"Oh, yes; thank you, Jay." Joshua left and Miss

Strong looked at us with disappointment on her face. "Sit down."

I didn't hesitate to obey.

"Would you mind telling me what the fight was about?"

"Hope wouldn't let me and Elijah play." Mia glared darkly at me.

"Is this true?"

I nodded.

"I see." Miss Strong crossed her arms and stared down at us as if she could burn a hole into us with her eyes. She was a nice woman, but not one to cross. I sniffled. "Now, we're cutting into our lesson time right now, so this better be quick. I want to know who started the fight, and why."

Mia cleared her throat, throwing her long, black, braided hair over her shoulder. "Like I said, Hope wouldn't let Elijah and me play."

"We were almost finished! It was the last pitch of the game and you ruined it!"

"We did not! You could have just put us in the game!"

"We were almost finished!"

Miss Strong stomped her foot. "That's enough! I don't care what the reason was. Mia is here to be like the rest of us, and she's very lucky. You will both stay after school and help me for a week, starting tomorrow. I don't want to see you two fighting again, is this understood?"

"Miss Strong, you know my pa won't let me stay after with her!" She was certainly crazy! This punishment would never happen with Pa. He wouldn't let me! The thought of having to tell him about it frightened me.

"That's part of the consequences of your actions." Miss Strong stood up and returned to her desk. "Mia, would you please ring the bell so we can continue our lessons?"

Mia nodded and walked outside. I sat, defeated, at my desk. What was Pa going to say when I told him what had happened? What if he already knew? I didn't want the school day to end.

When Miss Strong told us all to go home, I swallowed hard. I dropped my head and followed Elijah out of the schoolhouse. We had moved into our new home the week before, so maybe Pa would be in a good mood. There was only one way to find out...

It took us about fifteen minutes to walk to our new farm. It sat on a nice spot above the Link River and had good land for farming at the top of the hill. Smoke was drifting out of the small chimney, and we were surrounded by the smells of warm baked bread. Elijah went inside first, glaring at me over his shoulder. We had been fighting all the way home.

"Why, Hope, what's the matter?"

I fell into Ma's arms and cried. "Pa's going to be so mad at me!"

"What's the matter?" She stroked my hair and pulled me into her lap. "Come on, child. Tell me what's wrong."

I sniffled and looked up into her eyes. "I got into a fight during lunch today with Mia."

Ma, who was not one to scold us, gave me a disappointed look. That was worse than any punishment.

"Pa's going to be really mad."

"Well, what was the fight about?"

I didn't have a chance to answer. Elijah came back into the room and threw his lunch pail, slate, and arithmetic book on the table. "Because she's a big selfish loser, that's what!"

"Elijah James! You apologize to your sister this instant!" It was the first time in a long time that Ma had raised her voice at either of us. Elijah blinked at her.

He was silent for a minute, and then crossed his arms. For the first time I saw Pa in my brother. "No."

I widened my eyes at him as Ma got up and set me in the chair. This was getting bad...

She crossed the room to stand in front of him, taking him by the arms and forcing him to look up at her. "Did you just tell me no?"

He didn't speak. His face was a mix of fear for this new side of our ma, but also of stubbornness. He wasn't planning on changing his position any time soon. Ma shook him slightly, staring him directly in the eyes.

"This family does not call each other names, am I understood?!" She did not let down, and Elijah didn't either. "Go to your room, Elijah. Your father will speak to you when he gets back." He opened his mouth to protest, but Ma shook her head." I advise you to keep your mouth shut."

I was still sitting in the chair, half in shock at what I had just witnessed, but relieved. My brother might have been in worse trouble than I was, if that was possible. Ma went silently to the kitchen and pulled the hot bread loaf out of the oven. I wondered if I should step up and offer to help or if I, too, should retreat to my room.

Hesitantly I cleared my throat. "Ma?"

"Please, just go to your room, Hope."

I nodded and walked to my room without argument. I had never seen Ma so angry, and I hoped that Pa wouldn't be that bad. He was often worse than Ma, though. I didn't want to face him when he did come home. Just the fact that my fight was with the Indian girl would set him off, and I would have to tell him that she and Elijah were secret friends. I didn't want to betray my brother that way. Perhaps I would find a way to not tell him. Why did I have to open my big fat mouth? I sighed and fell onto my bed. I didn't want to think about anything, and rolled over. Within seconds I was sound asleep.

It was three days before Pa came home. He had been away making deliveries for the mercantile. I was pacing in my room, still not wanting to face him. How was I going to hide the fact that Elijah was friends with Mia? My heart was beating fast, and I felt hot. When I heard the wagon coming down the road I raced to the window to see if it was him.

My stomach dropped when I saw the familiar wagon at the barn and Pa jumping down. He pulled a couple of travel bags out and walked towards the house with a smile. He was in a good mood, and this lightened my worries just slightly.

I came out of my room to greet him, but Ma was already telling him about the incident. Elijah was cowering by his own bedroom door, and he looked to me for help. Why should I help? He was the one that got us into this mess in the first place.

"I didn't ask much about the fight. I was too angry with Elijah." Ma took his travel coat and hat and left us alone with him.

"Both of you come and sit down." We obeyed without argument, and neither one of us looked up at him. "I asked you not to give your ma any trouble while I was away, did I not?"

"You did, sir," we chanted.

Pa nodded. "And you did anyway. Explain yourselves." We both started in trying to explain, our words jumbling together. He held his hand up. "One at a time."

I swallowed. I would not get Elijah in trouble over his friendship with Mia, not if I could help it... "It was my fault, Pa. I got into a fight with one of the girls, and..."

"Who?" I did not expect this question so soon.

"Mia, sir."

Pa's face turned a slight shade of purple. "The Indian girl?" I nodded. "What did she do to you?"

"Nothing, sir."

"Don't lie to me, Hope. What did she do to you?"

I shook my head, a single tear running down my face. "Nothing, sir. She wanted to play in our base ball game, and I wouldn't let her."

"I see. Well, that was good for you to not let her play." I was somewhat relieved, but now the questions would be on Elijah. "And why did you call your sister names?"

Elijah didn't speak for a moment, and then finally he took a deep breath. "I told her just to ignore the Indian girl, but she wouldn't listen." He threw a quick glance at me, begging me to play along.

"Is this true, Hope?"

I nodded, my black curls rubbing against my ears as they bounced. "Yes, sir." I couldn't believe I had just lied to Pa, but Elijah would have been in terrible trouble if I had told the truth. Fortunately, he believed our story, and sent us to bed without dessert.

The last few weeks of school were a lot of fun for us. We were both doing well in school, and Pa had decided to take us on a spring camping trip before planting began. We were all looking forward to it so much, and because of it Elijah and I were very well behaved the rest of the month.

When Miss Strong told us we could all go home and to have a nice spring, we all rushed out. I raced after Elijah, but he stopped a few feet from the schoolhouse and stopped me. "Hope, please wait here for me. Give me ten minutes." I started to protest, but he was gone before I got the chance.

Elijah

I ran for nearly three minutes, into the trees behind the schoolhouse. The air was crisp and cool, the spring sun warm against my skin. I came to a clearing a few feet away. Looking around, I couldn't find what I was looking for. Where was she? "Mia?"

Mia reached out from behind the small hill where she had dug a hole in the ground, and pulled me inside. She smiled at me, a single tear running down her face. This was her secret place; it was where she came to get away from the reservation. I thought the reservation was a cruel punishment. I didn't like it at all, and had often encouraged her to run here.

"I wish you weren't going."

I smiled back and wiped the tear from her face. "I want to go, and we'll only be gone for two weeks. I'll be back before you know it."

49

Mia shook her head. "It's not good enough. School's out; what if I won't be able to see you?"

I hadn't thought of this before. My heart was sad. What were we going to do? There had to be a way to see each other more often. My mind ran through one idea after another, but nothing seemed to be good enough.

"I..." My eyes skimmed the small cavern under the earth. It was cold, but it was private, and no one else knew about it. "We'll meet here. If not more, I'll come here every...every Monday. We'll come here after everyone is asleep."

She shook her head. "The reservation is too far away, Elijah. That's too far to walk at night. I don't know how I wouldn't get caught. That's why I stay in town during the week, and when would I sleep?"

I fell back into my thoughts. The possibility of not seeing her for three months was killing me. Spring would be boring without her. "Well...I'll meet you halfway. There's that abandoned cabin just north of town, you know?"

Mia grinned. "Elijah! It's wonderful. Why didn't I think of that before?!"

There was a moment where we just sat, staring at each other with dopey grins. Well, I'm sure mine was. Hers couldn't be.

Our eyes met and I tried to ignore my racing heart. Mia's brown cheeks turned slightly darker and she kissed me quickly on the lips. I hadn't realized what hit me until I looked around at the rabbit hole and realized that she was gone. *What just happened?* I shook the thoughts away with a smile. Pa was waiting on us, and I didn't want to mess it up.

Hope

Spring in Oregon was chilly, but gradually warming, and wet. I was enjoying the campout with Pa and Elijah. We spent our mornings hunting, though we didn't find many deer this close to the end of winter. Our days were filled with fishing the wonderful river, with its white rapids and deep fishing holes. We were camped about two days east of Linkville. It was well-shaded by large pines and firs, which helped block out the rain, and our bedrolls and the campfire kept us warm at night. Our nights were quiet and comfortable, with our only fear the possible arrival of bears.

On our fifth night in camp, Elijah couldn't sleep. It was a Monday night, and he was staring up at the sky, deep in thought. I wondered what or who he was thinking about.

He rolled over in his bedroll. I pretended to be sound asleep as he kissed me on the cheek.

He got up and made the three-hundred-foot walk to the river and planted himself on the bank. Taking off his socks and shoes, he set them behind him, and slid his feet into the river. He sat staring into the fast-running water for quite some time before he heard my footsteps behind him.

He turned quickly and gasped as I got close enough to finally see him. "Hope! You scared me!"

I giggled and sat down next to my brother. I, too, took my shoes and socks off, not wanting to ruin the shoes Pa had spent a lot of money on, and put my feet in the icy water. "I rolled over and you were gone, so I came to check on you."

Elijah gave me a small smile and went back to

staring at the water.

"Elijah, I may only be eight, but I know when someone is thinking about someone they like. It's Mia, isn't it?"

Even under the moonlight I could see Elijah blush. I understood what he was feeling. What if he admitted it and I accidentally told Pa? So far I had kept their friendship a secret from everyone, including Pa. Wasn't that enough for him to trust me?

Finally, he pulled his feet out of the water and put his socks and shoes on. Apparently he wasn't ready to tell me...

"Let's go back to bed."

I dropped my jaw, pouting, and pulled my feet out of the water. How dare he not tell me! I snatched up my socks and shoes, not bothering to put them on, and chased after him. This, however, was a move I regretted. The ground was hard and pointy, and it stung my feet.

"Elijah! Wait up!"

He was already in his bedroll and asleep by the time I had caught up with him.

"Wow, he must have been exhausted. Stubborn old goat!" I sighed and brushed off my soiled feet. I slipped back into my socks and crawled back into my blankets. It wasn't long before I was lost in my own dreams.

Chapter 5

Sticky Buns

$\mathcal{M}$a and Pa had never really asked us to help with the planting before, but we were getting older and were expected to help more. Pa and Elijah left early in the mornings with their work clothes on. Ma and I spent our days mending buttons, hemming pants, and baking. We had acquired a milk cow from one of our neighbors and a few laying hens. While Ma milked the cow, I gathered the eggs.

On a good day, our nine hens would lay two eggs each. Those were the times we liked the most, because there would be enough for us to keep some and sell the rest.

Today was an exceptionally good day, because we got twenty eggs. I had already gathered twelve the day before yesterday, so when I brought Ma the basket, her face brightened.

"You run those straight to the mercantile. You can get a piece of candy for you and your brother and put the rest on our account."

I gasped with excitement. It had been a long time

since we'd been able to get candy. "Thank you, Ma!"

I raced into the house and grabbed the basket cover, sliding it over the warm fresh eggs. My work bonnet was hanging around my neck and I pulled it up over my black curls. Draping the basket handle over my arm, I skipped toward town.

The spring sun was bright, and shined off of the wet dirt road. My bonnet did little to shade my eyes, so I kept my head down, kicking at loose pebbles in the road. I knew the way into town very well after walking it every day for the last five months. It took about twenty minutes to get to the mercantile from our little house on the bank of the river, and I was enjoying the time away from the busy day.

I was daydreaming about fishing, holding the slimy, writhing worm while I skewered it on my hook and throwing it into the water for the unsuspecting fish, so I hadn't heard the thumping of the horse's hooves behind me. When the horse snorted at me, I jumped, nearly dropping my collection of eggs.

I turned around to face the brown thoroughbred and its rider. Joshua Tandra peered down at me, a dopey grin on his face.

I glared at him, trying to block the sun from my eyes. "Joshua Tandra, you scared me!"

"Beggin' your pardon, Miss. I didn't mean to by no means." He tipped his hat and dismounted his horse, dropping the reins to the ground. The leather dragged through the mud as the horse clomped behind him, not running away.

I looked at him, surprised by the calmness of his giant of a horse. "Wow, how'd you get him to stay like that?"

Joshua smiled at me, his pearly white teeth bright

against his ebony skin. "Trust, m'lady."

My cheeks flushed, and I looked away from his eyes. *'M'lady'? What was that about?* I shook it off. "Trust? That's it?"

He nodded. "And loyalty. Can't forget the loyalty."

I smiled a bit and shook my head, turning to continue on my way down the road. Ma would be expecting me back at a certain time, and I couldn't be gone too long. She'd need me to help prepare supper.

Joshua's large boots scuffed on the dirt as he moved alongside me. His horse followed obediently, clomping along through the dirt. "Where ya headed?"

I raised the basket up, careful not to disrupt the eggs. "Selling our eggs. We've been getting a lot recently. Ma said I could get some candy. I haven't had any in a while." I smiled, unable to contain my excitement.

Joshua nodded. "Yes'm. Candy is a good treat. You'd like my Ma's sweet buns. They's the best ones for miles."

They sounded delectable. I wondered if Ma would make some for us. I pushed the hope aside, realizing we wouldn't be able to afford it for a while. "You're sure lucky getting treats like that all the time."

He shook his head as we rounded the bend to cross the river bridge. "Nah, I don't get them much. We only get them if they don't sell out, an' they usually do. Some people don't get them just 'cause she runs out of supplies to bake more."

As we crossed the river, the sweet scent of baking bread and cinnamon filled my nostrils. Before I knew it, I looked up, and we were in front of Tandra Bakery. Surprised, I looked over at Joshua's horse, standing with me alone. Where was Joshua?

I shrugged and turned toward the mercantile.

I had just stepped past the front porch of the bakery when Joshua bounced off the steps and landed behind me. His horse neighed and trotted up behind us, falling back into his paced steps.

I looked up at Joshua, a bit surprised.

"Here."

I looked down at his outstretched hand. A sticky bun glistened in the sun, and the sweet scent of cinnamon and butter reached my nostrils.

My eyes widened. I couldn't break away from the bun. I stopped and turned to face him, torn. I really wanted to taste it. It smelled and looked so good.

Joshua chuckled, and I looked up into his brown eyes. "Oh, go on, miss. It won't bite."

I shook my head. I couldn't eat it all. It would spoil my supper. "Well, why don't you split it with me then?"

Joshua nodded. "Alright." His free hand reached up and broke the bun in half. One was slightly larger than the other, and that was the one he held out for me.

"You can have the bigger half."

He shook his head. "No, ma'am. Ladies first."

He never failed to surprise me. I didn't argue, and took the sticky bun.

The bread was still warm and the buttery cinnamon dripped onto my fingers as I grasped the treat. I brought it up to my mouth and took a bite. It tasted as good as it looked. I couldn't help but stuff it all in my mouth. Joshua chewed his piece carefully with a big grin on his face.

"Thank you, Joshua."

He nodded, pulling a napkin from his trouser pocket and handing it to me. I took it gratefully and wiped off the sticky mess.

He continued to follow me down the street, but neither one of us spoke. Finally, he cleared his throat. "Do you like to go fishin'?"

I nodded, forgetting who I was talking to. "I haven't been since we moved here, not around town anyway. I don't really know where to go. I'd love to go before school starts again."

I stopped as we came to the front of the mercantile, and Joshua faced me. "Why don't we go? When can you? I could show ya aroun'."

My heart thumped in my throat. I had mixed emotions about this. I knew what Pa would say if he even saw me standing here with him, and I didn't even want to think about what he would say if he knew we were fishing together, but I really, really wanted to go. How was I going to do this? Maybe I would talk Elijah into going with me. Then he could go spend time with Mia, and I could go fishing. What harm would that do?

"I don't know. Maybe next weekend?"

Joshua tipped his hat at me with a smile. "It be a date then." I watched him walk away, his horse clomping behind him.

A date? What did he mean by that? I shrugged my shoulders and headed into the mercantile.

The store was empty. Most folks were busy tending their fields. I went straight to the counter and put the basket on it.

Mr. Hunt, the shopkeeper, smiled at me from behind his spectacles. "Ah, Miss Hope. What brings you out here all by yourself?"

I smiled as I pulled the basket cover off, revealing the twenty brown and white eggs. I managed to get them all in without breaking them. "We got twenty today."

The shopkeeper smiled, pulling the eggs out one

by one and placing them in his own basket. "Well, your chickens must be very well taken care of. Twenty eggs will get you a whole quarter. How does that sound?"

I grinned. "A whole quarter?"

"Yes, ma'am. Shall I give you the quarter or do you want it on your account?"

"Ma said I can get candy for me and Elijah and the rest on the account."

The shopkeeper placed the basket aside and walked around the counter. He held out his hand and I took it, following him to the candy boxes. "These right here are just a penny. You get two of those and tell your Ma that I'll put the whole quarter on her account."

"You will?"

He just nodded and winked at me, heading back to his place behind the counter. I skipped to the candy jars and grabbed two pieces of long black licorice. I chomped on one and set the other in the egg basket. Then I waved at the shopkeeper and skipped out the door, heading for home.

Chapter 6

Fishing

Elijah and I had it all planned out. We would head for the river south of town after church on Sunday and split up. He would spend the day with Mia, and I would meet up with Joshua. This fact, however, Elijah didn't know about. I had told him I was giving him the opportunity to meet her just so I could go fishing. I wasn't sure if he believed me, but he agreed anyway.

Ma packed us lunches. We managed to talk her into two sandwiches each. That would give us enough for Mia and Joshua. When our fishing packs were loaded with lunch and bait, we grabbed our poles and headed south.

The spring sun was warm on our faces. Elijah ran ahead as we came to a small hill that would take us to the river. Mia was waiting anxiously near the bank, and skipped towards Elijah as he ran to meet her. I smiled, unaware of the bond they held. To me they looked like the best of friends, and perhaps that's what they were.

I continued on a little ways farther and found

Joshua waiting for me with his horse. He smiled when he spotted me, and I waved. Looking over my shoulder to be sure no one saw me, I stepped forward, and he pulled me up behind him. "How are you this afternoon, Miss Hope?"

I smiled behind him as the horse headed farther south. "I'm okay, how about you?"

He nodded under his hat, and the horse trotted on. Neither one of us spoke, and I took in the sights around us. We were outside of the town now. A few farms were scattered about, their fields freshly plowed. As we came down the side of the hill, I saw a river running nearby. "Is that where we're going?"

I heard him chuckle, and he asked his horse to go faster. As we got closer, he pointed across the water. "Over there be Whittle's Ferry. Not much, just a few people." The horse turned to follow the bank of the river, away from the ferry dock. "Good fishin', too."

We went about a mile upriver, where he jumped down. He turned to help me off, and I went straight to the riverbank.

It wasn't a large river, but still had potential. I could see several dark spots near the bank, and by rocks where fish were bound to be hiding. Excited, I didn't hesitate, and baited my hook. I threw the line in and waited.

"Well, you been fishin' before then? I figured I'da had to teached ya."

I chuckled, shaking my head as he threw his line in a couple of feet downstream. "No, I've been fishing before. Back in Rolla we used to go fishing every weekend, and we went over our camping trip, but that's all since we've been here. I guess Pa is just too busy to take us."

Joshua nodded, tipping his hat to shade the sun from his eyes. "Most folks are busy this time of the year. Don't worry, he'll take you, I'm sure of it."

There was a moment of silence. I stared into the water, the clouds above reflected on the surface. Joshua was the first colored boy I had ever met. Part of me was curious, as most eight-year-olds were. The other part of me, the part that was afraid of Pa's temper, knew I shouldn't be there. Yet, as the pole twitched in my fingers, I ignored that part.

The pole twitched again, and I felt the unmistakable tug of the line in my hand. My heart skipped, and I tugged on the line, ensuring my catch. Joshua pulled his line out, realizing I had a catch, and grabbed the fishing net from his saddlebag. I pulled on my pole again and pulled out a large fish. It had to have been at least a foot long. With a grin, I dropped the fish into the net.

Joshua reached in to grab my fish, but I was quicker. I wasn't afraid of the slimy thing, and pulled the hook out. He stared, a look of surprise on his face, as I pushed the fish onto the catch line my Pa had made me. I smiled and re-baited my hook.

"What?"

"You ain't afraid of no fish, are you?"

I shook my head, dropping my line back in. I liked this spot. "Of course not. Why should I be?"

"Well, I just figured you was since you're a girl."

"Well, you figured wrong, Joshua."

He laughed and dropped his line back in. There was a comfortable silence between the two of us.

We both caught fish and our lines were getting full, so we set our poles aside and sat in the shade of a juniper tree. I pulled Ma's sandwiches out of my pack and handed him one. He looked surprised, but smiled genuinely at me. "You really didn't have to do that, Miss Hope."

I smiled, unwrapping my sandwich. "I know."

Joshua pulled more sandwiches out of his pack and handed me one. "Well, least we be fed well." We laughed and ate our lunch.

Mrs. Tandra had made cold ham and cheese sandwiches and we even got a potato salad. Ma had made me peanut butter and honey. When we were done, my tummy was overly stuffed.

As we put away our lunch remains, I said, "Thanks for the trip, Joshua."

"Does that mean you're ready to go home, Miss Hope?"

I shook my head, looking at my catch of fish. I had seven, more than enough to feed us for dinner. I looked up toward the sun and guessed it was about three in the afternoon.

"Joshua, what's it like?"

"What's what like?"

"Being out of school, living on your own?"

Joshua smiled, picking up the wrappers and dishes. "It not be easy for sure. You enjoy being a child, Miss Hope. It won' last forever."

I didn't respond at first, thinking about Ma and Pa. They made being grown look easy.

"What do you want to be when you grown?"

"A teacher. My ma was a teacher, and I love the idea of helping kids learn to read."

"That be a large ambition for such a young girl."

"You don't think I can do it? How insulting!"

He shook his head, pushing his hat aside. "Not at all. You be anything you want to be. Not all of us are so lucky."

Now I was confused. "What do you mean, exactly?"

He smiled, laying back and propping himself on his elbows. "Where I come from, we work from the time we can walk. We lucky if we get food. If we don't do what we told, we get beat, almost to death. The old ones die from starvation and beatings. Sometimes we get traded for goods and services, sometimes we sold to other farms."

I was appalled. What kind of life would that be? Sold, starved, beaten? How could a human be so cruel? So, he had memories of that life, and they weren't pleasant.

"That's awful." That was all I could say. I didn't know what else to say.

"Ma took me away from there, and we come out here to have a better chance. Even here we get looked at funny, and some whites won't serve us."

Pa was like that. Why? I couldn't see anything wrong with Joshua. He had hopes and dreams just like me. How was he a bad person?

I looked at Joshua, studying his face. His eyes were chocolate brown, the spring sky reflected in them as he looked up into its depths. His black hair curled tightly to his head, and his hands were rough like most farmers' hands. The only thing different between him and other folk was his brown skin.

"Well, I think you deserve everything I do. Work, love, dreams. We're not that different, really."

"Yet you won't be tellin' your pa about our visit today, will you?"

I shook my head and looked to the ground guiltily. "No, I won't. He'd skin me alive if he found out."

Joshua smiled and stood up, packing away his things in his saddlebag. He pulled our day's catch out and handed me my string of fish. "Well, then it be our little secret." He squinted up into the sun. "It's getting late. 'Lijah will be looking for ya."

I nodded and stood up, taking my fish. He swung his leg over his horse and reached down to help me up.

On the way back I thought about our conversation. He seemed like someone I could really like as a friend, if only Pa would let me. *Yeah, sure. Never going to happen as long as I'm in his house.* With a sigh, I laid my head on his back, tired from the day of fishing.

Chapter 7

A Sewing Project

he first day of school went by fast, and I didn't want to return home. My parents had gone on a trip to try to find advance buyers for that year's crop, and Elijah had been left in charge. He was, after all, nearly a man...or so he said.

I scoffed. He was not a man when he wasn't even home to take care of his own sister!

I was passing Joshua Tandra's farm when I accidentally dropped my books. I cursed to myself and plopped onto the ground, not wanting to pick them up. I was frustrated with Elijah, wishing I knew where he ran off to every day since Ma and Pa had left. Even when they were there, he was sneaking out once a week, but why? I wished he had trusted me with something obviously so important. Since when did I tell on him? Well, there was that one time, but I was only four at the time! Maybe this had something to do with...

My thoughts were interrupted by the sound of a horse walking up behind me. I scrambled out of the road and turned to see Joshua's brown face smiling down at me. "Hey there, Freckles. How are you t'day?"

I gave him a quizzical look. "Freckles?"

He laughed, jumping off of his horse. "Aw, well, your face be covered with freckles, see?"

I nodded and looked at the black boy like he was crazy. Maybe he was...

"What the long face for?"

I kicked at the dirt and shrugged. "Nothing, it's just...my brother's keeping something from me." I'm not sure why I told him, but I had to talk to somebody.

Joshua nodded. "I see, an' does he usually tell you everythin'?"

I nodded, my curls brushing against my face as they bounced. "Yes." I looked into his chocolate eyes. They were warm and inviting, much softer now than when he had broken up my fight with Mia; they were the same eyes that told me of his past that day by the riverbank.

I sighed. "It's just...Elijah keeps sneaking off, at least once a week when Ma and Pa are home, but now that they're gone he sneaks off for hours every day and leaves me alone! I don't know what's gotten into him!" I kicked a rock on the ground and it bounced over Joshua's boots. I felt the blush color my face. "Sorry."

Joshua bent over and picked me up, setting me on his horse. He then picked up my books and led the horse towards his house. "I was hopin' a smart girl like you migh' be able to help me with somethin'."

I blinked, startled by the fact that he had just picked me up and put me on the horse. What would Pa think if he could see me right now? But he wasn't here, and I nodded. "Um, sure, I can try."

Suddenly, I was starting to enjoy this new freedom, with my parents not being around.

Joshua tied the horse to the post outside the little house and helped me down. I followed him into the cabin. It was nice, but definitely not made for more than one person. It didn't even have a bedroom; there was a small cot resting in one corner of the room. A small heating stove and cupboard was on the opposite side, and he seemed to have made a clothes trunk out of his floor. "Not much, but it be home." He closed the door behind us and poured two glasses of water.

I took it and sipped a few times, giving the clothes on the floor a dirty look. "If you brought me here to be your house maid..."

Joshua laughed. "No, no! I wanna start on a Christmas present for Ma, but I never done any sewin' before. Could you show me?"

Show him how to sew? Well, that was innocent enough. I smiled and looked around the room. "You got a sewing kit?"

He went to the other side of the room and pulled a small box from underneath his bed. "When I wen' down ta California ta make a delivery, I foun' this fabric in the mercantile. I thought Ma would love it, an' I wanna make her a blouse out of it, but I never even touche' a needle before an' I can't exactly aks Ma ta show me. I don't think Pa knows how ta either."

Joshua set the box on the table and opened it. Inside, a beautiful blue fabric fell out of its neat folds onto the table, and I found myself falling in love with it too. "In't wonderful?"

I nodded and took it into my hands. It was the softest material I had ever felt, and I envied Mrs. Tandra. She would love it! I set the fabric back down for fear of ruining it, and blinked.

"Well, the first thing you need to do is to borrow

one of your Ma's shirts. You don't want to go making the wrong size." I had seen Ma do this a hundred times.

Joshua nodded. "Ahea' of you there!" He threw some of the clothes on the floor aside and pulled up a simple blouse, one that I had seen on Mrs. Tandra many times. "I got dis from her dis mornin'...hopefully she won' have misse' it yet."

I nodded and pulled the small measuring tape out of the box. I measured the blouse carefully, and marked the measurements with pins on the blue fabric the way Ma always did. "Now you need to cut along the outside of the pins. Leave a little extra so you have something to work with."

Joshua blinked. "I won' run out of fabric?"

I shook my head. "Not if you're careful. I've seen Ma do it a million times!"

He scratched at his head. "I don' think I can do it."

"Sure you can; I've laid it out for you. You can use scissors, can't you?"

Joshua chuckled. "To be hones', I never had to." He looked between the fabric and me. "Woul' you be willing ta do it?"

I shook my head. "I don't think that's such a good idea, Joshua. If Ma or Pa caught me with something that belonged to you..."

He took me gently by the arms and looked into my eyes. "Please? I be willin' ta pay you for it. A nickel a week?"

This was a very generous offer, but still I hesitated. I wasn't completely good with a needle and thread myself, and the thought of what my parents would do if they caught me was scary. I looked into his pleading brown eyes, and something about them made me smile.

"I suppose so, but I'd have to hide it under my bed. It might get a little dusty."

Joshua shook his head with a smile. "I don' care! You're a life-saver, Hope Bryant!" He kissed me on the cheek, leaving me quite shocked, and replaced the sewing box and the fabric.

I clutched the box in my arms on the last day of summer school. I had grown very much attached to it and the fabric inside. There was something about it that I liked a lot, and I was a little sad that the blouse was almost finished. I had been working on it for nearly three months and would be getting more than a half dollar for my work—perhaps almost seventy-five cents if I stretched it out long enough.

It was beginning of October now, and the leaves were starting to fall off of the trees. School was out for the harvest, and the fall crops were being gathered. The men were heading out of town to sell their crops. Even I knew it had been a good year, and everyone seemed to be able to spend a little extra on Thanksgiving and Christmas this year. I was looking forward to my ninth birthday. Maybe I would get that new fishing pole I had been dreaming of for so long!

I was making my way down the road alone. Elijah had stayed after school to help Miss Strong clean up for the fall, or so he had told everyone.

I stopped when I heard the familiar sounds of a horse coming up behind me. "Hey there, Freckles."

I smiled and turned around. "Hi, Jay; how are you?" He nodded, eyeing his sewing box in my arms. "Oh, I've still got a bit of work to do on it. Give me a bit more time, alright?"

He nodded. "Oh yeah, of course. Woul' you like I pay you now?"

I shook my head. "No, it wouldn't be fair. What if you don't like how it turned out?"

Joshua smiled. "That woul' never happen, Freckles."

I returned his smile, and then looked around his horse. A familiar wagon was rounding the corner. "Uh oh! Ma and Pa are coming! I've got to get home and hide this box!" I left before he could protest, and ran full-speed towards the house. Elijah and Mia were standing outside the front door, and I widened my eyes.

I was right! It was Mia he had been sneaking off with! I had hoped, for his sake, it was someone else. There was no time to lecture him now; the wagon would be coming any second. "Mia, get out of here! Ma and Pa are coming! Pa will skin all our hides if he sees you here!"

Mia and Elijah exchanged quick but scared glances, and Mia ran up the hill behind the house. I ran into my room and shoved the box under my bed. Elijah ran in and started setting the table for dinner. When our parents came in, we were both sitting at the table with our reading books open.

Ma and Pa stopped in the middle of the doorway. "Is it just me, or do they look suspicious for some reason?" We ignored her comment, and they chuckled.

Outside it was cold and wet, and feeling very different from that of our house. Pa was already snoring in his room. I was lying in my bed, wide-awake, and waiting for the first sign that Ma had gone to bed too, ignoring the queasiness in my stomach. In the next room, Elijah was doing the same thing, though I didn't know it at the time. Ma would check on us both one more time before moving on to her own room. I was certain of this; I had asked Elijah how he knew it was time to sneak out. He hadn't wanted to tell me. Elijah was, he informed me, an expert at sneaking out of the house. I, however, was merely a beginner.

I was determined not to let my lack of experience stop me. Clutching the brown package under my blankets, I popped my eyes shut when the door opened and Ma walked inside. She bent down and kissed me on the forehead. I was a good actress, never flinching nor moving, until I heard the last lamp blown out and the third bedroom door close.

I threw my blankets back and scrambled for my socks and shoes. Then I drew up some clothes and pillows, and shoved them under my blankets so that it looked like I was still asleep in my bed. I pulled my winter coat over my nightdress and placed the package carefully inside.

I opened my door as quietly as I could. No one else was up, and I let out a relieved sigh. I tiptoed across the room and eased the front door open. It was raining pretty heavily. I wondered if I should wait, but it might have been raining just as hard the next day.

I shook my head. No, I just needed to do it.

"So, you are sneaking out!" I jumped and tried desperately not to scream. Elijah was coming towards me, and I slapped his arm.

"Don't scare me like that!" I glared at him and stepped into the rain.

He came out after me and shut the door quietly

behind him. "Hope! Hope, wait!" I stopped halfway down the road and tried to blink the rain away from my eyes. "Where are you going?"

"None of your business, Elijah James!" If he couldn't trust me, I wasn't going to trust him. "Where are you going?"

He sighed and went into the barn. I continued on down the road and stopped when Elijah's horse stepped in front of me. "It's Monday, in case you've forgotten. Now get up here and I'll take you!"

I shook my head. "No! I'm doing this on my own!"

"You'll be sick if you stay out here, Hope!"

I turned on my heel and continued down the road. "Then I better hurry, hadn't I?"

Elijah grumbled and kicked his horse. They ran past me and out of sight.

It took me nearly twenty minutes to reach Joshua's door. The rain was coming down so fast now that it stung my skin. I knocked on the door gratefully and tried not to cough. The pressure in my chest was almost unbearable.

When the door opened, I fell into Joshua's arms and felt the heat rise. I had never felt so sick in my life...

Joshua

It had been a long day, an' I sat down to relax with a col' glass of milk. I just pulle' my boots off when there was a knock on the door. I stood up, wonderin' who would possibly be callin' at my door so late at night. When I opene' it, I was shocked to see young Hope, drippin' an' coughin'.

"What on earth?" I pulled her inside the house an' pulle' her out of her wet coat. A brown package hit the floor, and my stomach gave a great lurch. It was instant guilt that had washe' over me when I realized what was in the package. "Please tell me you did not come in dis storm just to deliver that shirt."

Hope coughed, an' her whole body shivered. Her face was flushed an' her hair was sticking to her face. "Yes," she choked out. "I finished it yesterday."

I picked up the lumpy brown package an' threw it to my bed. Then I grabbed a clean flannel shirt from the floor an' held it out for her. "Get yourself out of that wet night dress." She took it from me an' I turned so I didn't see her change.

It was silent in the room, but I didn't want to risk turning aroun' if she wasn't finished. I was growing nervous. Surely she was done by now?

I sighed, an' there was a loud thud. I turned and saw Hope lyin' on the floor an' shiverin'. I hurried to her an' picked her up carefully, carrying her to the bed. Pulling the blankets over her, I ran to the stove. I dipped a washrag in the hot water kettle an' rushe' back to her. Then I knelt down an' stroke' her face with the hot, steaming cloth. "I wish you not come, Freckles."

She coughed as someone knocke' on the door.

My heart raced. What if it was her pa? He would kill me, an' what would he think, with her in my shirt? I was about to go to it when Elijah and Mia raced through the door.

"Where is she?"

I breathed a sigh of relief an' pointed at the bed. I was glad to see Elijah, but still a little worried.

He bent over an' took her hand in his.

"I told you not to do this on your own, foolish child." She couldn't stop coughin' enough to respon' to him. I could tell she liked to fall asleep, but somehow she was still awake. Elijah stood up an' turned to me. "Why did she come here?"

I blinked. "You don' know?" Elijah shook his head. "I hire' her to make somethin' for me. I was payin' her to sew a blouse for my Ma. She finishe' it an' was bringin' it to me."

Elijah looked at Hope. She was coughin' even harder now. Mia stepped closer an' took Elijah's arm. "She needs to get home, Elijah. You need to get her home." He nodded, a single tear runnin' down his face.

Mia turned to me. "They cannot get into trouble by their Ma and Pa. If I go with them, I know that's what will happen."

I shook my head. "No, Elijah. Get your sister home, an' quickly. Mia, you stay here until the rain clears. I be drivin' to town in the mornin'. I can take you to the reservation then."

Elijah shook his head, leaning over Hope. "Mia must be seen there before morning. We snuck out too."

I was confused, but I helped Elijah get Hope onto the horse an' went to get my own.

It was a long, rainy ride to the reservation, an' I was sure I would come down sick too, but returned Mia safe an' sound.

The rain was finally clearin' up as I stopped in front of Hope's house on my way home. It was dark inside, an' as far as I could tell it was quiet. I wanted to know how she was, but didn' dare knock on the door. The sound of her cough was ringin' in my ears. In that moment I regretted aksin' her to help me with the blouse; if it weren't for that, she would have kept out of the storm. I felt responsible for her bein' sick, an' once the truth come out, her pa would be on my door an' wouldn't never accept me or my family. I was even worried that he would somehow force me an' my family out of Linkville.

I growled as I put the horse back in the barn. Everythin' was such a big mess.

Chapter 8

Blind Fever

Elijah

*I*t had been three long days since I had returned Hope to her bed. I spent most of those days pacing the floor outside her room, listening to her cough. I had never seen her quite so sick before, and it scared me.

Pa had just come in from another day's work in the fields, preparing them for the winter, and I shivered. "Pa, do you think she's going to be alright?"

He sighed, taking off his coat and falling into the hard chair. He stared into the fire's flames before finally rubbing his face. "I don't know, Elijah. She's really sick."

I sat down next to him and we both sat in silence.

I jumped when Ma ran out of Hope's room. "Elijah! Quick! Run and get Doc Johnson!"

"Ma?"

"Now!" I didn't protest any further, but ran straight for the door, not bothering to shut it behind me.

Outside, it seemed like everyone in Linkville didn't have a care in the world. It was probably one of the last sunny days we would see dry for quite some time, and most folks were making the best of it. Some called out to me, but I didn't have time to be nice. I ignored everyone I passed, including Mia and the chief, who were in town buying food. When I finally made it to the doctor's office, I pounded on the door.

"Open up!" I pounded again, but still there was no answer.

"He not be in; what be wrong, child?"

I turned to face who had spoken to me, looking up into the face of Esther May Tandra. Joshua was standing behind her, looking particularly scared. I bent over to try to catch my breath so I could speak. My lungs were burning, and my heart racing. When my lungs finally slowed down I straightened up. "It's my sister; we need the doctor now! Where is he?"

Joshua's face went rather pale, considering its true color, and I met his eyes to confirm to him that the reason for my visit was because of the events of the other night.

Joshua nodded. "I know where he is! He was on his way out to the Carter farm to check on the new baby!"

My heart sank. The Carter farm was fifteen miles away! I collapsed, unable to stop the tears and unable to stand any longer. Hope could be dying! Why did Doc Johnson have to choose to leave then?

I nearly jumped when Esther May's soft hands folded around my arms. She pulled me up from the ground and wiped my face with her handkerchief. "If it be that urgent, let me go to her."

I didn't know what to do. What would Pa do if I

led Esther May into our house? If I didn't, though, Hope could die.

I cursed quietly to myself and ran down the street. "Come on! I don't know how bad it is!"

Esther May ran after me. Joshua tried to follow, but she stopped him. "You stay. Somebody need to be runnin' da store, Jay." He wanted to be there, but I was glad he stayed behind.

We were back at my house in five minutes' time, and I pointed Esther May to the room.

Pa nearly fell out of his chair when he saw her come into the house. He turned, red-faced, to me. "Explain yourself, boy!" Esther May was closing the door behind her, leaving me alone with Pa. I wished she hadn't.

I burst out in tears. My worst fear before had been Pa finding out about my relationship, not friendship, with Mia. Suddenly, my biggest fear was losing my sister and best friend. "I didn't know what to do, Pa! Doc Johnson isn't in town! Mrs. Tandra said she could help!"

Pa looked as though he could have blown steam through his ears, but when Hope coughed again, his face returned to its normal color. He went back to staring into the fire, and I, exhausted from my run, collapsed onto the floor in a fit of tears.

Georgia

I stroked my daughter's hair, crying into the pillow. Something was terribly wrong, and I was afraid I knew what it was. I had seen it once before, when I was just a girl. My sister had had it, and she had died within the week.

When the door opened, I jumped. "What are you doing here?"

Esther May held out her hands, hoping to calm me. "Please, honey. Doc Johnson be fi'teen miles from here. I only come to see what be wrong with da child. I could help until Doc come back."

I looked between the black woman and Hope. Hope was pale, and so hot. I nodded, and Esther May knelt down beside the bed. She felt her head and opened the gown to reveal the girl's chest.

"Oh, dear."

I flinched at those words. The examination moved on to Hope's mouth, revealing a strawberry-looking tongue.

"Oh, dear," Esther May repeated.

I sniffled. "She's...she's been too tired to get out of bed, and she's had a headache for about five hours."

Esther May nodded. "Mr. Bryant be around you or her very much?" I was surprised by this question, but shook my head. "You best send him into town to fetch ice from da ice house. Tell him to aks Mr. James at da mercantile to be puttin' it on my account. He must not be comin' back, and Elijah must be not leavin' dis house."

I was shocked to hear these words, but I covered my mouth with my apron and left the room. I did as I was asked, and sent Elijah to his room. When I returned to Hope's bed, Esther May was timing her heartbeat.

"Is it...?"

"Scarlet fever?"

I nodded, not wanting to hear the answer.

80

"I'm-a 'fraid so. It be very contagious. We be all stayin' here til da fever breaks or Hope be comin' out of it, whichever be comin' first."

I let tears pour out of my eyes. "But she will get over it?"

"We be catchin' it early. I sure hope so."

Elijah

Pa came to the house every day to see how Hope was doing. Every day for three weeks I turned him away. I spent most of my time staring into the flames of the fire. I was not allowed to leave the house until the fever was gone, and it gave me time to think about my family and myself.

I had grown up believing colored folk were horrible and worthy only of enslavement. Now it seemed as though the colored woman was going to save my sister.

This wasn't the first time I had questioned the things my parents had taught me. I had also been told that the Natives were savages and mean. Perhaps some of them were, but ever since the first day I had laid my eyes on Mia, my world had changed.

I saw the world in her eyes. She saw the world so much differently than everyone else. To her, it was a place of discovery and passion. She was the only one in any of the Linkville tribes who ventured out of the reservation because she wanted to. Most of the other Natives only came into town if they had to. Mia wanted to be in school. She wanted to learn so she could teach others, and she had put her trust in me. I was glad for it.

Ma and Esther May emerged from Hope's room, wiping their faces on their aprons. Esther May knelt in front of me for my daily check. "You feel sick?" I shook my head out of habit.

"Open your shirt."

I did without hesitation, but knew I didn't have the fever.

"Skin be clear; mouth?"

I stuck my tongue out.

"Good."

She paused. "I got good news for you."

I picked my head up immediately and met her friendly face. She was smiling back at me brightly.

"Is she...?"

Esther May patted my hand. "Fever broke. Couple more days to be restin' an' she be good as new."

I grinned and jumped out of my chair, nearly knocking Esther May over.

"Oh, sorry. Can I see her?"

Ma shook her head. "Not yet. She hasn't woken. Let her sleep."

My excitement deflated a bit. I wanted Hope to get better, but I needed to see for myself that she was okay. "Please, Ma. I promise I won't wake her up. I just want to see her."

Esther May smiled. "Let da child see his sister."

Ma sighed. "Oh, alright."

I grinned and raced for the door.

"Quiet!"

"Sorry, Ma," I whispered.

I opened the door and closed it quietly behind me. Hope still looked so helpless and weak. I sat on the bed beside her and took her hand in mine. "You gave us a scare, you little brat."

She squeezed my hand and stirred uncomfortably. "Hope? Are you okay?"

Hope stirred again and yawned. Slowly she opened her eyes.

A look of fear wormed its way across her face and she struggled to find me. "Elijah! Ma! Pa! Help me!!!"

Georgia

I hugged Esther May, something I never thought I'd do. The last three weeks were frightening to me, and Esther May was the only person who had gotten me through it. "Thank you, Mrs. Tandra."

"Oh, honey. Call me Esther."

I wiped my eyes with my apron. "I don't know what would have happened if Elijah hadn't brought you home."

Esther May smiled. "Listen, honey, I knowed your husban' won' be speakin' to me, but when Hope be feelin' better, you bring her in to da bak'ry an' I give you a righ' big meal, ya hear?"

I was about to respond when I heard Hope yell from inside her room.

"Good Lord!"

Hope

I felt someone sit on the bed beside me. I recognized

Elijah's touch, and when he spoke to me I squeezed his hand. I felt like I had been sleeping for weeks.

I released his hand and stretched, letting the air seep into my lungs like it was my first breath. Slowly I urged my eyes open...or had I?

Was it night? The room was dark, and I couldn't see anything. Outside my window I could hear birds chirping, something that rarely happened during the night. What was wrong? Everything was so dark, and my heart raced. The darkness, the horrible, sickening darkness, overtook me, and I felt like screaming. I groped awkwardly and frantically for my brother. "Elijah! Ma! Pa! Help me!!!"

I tried to jump off the bed; something hit the floor and Elijah's arms wrapped around me, holding me down.

The door flung open.

"Good Lord, child, what you doin'?!"

Someone pulled Elijah off of me and sat me up in bed.

"Calm down, child; everythin' be alright."

I groped at the woman's face to confirm the voice I was hearing. I could hear Elijah crying as the woman in front of me stroked my face. "Listen to me, darlin'." I stopped and sat there, listening. "Hope, honey, you know who I be?" I nodded, my eyes never moving. There was nothing more to focus on. "Who I am, child? An' how you know?"

"You're Jay's ma; I recognize your voice."

Ma broke into tears to match Elijah's sobs. Esther May laid me back on my pillow. "Go to sleep, child; everythin' be alright."

The exhaustion was taking over then. I knew the darkness was permanent, and it tired me. I closed my eyes and took a deep breath. I heard feet shuffling around, and Ma gasped.

"Da fever be takin' her sight."

Esther May

I walk to da bak'ry. I be so tired dat da smell of cakes, pastries, an' bread made me sick. Da store be empty, so I turne' da OPEN sign an' locked da door. My customers would be understan' why, when they found out about da poor Bryant girl.

It be alarmin' how somethin' as simple as a sore throat an' cough could turn so wrong. Scarlet fever come comin' to many, but it be rare to be so strong as to take someone's sight. I had had da fever myself when I be a girl; that be how I knowed to recognize it. Never before had I be seein' it so severe. I shook my head an' went to da stairs.

My legs be feelin' like they filled with lead, but I manage to climb to da second floor. Joseph an' Joshua be sittin' in da upstairs parlor in silence. As soon as he saw me come in, Joshua be rushin' out of his seat.

"How is she, Ma?"

I urge him to sit back down, then I sit down in da chair next to Joseph. I wipe' da tears from my face. Joshua be lookin' me in da eyes, an' I frowne'.

He be blamin' himself for dis. He come to da house last week to brin' more ice an' tol' me why Hope be gotten sick. Joshua be sensitive, a trait I possesse'. He be not takin' the news well. I dry my face an' after more silent moments, I cleare' my throat. "Da fever be takin' her sight."

Joshua

I blinke' at my ma. Had I heard her right? Had she just tol' me that the innocent little girl lost her sight? It was my fault. If I had only aks someone else to make the shirt for me; why her?

I didn't say anythin'; I couldn't. I kissed them goodnight an' left for home. My horse took me home slow an' steady, an' my mind wandered. Hope had slept through her birthday yesterday, an' she would probably think of this November as the worst ever.

I couldn't stop thinkin' 'bout her beautiful green eyes. She was the most bright-eye' child I knowed, an' now they were merely there for decoration, or so it seeme'. Would she ever be the same Hope again? The answer to that question would only come wif time.

My new question, however, was if the Bryants knowed why Hope had gotten so sick so suddenly. If they didn', would they fin' out? What would they do if they did?

I stopped the horse a few feet from the Bryants' house. From this spot I had a clear view into their window. Mr. an' Mrs. Bryant were cryin' in each other's arms. I wanted to run in there an' apologize, but Mr. Bryant already didn' like me.

"I want you to know that Ma and I don't blame you."

I jumped an' moved the horse aroun'.

Elijah was walkin' up the frozen road, a letter

clutche' in his hand. "We don't blame you, and you shouldn't blame yourself."

I shook my head. "If I hadn' aks her to make that blouse, she never woul' have been out in that mess."

Elijah walke' closer, an' petted the horse. I had always seen him as an image of his father, but this was certainly somethin' Mr. Bryant wouldn't have done. "You know Mia?"

I nodded.

"I might only be twelve, but I know what love is. I love Mia. I haven't told her, and my parents don't even know that I'm friends with her. Pa's likely to skin me alive when he finds out, but I don't care."

I smile'. I admire' Elijah's honesty. "Get yourself in the house before you come down with the fever."

Elijah nodde' an' heade' for the house.

"I'm-a help her somehow," I mumble', more to myself than to Elijah.

I waite' until he was safe in the house an' headed for my farm. Somehow I would make it up to that child, even if I lost the farm in the process. I had to make up for what I had caused.

Chapter 9

Dance in the Pacific

Hope

O ur second Christmas in Linkville had come and gone, and I still had barely left my room. I was too scared. It took me weeks to figure out how to find my way around the house, and it wasn't even that big. I still needed help finding the outside. The thought of venturing out into the outside world that I could no longer see frightened me more than anything.

Still, this day was special. It was January 15, and Elijah was turning thirteen.

He spent a lot of time in my room, reading me books and just talking. I was grateful, but I knew he hadn't been going out to see Mia because of it. I knew Elijah liked her, because of the way he talked about her, and it was a secret I kept to myself.

"Hope, honey. Come on out; it's time for dinner."

I sighed and groped for my slippers. I put them on the wrong feet, but they were on (it was an improvement).

I shuffled out of the room, my hands flopping around in front of me.

I had never wished I could see a stupid old door more than I did right then. I didn't feel like a nine-year-old anymore; I felt older...much older, like a helpless old woman who couldn't take care of herself. Somehow it didn't seem fair.

I felt a warm hand grasp my arm, and I was thankful for the help.

"Thanks, Pa," I said as he led me to a chair at the table. I sat, and he kissed the top of my head and walked away.

I was listening intently to the sounds around me. There was stew cooking on the fire, and Pa was rocking in Ma's rocking chair. Elijah came out of his room and gave me a hug. I was about to wish him a happy birthday when there was a knock on the front door.

"What are you doing here?" Pa had answered the door, and he obviously didn't like who it was.

"Please, sir, I come wif respec'."

I smiled for the first time in two months. It was the first time I had heard Joshua's voice since the night I had fallen into his arms. I wanted to apologize to him, to tell him it was my fault, but I couldn't without getting me and him both in trouble.

"I wondere' if I could speak wif you an' Mrs. Bryant. It about Hope."

I was curious as to why everyone was so quiet, and then there was a creak from the front door. I heard the strong footsteps cross the floor and knew that Pa, remarkably, had let him in.

Ma cleared her throat and put her hand on my shoulder. "What can we do for you, Mr. Tandra?"

Joshua cleared his throat next. I sensed the

uncomfortable feeling from everyone in the room. "I been sendin' telegrams an' I just gotten a reply. I been askin' about schools, special schools for the blind. There be one in St. Paul."

Ma gasped. "That's clear in Minnesota!"

"They can teach you to read an' write, Hope. They can teach you to cook an' clean an' play music, jus' like you did before."

I was a bit surprised that Joshua was addressing me. Did he know that Pa was still in the room? I blinked my useless eyes.

"Please do it, Miss Hope."

Pa slammed his fist on the table angrily. "And just how do you expect her schooling to be paid for, boy?"

Joshua was silent for a moment, and then he cleared his throat again. "Fidteen percen' of the Tandra Bak'ry profits will go to Hope's schoolin'."

I blinked my green eyes, not that it did any good; it was only darkness in front of me now. It seemed like years ago that I lost my sight, but in reality, I had only been blind for a short few weeks. My life was so different now; I hadn't been outside except to use the outhouse, and it seemed all of my friends from school had forgotten me. I wanted to scream. I no longer felt like a child. It was as if something had ripped out my inner being, and it hurt. I felt like my lungs were on fire.

I no longer knew if it was night or day, nor did I care; I only knew I had just woken up. Visions of the summer sun and watching the pelicans in the river flashed before my blackened eyes. They tormented me, took me to a time and a place I never would see again.

The sounds of children laughing as they played base ball were deafening. Why did it have to hurt so badly?

I felt around me, the soft fabric of my bed-quilt moved across my fingers. Why was there nothing to throw? I growled, not wanting to wake my parents if they were asleep. My heart beat in my chest strong and proud. Why wouldn't it just stop?

I fell back, dropping my head onto the soft feather pillow. The silence consumed me, almost ringing in my ears, and then a door creaked in another part of the house. Soft footsteps moved across the wood floor, and I heard a knock at my door.

"Can I come in?" Ma's voice was soft and caring.

"What?" My response was cold and short, a clue as to how angry I was. I just wanted everyone to leave me alone.

The door gave a creak and Ma walked in, shutting the door behind her. "Are you packed, dear?"

I shook my head, trying to hide the salty tear I felt drip from my eye.

"Hope, we're leaving in a few minutes. Today's the day we leave for Minnesota. We can't miss the stage."

I felt a lump in my throat. I had forgotten. Joshua didn't mean to interfere, and I did appreciate his effort in arranging the blind school. My stomach turned, my head swimming. Why did it have to be so far away? A deep hatred formed inside me, and I wanted to throw something again. This was his fault!

Then I felt warm, and slightly sad. 'This must be guilt,' I thought as I shook the thoughts away. Of course it wasn't his fault.

"I'm sorry, Ma. I didn't pack."

I heard Ma moving around, and something was set on the bed beside me. "Well, we just have to hurry.

Tell me what you want."

Fear consumed me again. What would I do alone in Minnesota? No, I wouldn't go, but I had to. Joshua had sacrificed so much.

I told Ma to put my bonnets and socks in, my dresses, and a sweater. She closed the travel bag and took my arm. It was when I made it to the door that I turned around to the black room, my mind on my secret friend. I didn't know how with my condition, but I wanted desperately to write to Joshua while I was away.

Holding my hand in front of me I reached for the dressing table. My fingers fell upon the cold, smooth leather and the pencil lying next to it. It was my writing book, and I clutched it tightly. A whole stream of emotions washed over me. Fear, sadness, and excitement. I couldn't keep up. I handed the leather-bound book to Ma and left the room.

Pa took my arm once I was outside, and led me to the wagon. "Your Ma's in the wagon. Just reach up and she'll pull you up."

I didn't want to go yet. Where was Elijah? I listened intently for any sign of him. "Where is he?"

Pa sighed. "He's already gone to school."

A tear fell down my cheek. My own brother wasn't even here to say goodbye. It was going to be a long stage ride to San Francisco, and it would be even longer before I would speak to my brother again.

"Pa, is he staying alone?" I reached up clumsily and found Ma's hands. She helped me as I struggled into the wagon, and Pa climbed up next to me. I nearly fell over the back of the seat when the wagon lurched forward. I didn't like not being able to see where we were going.

"Pa? You didn't answer my question." I felt like I

was being ignored.

"No, darling. He's staying with Miss Strong."

The wagon ride into town wasn't very long. In fact, I was surprised at how short it was. The cold air nipped at my face, but it didn't cover up the wonderful smell of the Tandra Bakery. It was the one thing I would always remember about Linkville.

It was two weeks before Ma and Pa had finally agreed on letting me go to the blind school. Pa didn't want to take the money from the Tandras. The fact that he had was a big step for the otherwise prejudiced man. I, however, wished he hadn't taken it. It meant that I had to leave my home for possibly several years. We had only been in Linkville for a little over a year, but I loved it.

Pa helped me down from the wagon and then into the stagecoach. I had never been on one before. The seat was soft but thin, and I had a feeling it would become very uncomfortable very soon.

I expected my parents to sit down beside me, but they hadn't come into the stage yet. I wondered where they were, but stayed silent, listening. People were driving by in their wagons and the children at the school were outside playing. I wondered if Elijah was out there, and if he'd come to say goodbye. It pained me to think about not saying goodbye to him before I left. Perhaps he was off in his secret hiding spot with Mia. I hoped it would work for the two of them.

Finally, the stagecoach moved and I felt my parents sit beside me. Ma put her arm around me in a hug. "Mr. and Mrs. Tandra just gave us the money for the train and for the first month of your schooling. Elijah will take the horses and the wagon to Miss Strong's house. They wish you the best."

I gave a weak smile. "Am I going to get to say goodbye to Elijah before we leave?"

Pa took my hand in his. "He felt it best that he stay at school. He doesn't want you to go, but he knows you need to."

I nodded and fell silent. I hated the darkness. No matter what I did, the blackness enclosed me. I wished I could have taken that day back. I wouldn't have gone out in that storm, but it was done, and I couldn't change it now.

The stage lurched forward and bounced along the dirt roads. Pa said it was a long way to San Francisco, and I wished I was at home and in school with my brother and the other children.

It took the stagecoach nearly a week to reach San Francisco. The air was different there, cold and salty. As I was helped out of the stage, I noticed there were a lot more people. San Francisco was big. The last time I had heard this many people, we were in Virginia City.

I was led up a hill, and then down. We went up a second, and a third. It was a very tiring, uncomfortable walk. We passed many people; I heard them whisper about me. They told each other to get out of my way so they wouldn't hurt me. I wanted to cry, but I wouldn't give in to their rudeness.

Finally, my parents stopped, and I was guided to a bench. Ma sat down beside me and squeezed my hand.

"We're at the train station. Your Pa's gone to get the tickets. We're just waiting here for him."

I shifted on the bench. I was tired, and fell on Ma's

shoulder. People were walking by and talking about the train rides they were preparing for.

The sounds of people were normal to me, but there was something different here. It was a strange sound. It was like a fierce wind was coming and going. It would get louder, and then softer until it was gone, and then it would come back. In the distance, birds were squawking and children playing, but that wind... or was it wind? I didn't feel it on my face. It seemed as though it was calm and quiet, but this sound was there, and I didn't know what it was.

"Ma, what's that sound?"

Ma stroked my hair. "What sound, dear?"

I listened again, trying to figure out a way to describe it. "I'm not sure. It gets louder, and then it goes away, and then it gets louder again. It sort of sounds like the wind, but it doesn't. Do you hear it, Ma?"

Ma squeezed my hand; it was her way of smiling at me. "I think you're talking of the ocean, child."

My eyes widened. I had dreamed about coming to the ocean since I first heard about it from my teacher back in Rolla. It made me angry that I was here now and couldn't see it, but I wanted to be close. I needed to experience it in any way I could. "Ma, take me to the ocean. Please?"

Ma sighed. "I don't know if that's a good idea, Hope."

I sat up, a new excitement flowing through my veins. "Please, Ma."

Pa walked up then, and sat down on the other side of me. "What's the matter, Hope?" I turned to face him and felt for his hands. When I found them, I squeezed.

"Pa, I want to go to the ocean."

He sighed.

"Please, Pa. I want to do it before we leave."

Ma took my hand. "Do we have time, Thomas?"

He didn't answer, but pulled me up. I grinned and followed him back outside. He led me up and down three hills, and then down a long flight of wooden steps. When we reached the bottom, he stopped me on the last one.

"Listen to me, darling." I stayed silent. "When you take the next step, it's going to be very different. It's not like normal dirt. It's sand, and it's very soft until we get closer to the water." I wondered how he knew about it. I didn't think he had been to the ocean before, but perhaps he had. Or perhaps he had heard about it from someone else.

Ma put her hand on my shoulder to draw my attention. "Thomas, let the child experience the sand between her toes."

There was silence before he helped me sit down on the steps. "Take your shoes off, Hope." I obeyed, and struggled to untie the laces. When I managed to get them off, I took my stockings off too, and put them inside my shoes.

Ma scooped them up out of my hand. "You'll enjoy the sand this way."

I smiled as Pa pulled me back up. "Are you ready?"

I nodded and he continued out off of the steps. I stepped out, too, and the sand hit my toes. It surprised me at first, and Pa stopped so I could get the feel for it. I wiggled my toes and the grainy sand wiggled its way around my feet. It was soft, yet scratchy; I couldn't tell if I wanted it on my feet or if I wanted to shake it off. Pa led me farther out, and the more I walked through the soft sand, the more I liked it. It was dry and difficult to walk in, but I wouldn't have passed it up for anything.

As we went on, something changed, and I was confused. The sand was getting colder, and my feet weren't sinking so far. "Pa, where are we? What am I walking on?"

He squeezed my arm to reassure me that everything was okay. "It's the sand, darling. We're close to the water now, so the sand is wet." I nodded, understanding the sensation on my feet. I could feel the water over the sand. I was listening intently to the sound of the ocean, until Pa spoke again. "I'm going to take you a little ways further, and I still have my shoes on, so I'm going to let you stand there and I'm going to back up. If you get scared, or you want to come back, let me know and I'll be right there to get you, okay?"

I nodded, and Pa led me a few feet farther. He let go, patting my arm to reassure me, and then he was gone.

I stood there listening to the sound of the ocean. It was growing quiet, and after a short few seconds, it was getting louder. I nearly screamed when the water hit me. It was cold and came nearly to my knees, and it was gone almost as quickly as it had come. It was a weird feeling. I felt like I was moving. I felt as though the ocean was taking me with it, and I started to get scared, but the water was gone, and so was the sound. It was coming back, louder and louder, and the water hit my legs again.

I smiled. It was amazing! It was like the water was being swished back and forth in a bowl. What made it do that? Why did it constantly come in and go out? How I wished I could see it.

A small wind blew through my hair, and I closed my eyes. I took a deep breath and suddenly realized that the strange smell was of the ocean. It was strange, yes, but it was beautiful to me.

I wished I didn't have to leave, but Pa had come and taken my arm, leading me away from the stunning motion and sounds of the water that had been surrounding me. I closed my eyes, trying to imagine what it all looked like. I had to remember this; it might very well have been the last and only time I would be here. In a short time I would be on the train going back east to St. Paul. My parents were leaving me behind, and it made me angry.

Chapter 10

The Moon's Flight

Elijah

I couldn't sleep. It was a strange bed and a strange house. Nothing was normal anymore. Part of me wanted to blame myself for Hope's loss of sight. The other part knew it was silly. Mia kept reminding me every day that it wasn't my fault, and perhaps she was the only thing that was keeping me in reality throughout this whole ordeal.

There was a knock on the door, pulling me out of my thoughts, and I jumped. "Uh...come in."

The door opened, and Mia walked in. She tipped her head and smiled at me.

I sprung up off of the bed with a smile. "Mia! Wait, what are you doing here? It's Friday night; aren't you supposed to be on the reservation?"

Mia sat down on the bed beside me. "I told the chief I needed help with some homework that I needed to turn in Monday. No one on the reservation can help me, so Pa let me come."

"But we don't have homework due Monday. We're almost done for the winter."

She chuckled. "I know that, but it worked to get me here, didn't it?"

I gave her a weak smile. "Yeah, it did."

"She's going to be alright; she's a strong child."

I laughed. "You know, it's only been four years since we were her age, and already we call her a child."

I met her eyes, and we stared at each other for a few moments, my heart racing. Should I ask? What would she think of me?

My heart skipped. It was now or never... "Mia, have you ever thought about getting married?"

She blushed and looked away, staring at the floor silently. "The chief says I'm to marry someone in the tribe."

I felt a twinge of jealousy and pain. Someone marrying my Mia! I couldn't stand the thought of her with anyone else. "Oh." It was all I could manage at the moment.

She took my hands in hers, and I looked up into her brown eyes. "I don't want to, Elijah James. Rescue me!"

A tear rolled down her brown cheek and I wiped it away. I leaned forward, my heart beating even faster, and kissed her. It was a new feeling, but it was short and sweet.

My spine tingled. She smiled at me.

I took a deep breath. "Marry me?"

Mia

I blinked. Surely I hadn't heard him right. Maybe my understanding of the English language wasn't as good as I had thought.

My heart was racing. Elijah made me feel good about myself. I saw the world exactly how I wanted to see it when I looked in his eyes, but surely he couldn't love me. Our worlds, as much as I hated to admit it, were very different. I was the daughter of the chief, a princess. He was the son of a farmer, a white boy.

I couldn't see how it would work. We would be banished from our families. Things were not well on the reservation as it was. It had only been three years since the end of the Indian war, and some of the men were still hostile about it. So far, I had kept that part of my life secret from everyone, including Elijah. Still, I couldn't see living life without him. He encouraged me to do things I might have never done before. He was my life.

A smile broke onto my face, and I hugged him. I wanted this, but I also needed to be sensible. We were, after all, only thirteen. "I will, but not just yet."

Elijah pulled me out of the hug and our eyes met. "Mia, I love you."

I smiled and gave him a quick kiss. Then I got up and left the room, leaving Elijah to himself.

I would like my walk home tonight.

Elijah

I came out of my new room to go to school with a yawn. I

hadn't gotten much sleep; I had been too busy thinking about what had happened between Mia and me.

It had been three weeks since my parents had left for St. Paul with Hope, and I wondered when they were coming back. I had received a post from them a little over a week before, to tell me they had arrived in San Francisco and were leaving by train for St. Paul. I missed my sister, and part of me regretted not saying goodbye to her. Yet I also knew that it would have been too hard for the both of us, and I couldn't bring myself to walk over to the stagecoach that day.

I knew she'd be okay. Hope was a strong girl, and she adapted easily to things. It wouldn't be long before she'd be home, and I would scoop her up in my arms and give her the hug I so desperately wanted to give her.

I sighed when the schoolhouse came into view. The only good thing was that I'd be seeing Mia in a few minutes. It was still early, and she probably hadn't arrived yet.

I sat down on a log nearby and set to picking at the bark. The morning sun was glaring off of the late-February snow and I had to squint to see anything. Some of the boys were walking up to the schoolhouse, and they immediately raced for the balls sitting on the top step. I smiled. Hope would have been right in there with them.

The boys started to play, and I watched them for lack of not knowing what else to do. Ten minutes went by, and then they spotted me. They stopped the ball game and walked towards me.

"Hey, Elijah, you heard about the savage girl?"

I fought the urge to hit him for calling Mia that. What were they talking about? Was she alright? My heart pounded for the thought of it. "If you've got something to say, then say it, Jared!"

Jared gave a mischievous grin. "Just thought you'd like to know your little Injun friend isn't coming back to school anymore."

I stood up, ready to defend her if I needed to. Jared obviously knew something I didn't. "Get on with it!"

Jared and the other boys laughed. "So it is you. See, we heard the Injuns are keepin' her locked up in one of their teepees because she's been sneaking off the reservation when she's not supposed to. It's you she's been runnin' off to see, isn't it?"

"What's it to you?" I inched closer; I didn't like the way this was going.

"Come on, you love that Injun, don't you?"

I couldn't take it anymore. I leapt onto Jared and hit him in the face. We fell to the ground and I tried to hold him down. Jared put up a good struggle for being half my size, but my adrenaline gave me strength. I hit him again, and blood oozed out of Jared's nose.

Feeling satisfied, I released him and went into the schoolhouse. I was going to tell Miss Strong the truth before the boys had a chance to stretch it.

"Miss Strong, I've got something to tell you."

Punished...I can't believe my own teacher punished me! I slammed the small cabin's door shut behind me. Miss Strong had stayed behind to talk with Jared's parents. I wasn't allowed to leave the cabin save for going to school and the outhouse until my parents got home.

"Yeah, who knows when that will be?" I flung myself onto my bed, thinking and worrying about how

Mia was.

Maybe I would sneak out and try to rescue her tonight? I shook my head. Miss Strong slept like there were rocks under her sheets. Any small sound and she was out of bed checking the house. It drove me mad.

I sighed. There was absolutely no way I could get away with it. I would have to wait, and hope that nothing happened to Mia. In that moment, I made myself a promise. I would be there to get her, no matter what it took.

I just hoped I wouldn't be too late.

It was the end of March, and I sat atop Pa's wagon. I was waiting for the stage in front of the hotel. Hope was at her new school, and Ma and Pa were expected to come back on the stage.

I still hadn't seen Mia. As each day passed, my worries got stronger. Whether she was okay or not, I didn't know. Deep down, I knew she was probably angry that I hadn't come to get her yet, but living with the teacher did not make it easy to get away.

A horse neighed at the other end of the road, and I spotted the stage crossing the bridge. I smiled and jumped off of the wagon.

The coach stopped in its usual spot, halfway between the hotel and the doctor's office, and I smiled when my parents climbed out.

"Ma! Pa!"

Ma let out a sigh of relief and hurried towards me. I grunted when she hugged me, but I hugged her back excitedly. "Two months is far too long to not hear from my son. What have you been up to?"

I blushed. "I...I got into trouble." It sounded funny to tell my Ma that someone else had punished me, but I was sure Miss Strong would if I didn't. "I got into a fight."

Pa gave me a disappointed look. "I hope that teacher of yours gave you extra homework." I smiled and hugged him. "Missed you, son."

We spent the wagon ride home in silence, and I helped them get settled back into the house. There hadn't been any life in it since they left in early February, and even the fire mantle had icicles on it. Pa started a fire, and Ma served the meal we had bought at the restaurant.

Pa joined us at the table, and the three of us took each other's hands for prayer. "Lord, we come to you tonight, not to ask for ourselves, but to ask for the one who should be sitting with us at this table. Hope will need your strength. It won't be easy, and we'll miss her dearly while she's gone. Bless this food and this family, all present and not present. Amen."

Ma and I repeated the last word before starting our meal. It was silent for the most part, and then I looked up at them.

I debated whether to tell them of my worries about Mia. What would Pa do? I'd have to tell them why I was worried. If I did that, it would lead to the reason Hope was out in that storm, and I didn't want to be the one to let that slip. I took a drink of my milk instead, and then Ma cleared her throat.

"Elijah, honey, we have something we'd like to tell you."

I put my glass down and looked up at her.

"We had a visit to a doctor before we headed home, and he told us that we're going to have a new baby in the family."

My eyes widened. How could they? Had they forgotten that Hope would be back some day? It's not like they were leaving her in St. Paul forever! I slammed my hand on the table; it stung, but I went on. "How could you?! Have you forgotten that you still have Hope?!"

Pa stood up and pulled me in front of his face angrily. "Don't you dare speak to us like that, Elijah James! We love your sister, and this baby is not coming to replace her! Are we clear?"

I felt a tear roll down my cheek, but I didn't say anything. My emotions from not seeing or hearing from Mia were getting to me, and I didn't have a response to my parents.

Ma put a hand on Pa's shoulder. Pa let go, and I went on to my room.

I spent the next hour pacing. I had to get to the reservation. I had to get to Mia. Where would we go once we were out of there? We had to go somewhere.

I started picturing the places I had seen during our move to Linkville. The one place that stuck in my memory the most was Virginia City. People of all ethnicities were free to live and work there. Mia would be safe there.

I slipped into my bed and started the wait until my parents were asleep in their room next door.

I woke with a start. I hadn't meant to fall asleep, but my worries had left me exhausted. I rolled over to look out the window, hoping it was still dark outside.

The moon was shining brightly through the glass, and I sighed with relief. I still had time to get out of the house before my parents would catch me. Pulling my travel pack out from under my bed, I put my clothes and a bedroll inside. I would take the horse I had gotten for my birthday; no one would miss it. I looked around the room and, satisfied with what I had packed, left my room for the last time.

It was still chilly outside, and I was glad I had put my coat on. Saddling my horse, I climbed on and raced away from my home.

The town was quiet. It was still late in the night and it would be hours before anyone discovered I was gone. This I was thankful for. I would need the head start to ensure our escape.

I sighed when I reached the end of town. I hadn't been discovered yet. Now I just needed to make it the two hours to the reservation without being seen.

The horse carried me to an old abandoned cabin, but suddenly stopped. "Come on, we're not saying here tonight. Let's go." I urged the horse on, but he didn't move. I growled and jumped off; maybe he was stuck.

"Elijah, please say that's you."

I looked up to the door of the cabin. Mia was standing there, dressed in nothing but the old holey blanket off of the cabin's bed. I tied the horse to the post and ran up the cabin's steps, scooping her up in my arms. I then carried her back inside and shut the door.

"Elijah, I got away, but they're looking for me. They nearly found me today."

I set her on the bed and took her face in my hands. It was bruised, but otherwise she looked okay. I kissed her gently on the lips; my stomach flipped.

"I'm so sorry. I didn't mean to take so long."

I looked around the cabin, trying to find clothes for her. There was an old pair of pants and a flannel shirt. I grabbed them and threw them to her. "Put those on. We need to go." When she was ready, I made sure it was safe for us to leave. I led her out and climbed back on the horse, pulling her up behind me. Then I took a deep breath and kicked. We needed to get as far away as we could. If we were lucky, we would reach Virginia City in a little over a week.

A week had come and gone, and Mia and I had not yet arrived in Virginia City. Mia had gotten sick about halfway through the week, and I thought it best to stay in one place for a few days. We were only a few miles from the town now, and Mia was leaning on my back, sound asleep.

I slowed the horse and took in the smell of the air around me. The weather was warmer in Nevada, and I liked the idea of being on my own. I knew it would be difficult for the both of us at first, but we would make it.

The horse began the climb up a mountain, and as the sites of mines and houses came into view I shook Mia awake gently. When she woke, I smiled. I only wanted to make her happy. "Welcome to Virginia City, Mia."

Chapter 11

Letters

Hope

I yawned, feeling the sun on my face from the window. It must have been morning.

I had been at the school for nearly five months, and still refused to listen to the teacher. So far, the teachers had been patient, and kept feeding and bathing me. Still, I was unhappy. Life without my sight felt dumb and pointless, and I wanted to go home and hide in the corner of my room like I had done before. At least then I'd be with people who cared for me. Sure it was childish, but that's how I felt.

There was a knock and I growled. "Who is it?"

The door opened, and the soft, strong footsteps of my teacher, Jenny, filled the room. "It's time for breakfast." Her cold hand slipped over mine, and I pulled away. She sighed. "I thought I'd tell you that a letter arrived for you this morning."

I sat up and groped around the bed for my

dressing robe. "Well, who's it from, then?" I struggled to get the robe on, and Jenny sighed again.

"We don't know. There was only your name and the name of the school on it." She helped me into the robe. "Just says it comes from Virginia City."

I was confused. Who would be writing to me from Nevada? I didn't know anyone there, at least not that I knew of.

"If you want to know who wrote the letter, you're going to have to learn to read it yourself. It's written in Braille." Jenny walked out of the room and shut the door.

I growled and tapped my fingers on my leg. The whole thing was frustrating. I hadn't worn normal clothes since the day my parents left. No one would help me get my clothes on. In fact, I was pretty sure I was lucky to be getting baths and food.

I wanted to know what that letter was. I sighed and fumbled around the bed on the floor, looking for my shoes. I found them and placed them on the bed to be found easier. Putting my hands out in front of me, I clumsily felt around, shuffling towards the room's wall.

"Ow!" I had found the bedside table and fell to the floor, grasping for my throbbing toe. When the pain subsided, I punched the floor and stumbled to my feet. After a few more hits to the toe from various objects around the room, I finally found the wall. I walked around, sliding my fingers on the cold wood, until I found the dresser. I sighed and opened the top drawer.

The first drawer, after some struggling to get it open, contained socks and my undergarments. I didn't need those. Moving onto the second, which was just as stubborn as the first, I found dresses and bonnets. Which ones matched, I didn't know. I fumbled around and managed to get my dress on right. Then I slammed the second drawer and turned back, shuffling for the bed. I managed to find my shoes again without too much trouble, so I fell onto the bed with a grunt and shoved a foot into my shoe. Thankfully it was the right foot in the right shoe, and I shoved the other foot in the other one.

I rose ineptly to my feet and shook my head. I wasn't going to make it out of that room without help, and I clutched the bedpost in an attempt to stay on my feet.

"Jenny!" There was no sound; the room was eerily quiet. If something had touched me or if there was a noise, I would have screamed.

I listened carefully. After a few more silent moments, I cleared my throat. "Jenny!"

The door opened and I jumped. Jenny came into the room and laughed. "I'm sorry; I didn't mean to scare you. Everyone just finished breakfast." I glared at her. "Well, is our little princess finally ready to join the living?"

"Very funny."

Jenny chuckled and put my arm in hers, leading me out of the room. "Since you're ready to cooperate now, I'll warn you that it won't be easy."

I sighed when Jenny ushered me into the empty chair. There was a clang somewhere behind me, and Jenny came back. "Your breakfast is in front of you." She took my hands and placed them on the table. "No more being fed. It's time you learned to feed yourself. Your knife is on the left, spoon and fork on the right."

I nodded, moving my fingers up and down the silver. Jenny moved my hand to the top of the plate. "Your meals are set like a clock. Scrambled eggs at twelve, sausage at three, bacon at six, and toast at nine." My hand was redirected to the top-right of my plate, and my fingers bumped against the glass. "We drink orange juice for breakfast. You will find your glass in the same position every meal." Jenny let go of my hand and sat in the chair beside me. "If you want butter, syrup, or anything else, you ask for it. Someone will give it to you. Understand?"

I nodded, trying to picture my plate and glass in my mind. It seemed simple enough, but this was just breakfast. How would I know about the other meals? I heard Jenny clearing the table from everyone else's breakfast and I sighed. This was going to be a long day...

Three days had gone by, and I was exhausted. It was tiring trying to learn how to take care of myself. I never had to do this much work when I could see! The hardest part was making the bed. If the blankets weren't perfectly smooth, Jenny...stubborn Jenny...pulled the blankets off and made me do it again. It usually took me about four tries before I had it good enough to meet Jenny's approval.

I had learned how to find my matching bonnets. They were arranged by color; alphabetical order. Blues were first, then brown, green, red, and yellow. I had finally learned the layout of my room; my toes were thankful. My favorite thing about the house was the indoor outhouse, or water closet. I didn't have to venture outside to do my business; all I had to do was walk fifteen steps to the left from my room! It was simple things like these that I had always taken for granted.

The end of summer was coming, and I was suddenly looking forward to going to school with the five other children in the house. I'd have to learn to read and write first, though.

Jenny would be up soon to get me for my first lesson, but I was ready for her. I made my way to the top of the stairs, and when I heard Jenny take the first step, I cleared my throat.

Jenny stopped and gasped, startled. "Why, Hope! You're dressed and out of your room without me!"

I gave Jenny a smile and nodded. "I figured if you were already in the classroom I shouldn't make you come and get me." I clutched the banister tightly and took the first step for the first time alone. At the bottom, I was taken into a hug.

"Jenny...can't....breathe."

Jenny let go and held her arm out. I took it, and was led into the small classroom. It was thirty steps from the staircase; ten steps to my desk. I sat down, ready to begin my first reading lesson. I had always liked to read, and was curious how I would still be able to do it.

She set a book in front of me and I placed my fingers on the soft, warm, leather cover. There were bumps on it, and I tried to wipe them away like dust.

"No, honey. That's called Braille. It's how you're going to be able to read."

I shook my head, running my fingers along the cover. "I don't understand."

Jenny opened the book and pulled my hands away from it. "Just listen for a moment."

I set my hands on the table and turned my head slightly to let Jenny know I was listening. "About 47 years ago, a blind Frenchman by the name of Louis Braille decided that he wanted to be able to read, just like everyone else. So he invented a system of a rectangular six-dot cell. You read it with your fingers, according to the combination of the six dots." Jenny took my hand and placed it on the first page of the book. "What do you feel?"

My finger was sitting on six dots. They were set in two columns and three rows. "There's six dots."

"Good. That's a Braille cell. You read them from the top to the bottom, and as the dots change so do the letters." She moved my fingers over a little. "What do you feel now?"

I moved my fingers around. It felt like somebody had carved the letter 'A' into the paper. "The letter 'A'."

"Good." Jenny moved my hand over again, and my fingers were resting on a single dot that would have been in the top left corner of the six dots. "That is how you read the letter 'A' in Braille." She moved my hand over again, and my fingers were now sitting on two dots, one right over the other. "This is the letter 'B'." She moved me over again, and the dots moved from one over the other to side by side. "'C'." Now there were three dots; two next to each other and one below the right one. "'D'." Now there were two dots, one on top and one diagonally to the right below it. "'E'." Now, three dots. This time two next to each other, and one below the first one. "'F'." Now, four in a square. "'G'."

My eyes lit up. This was perfect! I'd be reading in no time! It certainly was easier than it sounded, and I couldn't wait to read my first book!

My reading lessons continued on through October, and I was reading nearly as fluently as I had before the fever. I was also learning to write, both with my Braillewriter and with a pencil.

I had already written my first letter to my parents, and Jenny had gone off to send it, along with the mail the other students had for her.

I was resting; the whole school had gone on a picnic, and I had learned to fish again! It left me tired and I need a nap. I was just about to fall asleep when someone knocked on the door.

I popped my eyes open and sat up, rubbing my tired face. "Come in."

The door opened, and I recognized Jenny's footsteps immediately. "Hope, I don't think you remember, so I brought you that letter that arrived a few months ago. You never asked for it."

The letter! I had forgotten about it completely.

Jenny laid it in my outstretched hand, and I tore the envelope open. Inside, I found a letter typed in Braille. I unfolded it and ran my fingers across the paper:

Dear Hope,

I know this will probably be quite a shock for you, but this is Elijah. Mia was being abused by some of the Indians, so we ran away. We're living on our own in Virginia City now! I thought you might like that, because of how much you liked the town when we passed through it during our move to Linkville.

If you're wondering, I met a man who works at the mercantile, and he's blind! He told me about this Braille stuff and when

I told him about you he urged me to let him teach me how to write a letter to you. So here I am, and I hope I've written it okay!

Mia says hello and we both miss you a lot. If Ma and Pa never told you, they're having a baby. I feel kind of bad because the night I left I told them they were trying to replace you. Oh! Please don't tell them where I am! I haven't written them yet, and I'm not going to until Mia turns 14. She says once she's fourteen she can choose to leave the tribe, but I'm afraid they'll come after her if they find out.

Well, I don't want to wear out your fingers (I laughed at this remark; Elijah was happy again, and I was glad) so I'm going to let you go. I hope you're doing well, and we love you.

Your brother, Elijah (and Mia too!)

I folded the letter carefully and put it inside my bedside table drawer. I had forgotten Jenny was in the room until she spoke. "Who's it from?"

I gave Jenny the biggest, brightest, happiest smile I had had in a long time. "From my brother."

November had snuck up on me, bringing with it the various illnesses of cold weather, and I was sick with a horrible headache. It literally felt like my head was going to explode. The sun was shining on my face through the window and I rubbed it.

"Jenny!" I rolled over and covered my head with the pillow.

Jenny's footsteps came down the hall and the door creaked open. "What's the matter?"

I groaned. "I'm sick." Jenny pulled the pillow off of my head. "I feel like my head is going to explode."

Jenny laughed softly and rolled me onto my stomach. "You have a migraine."

She rubbed my back and neck for nearly an hour and when she was done, I rolled over. "Feel better now?"

I nodded. "A little."

Jenny patted me on my knee and stood from the bed. "You have a birthday party in two hours, if you're up to it." Her footsteps crossed the room and stopped before the door opened. "Can we expect you? The other girls are looking forward to it."

I smiled and sat up on my bed. I had almost forgotten it was the 20th of November. "Yes. I think I'll just rest for a while. Maybe I can get rid of this headache."

The door creaked open and Jenny left the room. When the door shut again, I groaned and fell onto my pillow. I should be happy about my tenth birthday, but so far it seemed my parents really had forgotten about me. Perhaps the baby, who was probably healthy and could see, really was taking my place.

I pushed the brush through my soft black curls. I could no longer feel the sun on my face and knew it was dark, or just before dark.

There was a knock on the door and Jenny came in. "I'm almost ready, Jenny." I walked to the bed (three steps from the dresser) and bent over. I slipped my feet into my shoes and walked over to the table (ten steps) that held the wash basin.

"You really are doing wonderfully, Hope."

I continued washing as though Jenny hadn't said anything. I was too afraid of yelling about my parents. Still, Jenny knew something was bothering me, and she sighed. "Hope, honey, please tell me what's wrong?"

I slammed my hand on the table. "Nothing is wrong, Jenny! It's my tenth birthday and my parents don't care anymore! Everything is fine!"

Jenny put her hands on my shoulders. "Hope, we received a telegram from your pa this afternoon." I glared at nothing in particular, not sure I wanted to hear what my pa had said. Jenny sighed. "He sent his love and apologized for not being here for your birthday, but your ma had the baby early this morning."

I swallowed the lump in my throat. I felt like someone had hit me hard in the stomach. Suddenly, I was mad at myself for being angry at that baby.

A tear fell down my face and Jenny wiped it away. "Did...did he...did he say what the baby was?"

"No. He said he'd send a letter to you soon." There were a few moments of silence, and finally Jenny wrapped her arms around me. I returned the hug. "You have company for your birthday, though."

I pulled out of the hug and sniffled. "Who?" I wasn't sure who would have come to see me. I didn't think it would have been Elijah...he probably wouldn't have had enough money.

"Well, I will warn you that he was only allowed in because Mrs. Brinks isn't here." Mrs. Brinks was the house mother, and she reminded me a lot of my pa, only worse. "Come on, dear."

Jenny led me out of the room and down the stairs.

We stopped in front of the front door, and Jenny left me alone. Finding the room eerily silent, I cleared my throat. "Hello?"

Three strong footsteps moved toward me, and someone took me into a hug. "You look wonderful!"

I recognized Joshua's voice immediately, and I suddenly understood why Jenny was so worried about Mrs. Brinks. "Hello, Jay. How are you?!" It was so good to hear his voice, and it was hard to contain my excitement.

Joshua let me go. "Can we sit and talk somewhere?"

I didn't think he should stay long, and shook my head. "I don't want to get Jenny in trouble with our house mother or anyone else. We should go somewhere else to talk. Wait here." I held my hand out to my side and walked (twenty-five steps) down the hall to the sitting room, running my fingers along the wall. "Jenny?"

"Yes, Hope? Is everything okay?"

I nodded, wishing Jenny wouldn't sound so alarmed. "Yes, everything is fine. I was just wondering if I could go out and..." I wondered what to say. I wasn't sure if Jenny was alone.

"Yes?"

"And get a drink."

"What about your party?"

I put a frown on my face. Jenny wasn't going to let me go, and I really wanted to talk to Joshua. "I won't be gone very long. A few minutes at the most." I gave Jenny a pleading look, hoping it was convincing enough.

Jenny let out a sigh. I heard her get out of her chair and cross the room, speaking softly. "I will be in a lot of trouble if Mrs. Brinks finds out about this. Why don't I make up some hot cocoa, and you can take your guest into the garden. It's warm enough for that for a few minutes."

I smiled.

"I'll be right back, children."

Jenny left the room and I returned to the front door. "Jay?"

"I'm still here."

I smiled and went to the coat rack to find my coat. I felt Joshua's hands reach to help me. "Thank you."

Jenny returned and led us around the house to the gardens. There was a wooden bench under a tall gazebo somewhere in the middle of the grounds. I sat and Joshua sat down beside me.

"I wasn't expecting it to be you." I smiled.

"I know. I come to deliver a crop and get somethin' for Ma's bak'ry an' a few thin's for the mercantile. I hope you don' min'."

I shook my head. "I don't, but I can't say that for everyone else in the house."

Joshua sighed. "I know. You won' be in trouble?"

Jenny re-emerged and she handed us both a steaming cup of hot chocolate.

"Thank you, Jenny." She left, and I took a sip of the hot liquid. It stung my insides, but tasted good. "The house mother is the one to worry about, but she's not even in St. Paul, that I know of."

Joshua sipped his hot chocolate before speaking again. "You okay?"

I didn't answer, curious why he was asking me such a question.

Joshua sighed. "It just...I guess I feel responsible, an' I wan' to make sure you doin' alright."

I smiled. I wished that everyone cared as much as this man did. I put a soft hand on his. "Jay, I don't want you to blame yourself. I would have gotten sick whether

I had come over or not."

He took another drink, and we spent the next several moments in comfortable silence, drinking our treat. Finally, Joshua spoke. "Did you knowed your brother is missin'?"

My face went pink. How was I going to get through this conversation without telling him that I knew where Elijah was? Somehow I had to. I couldn't let anyone know I knew where he was, not for two more months, at which time Mia would turn fourteen. I retreated to finishing my hot chocolate. "Yes, I did know he was missing." I pleaded silently that this would be enough for him.

He cleared his throat, but I stood up and pulled him up too, stopping him from saying whatever he was going to say.

"What you doin'?"

I didn't answer, but pulled up a loose board on the bench. There was a secret hole I had discovered months ago, when Mrs. Brinks started acting funny about my writing, and I reached my hand inside. I pulled out a small book and a box and handed it to Joshua.

"What be this?"

"Don't open it now. The book is a Braille book. Inside the box there's a Braille-writer. Take it home, and I want you to promise you'll write to me. I can write to you, and..." I stopped in the middle of my sentence. What if he didn't want to write to me? What if no one wanted to write to me anymore?

Joshua kissed my cheek. "Thank you, Miss Hope. I will, I promise."

I smiled, and we stood in another few moments of silence.

He had just cleared his throat again to say

something, when Jenny slammed the back door of the house and ran to us.

"Hope! You have to get up to your room, now! Mrs. Brinks is home early!"

I'm sure the look now on my face was one of terror, and I nearly fell over. Jenny caught me and stood me back up.

"I'm-a write, Hope, I promise." Joshua squeezed my hand, and then he was gone.

Jenny was running back towards the house so fast that she nearly picked me up off the ground. Somehow, she managed to get me back to my room just in time for Mrs. Brinks' footsteps to come down the hall and knock on the door.

"Come in." Jenny was helping me tie a dress apron over my dress.

The door creaked open, and the eerie footsteps that belonged to the house mother came into the room. "Well, don't you look pretty, Miss Hope."

I smiled into the wall I was facing. "Thank you, Mrs. Brinks."

Jenny finished tying the apron and turned me around. "She's ready for her party, Ma."

"Wonderful." Mrs. Brinks clapped her hands and pushed Jenny out of the way. She took my arms and pulled me into a hug. "I was so worried I was going to miss your birthday."

I shook my head. "That's okay, Mrs. Brinks."

The woman chuckled. "Oh, dear, call me Ma."

I shook my head. "No, ma'am. I won't do that."

Mrs. Brinks scoffed. "Why not, child?"

I wondered why Jenny wasn't back to my side. My stomach dropped, but I shook my head anyway. "I already have a ma and pa."

Mrs. Brinks chuckled again. "Your ma and pa have replaced you by now, child. Why do you think they dropped you off and left you here? You're useless to them."

I let a tear slide down my face. I could feel Mrs. Brinks' eyes boring down into mine, and I didn't like it. Where was Jenny?

"That's not true."

"Yes it is, child. Your parents don't need you anymore."

"Mother!" Jenny's voice echoed down the hall, and I jumped. I had never heard Jenny sound so angry. "How dare you say that to this child!"

"It's true, you worm. Once the girls are checked into this house, they never leave. The parents never come back; they have new babies to replace them."

As the tears burst out of my eyes, I heard Jenny slap her mother. "Get out! I should have done this a long time ago, but I took pity on you! This is not your house! Pa left it to me, and I want you to get out of my house!"

Mrs. Brinks laughed. "You're just a stupid seventeen-year-old girl who doesn't know how to take care of herself."

Jenny stomped her foot. "I will call the sheriff, Ma! GET OUT!"

I flinched when the door slammed shut. Jenny ran to me and took me into a strong hug. "I'm so sorry that had to happen, Hope. I should have done it a long time ago. Don't you dare listen to what she said."

I sniffled and pulled Jenny out of the hug. "Don't I have a party to attend?"

Jenny squeezed my hand. "I never would have had the strength to do that if you hadn't come here."

I hugged her, and we left the room to join my birthday party.

About a week had gone by since Jenny's outburst, and the house seemed really quiet. The other children were much more talkative without Mrs. Brinks around. I even found myself laughing in Jenny's company, and I hadn't done that for a long time. Still, her words replayed over in my head. Had I really been forgotten and replaced by the new baby? Why else would they have brought me here?

With a sigh I stumbled around my bed and kicked off my shoes. I'd probably regret that in the morning while I was searching for them, but I was too tired to care. I opened the drawer for my nightdresses and pulled one out. Shutting the drawer, I slammed it on my finger. Stifling the scream and curse I wanted to yell, I plopped on my bed and began undressing.

Slipping the nightdress over my head, I pulled back my covers and slipped in.

A cold breeze blew in through the window. I shivered. How did that get open? Oh well, not getting up now. I pulled my blankets up tighter around my chin and ignored the crisp November air. I closed my eyes and tried to turn off the thoughts in my head so I could sleep.

The house was quiet. Everyone seemed to be asleep, but my stomach flipped annoyingly, and my head swam. Was I getting sick? I turned over, snuggling even farther under my blankets away from the cold, and took in a deep breath. Sleep, I just need to sleep.

A floorboard creaked nearby and, not that it

did any good, I popped my head out of the blankets, listening. Another creak, and my stomach flipped again. "Hello?"

The room was quiet, except for the pounding of my heart in my ears. Adrenaline raced through my veins as I took a deep breath and laid my head back down, hiding under the blanket. The room went quiet again and my lids closed, their tired heaviness winning out. I was about to doze off, and there was another creak!

This time I nearly jumped out of my bed, my heart thumping loudly in my chest. I felt a cold hand clamp over my mouth, and I tried to scream. A rag was shoved in between my teeth, stifling any sound that might've escaped. I tried to run for the direction I thought the door was, but familiar arms grasped mine, and pulled me into a tight hug. The cold, wrinkled hand stroked my head.

"There, there, child. Mommy's here." Her voice was vile and desperate, and I tried again to run out of Mrs. Brinks' grasp. She only held tighter and led me quietly down the stairs. The front door gave a quiet squeak as the cold, crisp air stung my cheeks.

I tried to spit my gag out, but it wouldn't budge. The cloth was dirty and tasted of cooking grease. Mrs. Brinks patted my shoulder and pushed me into the back of a wagon. Something large and heavy wedged me in place, and a moment later the wagon lurched forward. I couldn't move, stuck in the middle of the junk.

I don't know how long I was in the wagon. It felt like days, but it was probably a few hours. I could feel the warmth of the morning sun shining on my face when it finally stopped. Mrs. Brinks pulled the gag out of my mouth before helping me down. I opened my mouth to scream and she shoved it back in.

"Don't bother, child. We're in the middle of nowhere. No one can hear you."

She again removed the gag and I screamed. She only laughed. Angry, I closed my mouth and told myself not to talk to her again. Somehow, I would figure out how to get away.

I was led through a door, my feet scraping across a dirt floor. She set me down on an old, splintered chair. "Now, how about's some breakfast." I didn't answer. "Come on, Jenny, have a spot of breakfast. I'll heat up some porridge."

Jenny? Who did this woman think I was? She's insane. I refused to eat, and she went about her day, humming and whistling as she moved around me. I never moved, my mind racing. How was I going to get away? It was pointless to even try. With a sigh I sat in silence, waiting for the psychopath to tire herself.

She tried a few hours later to feed me again, and again I refused. I turned my face towards the warm sun shining through a window and wondered where we were. Obviously we weren't in the city any more. There were no sounds outside.

As the sun began to set, she again tried to feed me, and again I refused. My stomach growled furiously, betraying my vow of silence. "There, you see? You need to eat, child. Have some ham and potatoes."

With another growl of my stomach, I crossed my arms and closed my eyes. I'd rather starve to death than live with this woman.

"Fine, starve then, but don't blame me!"

Mrs. Brinks began slamming dishes and pots around in her anger. A few things flew past my head, but I barely noticed. When she stood me up a short time later, she ushered me into another room and laid me down on a cot. I didn't sleep, but stared blankly.

Would Jenny find me? I hoped so. My stomach was loud, and I wanted food. My mouth was dry and I was sure my voice would crack from lack of water in 24 hours. Tired and hungry, my eyelids began to droop, and I started to fall asleep.

A moment later there was a loud pounding on the door of the cabin. Mrs. Brinks ran to my side and put the gag in my mouth. She ran out of what must have been my bedroom and shut the door.

"Who is it?" Her voice was shaky and muffled.

"Sheriff, Mrs. Brinks. Open the door!"

There was a creak of the front door and three sets of footsteps entered the cabin. "Goodness, what is all this about?"

"A child's been kidnapped from the blind school. What do you know about it?"

Her gasp of shock was so fake it was pathetic. "Oh dear! That's terrible. Surely you don't think I did it? My daughter kicked me out."

"Precisely, ma'am. Please show me the house."

"Of course."

Their footsteps shuffled through the house, but the door where I was hiding was never opened. I waved my hands around weakly, looking for something to make noise.

Outside my room, the sheriff tapped on the door. "What's in there?"

"Just a food closet. It's empty. All the food I have right now is right there."

I found a lantern near the bed and knocked it on the floor. "What was that?"

"Oh, that must have been the cat."

"Move aside, madam."

More shuffling of their feet indicated a scuffle. She was obviously trying to keep them out. The door gave a groan as it swung open, and strong, masculine arms scooped me up. The gag was pulled out of my mouth and I let a tear slide out. "You okay, Hope?"

I smiled at the deputy. "Just a little hungry. I wouldn't eat her food."

He chuckled and carried me out of the house. As he put me into the front seat of a wagon and wrapped me in a blanket, I heard the Sheriff and Mrs. Brinks arguing. "Sheriff, I don't know how she got there!"

"You're joking right? You're going to jail, ma'am. You kidnapped and gagged that child!"

"You have no proof it was me!"

"I have a statement from your daughter saying she saw your wagon pass by the house last night. Witnesses saw you carrying the girl out."

"Lies! All lies!"

I sighed as the wagon jumped forward. "Let's get you home now."

Home. Oh how I wished I could go home...

The time in the blind school turned out to be absolutely wonderful without Mrs. Brinks in the house. It was Jenny at the head of the table during Christmas dinner that year, and the atmosphere was much more joyous and happy.

It had only been a few weeks since I had seen Joshua, and already he had written me a letter with the Braillewriter. He had sent his Christmas wishes, as well as his parents', and I replied with the same. They were, after all, responsible for me coming to the school in the first place.

I had received a blanket from my parents for Christmas, along with a letter. The baby was a girl, and they had named her Cassandra Marie. It was what I had named my doll before we moved to Linkville, and it proved how much my parents loved and missed me. I couldn't wait to finish my schooling so I could return home and meet my new sister.

I decided my Christmas would only be better if I had heard from my brother. I hadn't heard from him or Mia since that first letter, and I wondered if everything was okay. I couldn't help but wonder if Mia had been found by her Indian family and forced to go back. If that was the case, what would Elijah have done? I knew how much he cared for the Indian girl that Pa had found hiding in the schoolhouse our first winter in Linkville. It seemed almost unrealistic. Then again, Elijah had always had a fascination with the Indians we were learning about in school before then, so it made sense.

When we had finished our dinner, I returned to my room. I found some paper and a pencil on my desk and sat down. Putting the pencil to the paper, I sighed, now glad that Jenny had taught me how to write again.

Dear Elijah,

I know you don't want Ma and Pa to find out where you are, but I hadn't heard from you and I was starting to get worried. I got a letter from them and a blanket for Christmas. The baby was born on my birthday. It was a girl and they named her Cassandra Marie.

It's been a good Christmas, and I'm

tired. Sorry this is so short; please write soon. Happy Christmas.

Love, Hope

Chapter 12

A Father's Mistake

Thomas

*I*t was February, and winter in Linkville was still going strong.

The sun hadn't come up yet, but I was already knocking on my neighbor's door, clutching the crumpled letter in my hand. I knew the expression on my face was cold and unfriendly, but I didn't care. When nobody answered, I knocked again, harder and louder this time. The door opened and I found myself staring into the barrel of a shotgun.

"Put your gun away, old man. It's just me."

The shotgun dropped and the door opened the rest of the way. "Hell, Thomas, you scared us to death! Do you know what time it is?"

They let me in and I shook the snow off my coat. "I'm sorry, Jeb, Sarah."

Jeb's wife came out of their room, clutching a robe around her. "Is everything okay? The baby?"

I nodded. "Georgia and the baby are fine. I came to ask if you could check in on them for a little while. I've got to go away for a bit."

Sarah shook her head. "At this late hour?"

I nodded.

"Why?"

I sat and slid the crumpled letter across the table. Sarah opened it for her and Jeb to read in the light of the fireplace:

Dear Ma and Pa,

I want to apologize that it's been nearly a year since I spoke to you. I left the house that night to find Mia. I had found out at school that she was being held against her will on the reservation, and I had to make sure she was okay. When I found her, she was hiding in an old abandoned cabin, covered in bruises. Some of them were abusing her, and I was afraid they were going to kill her.

I didn't know what else to do, so we ran away. I took her to Virginia City, and we've been here ever since. I couldn't tell you where we were because I was afraid they'd find out. Pa, I know you don't like the Indians, but please give Mia a chance. She's not like them. She's kind and gentle and she just wants to be treated like everyone else. We're fourteen now, and she gets to choose where she wants to be now.

I'll understand if you hate me.

Love, Elijah

Sarah slid the letter back across the table. "What are you going to do?" She had a look of terror on her face. She knew I didn't like the Indians. Perhaps that scared her.

I put the letter into my coat pocket. "I'm going to Virginia City. I'm going to knock some sense into him and bring him home."

I stood from the table. "That's why I'm leaving now. Georgia doesn't know about this letter, and I don't intend to tell her about it until I have Elijah home again." I opened the door, but before I left, I pointed a finger at my two friends. "No son of mine is going to be with a savage. I will not stand for this." I shut the door hard and climbed onto my horse, giving my home down the road a loving look before riding off into the darkness.

Mia

Elijah rolled over and I smiled. I loved watching him sleep. He looked so peaceful and so happy...

...and I was scared to death.

I'd been sick for a while, and something just seemed different. I hadn't told him, of course; he would worry too much.

It was time for him to get up, and I crawled beside him on the bed. I wrapped an arm around his waist and kissed his ear. "Good morning."

He smiled over his shoulder and squeezed my hands. "Good morning, what's for breakfast?"

I pulled away from him. "Is that all I'm good for? To cook your food?"

Elijah blushed. "No, honey, you're good for a lot more."

I smiled knowingly at him, and turned back around. He wrapped his arms around me and we kissed.

After a few short moments, I pulled away from him and went downstairs. I was going to treat him to breakfast from the hotel this morning, trying to butter him up. I would pay a visit to the doctor, and hopefully he would tell me something else was wrong, not what I thought it was, relieving the fear I had been carrying for the past couple of weeks.

I returned with two platefuls of pancakes, eggs, and bacon, and I sat down at the table. "When do you work today?"

Elijah took a bite of his pancakes and shrugged. "I know I have to be there at nine. Don't know how long they'll keep me down there this time."

I ate my breakfast without another word. Elijah was working in the silver mines. It was a job I wished he hadn't gotten. He was usually hundreds of feet below ground for sometimes hours at a time. What if the tunnels caved in on him? Would he survive? Would he come back to me? What if he got sick from the blistering heat while he was down there? Every time he left our room to go to that job, I sat waiting for him to return.

Elijah finished his breakfast and juice, and stood to put his jacket on. I wrapped him in a hug, as I normally did before he left, and kissed him on the cheek. "I'll be home when I get done."

I gave him a weak smile, and he left our boarding-house room. I let out a worried sigh before cleaning up our breakfast dishes. When I was satisfied with my cleaning work, I blew out the lamp and left for the doctor's office.

Virginia City was warm that day, and the sun glistened off the white snow. It stung my eyes as I tried desperately to navigate my way around the people visiting town. Finally, I reached the office and stepped inside.

"Doc Parker, are you in?"

A tall, blonde man came into the front room, glasses on the tip of his nose and a medical book open in his hands. He looked at me over the glasses and smiled. "Hello there, Mia. How are you today?"

I blushed and swallowed. How was I going to say this? What would he think of me if my suspicions were right? I shook the thoughts away.

"Well, I...I was wondering...I've been sick for about two weeks. I think..."

Doctor Parker raised his hand. He didn't need to hear any more, to which I was thankful. He motioned for me to go into the exam room, and he locked the door.

I had never been in a doctor's exam room before. It looked absolutely frightening to me. I couldn't bear to look at the tools, so I stared at the wooden floor. There was an exam gown folded on the table, and I changed into it quickly.

The doctor came into the room and pulled the curtain shut behind him. "Okay, Miss Mia, jump up on the table please."

I did as I was told, and the doctor went on to poking and prodding me in ways I thought no man should have done. It was uncomfortable and a little painful, and when he was finished he went to the counter and washed his hands. I struggled back into my dress and sat patiently for the doctor to tell me.

"You're going to have a baby, Mia. I expect you have another six months, probably around August sometime."

My stomach dropped. What was I going to do? I was only fourteen, barely learning to take care of myself, let alone a baby. And what's worse...how was I going to tell Elijah?

Elijah

I dropped to my knees onto the hard rocks and took a drink from the water bucket. I wiped my brow and stood back up, wishing we would be allowed to go soon. Something was worrying me today, and I wanted to get home to Mia.

I had a surprise for her; we would be able to buy the house she wanted now. I had been saving half of my earnings secretly for months, and finally I had the $200 I needed to buy the small-sized mansion that sat above all the other buildings at the top of the hill.

Two more hours had gone by before we were finally told we could go home for the day, and I climbed out of the tunnel. The sun was starting to sink into the horizon, and I dumped two ladles of water over my head. The days down in the mines were hot and tiring, even in the middle of winter, but I enjoyed bringing home the money. It made me feel important. It made me feel like my life was worth something, and I liked taking care of Mia. She deserved a normal life.

I looked up and found that the saloons were already in full swing. I decided to see if the sheriff, who owned the house and was willing to sell it to me, was still around.

I walked down the boardwalk, looking out over the valley far below; I really did like it here, but a part of me wished I was back in Linkville with my family.

I arrived at the sheriff's office and walked inside. "Elijah, m'boy! How's the mining today?"

I grinned. "We did alright. How are you?"

The sheriff walked in front of me and put a hand on my shoulder. "To be perfectly honest, I'm glad to see you. There was a man in here looking for you today. I told him you were probably in the mines, and sent him to the hotel."

My stomach dropped. What if it was one of the Indians looking to take Mia away from me? My fear must have shown on my face.

"It wasn't any of the Injuns. I think it might have been your Pa."

My heart sunk. That was even worse.

"Thank you, Sheriff." I turned to leave, but he stopped me.

"Wha'd you come in here for, son?"

I smiled; I had almost forgotten! I pulled my money bag out of my pocket. "Here's the $200 we agreed on for the house. I told you I'd have it by spring."

The sheriff, surprised, took the moneybag and opened it up to count the coins and bills inside. When he had finished, he closed it and put it in his pocket.

"Well, I can't say I'm not surprised. It's remarkable for such a young boy, really."

I grinned, happy if but for a few short moments, before I would go to look for Pa. The sheriff went to the desk and signed a crumpled piece of paper, handing it to me when he was done. "Congratulations, home owner. Don't forget to take the bill of sale to the county clerk tomorrow."

I smiled and slipped the paper into my pocket. I said goodbye and headed for the saloons down the street, hoping that I would find Pa at least a little drunk.

I walked into the disgustingly loud saloon. It was Friday, and the men were celebrating. It seemed exceptionally rowdy that night, but I fought my way through the crowd to the hotel's stairs. I would be able to see into the saloon from the top of them, and hopefully...well, I needed to find my pa.

I scanned the crowd, and found a man sitting by himself at the far end of the bar. He was swishing around the gold liquid in his glass.

I sighed. That was him, and he was definitely not in a good mood. I straightened my clothes and tried to brush the dirt off of them. That was an impossible feat and, giving up, I made my way across the saloon to my pa's side.

"Hello." I tried to sound confident and manly, but inside my stomach was turning.

Pa gripped his glass and turned to face me. His face was cold, and there was no emotion on this face. "Elijah, you don't seem surprised to see me."

I shook my head, moving out of the way of two brawling men headed my way. "The sheriff told me you were here. Let's go outside."

Pa wasn't going to leave the bar, but I gave him no choice. I led him out to the boardwalk. "What are you doing here, Pa?"

He glared at me. "Where's that savage you're smitten with?"

I took my pa's shirt in my fists and pushed him

against the wall of the saloon, my anger finally showing through. "Don't you EVER call her that! I'm not afraid of you, Pa!"

He seemed taken aback, but obviously wasn't going to let me intimidate him. He pushed me back, and we stood staring at the ground for a few moments. "Where is she?"

"She's at the boarding house on the other side of town."

Pa sniggered. "You're not even able to buy her a house?"

I threw my cold glare at the ground instead of at him. "For your information, I just bought her a house a few minutes ago. Believe it or not, I can take care of myself!"

Pa sniggered again, but was interrupted by Mia running down the street.

"Elijah!" She jumped into my arms and kissed my neck. "I was so scared something had happened to you in the mines! Are you alright?"

I pulled myself out of her tight grip and turned her around. Mia's face fell when she saw him, and I could tell she wanted to run, but I held her still.

"Mr. Bryant."

He glared at her, and then diverted his eyes back to me. "Well, you haven't killed her yet. Maybe they'll take her back on the reservation."

Mia glared at the man before her. "I'm not going back there, sir."

I squeezed her arms and pulled her away from Pa. I looked deep into her eyes. "I won't let him take you away."

She took me into a tight embrace and kissed my ear. "Elijah, I'm pregnant. Don't leave me."

I nearly fell over when I heard the words escape her lips. I pulled her out of the hug and peered deep into her eyes as if trying to see into her soul. Was she just saying that, or was it true? A small smile crept onto her face and I knew her words were genuine.

I took her hand and returned to Pa's side. "Neither one of us are leaving, Pa. We are getting married, and there's nothing you or anyone else can do about it."

The last thing I remembered was Pa's hand going up in the air, and then my world went black.

Chapter 13

Power of the Moon

Thomas

I woke that morning in a cold jail cell. I couldn't remember much of anything from the night before. The only thing I remembered was hitting my son over the head after Elijah had announced his engagement to Mia.

I couldn't believe he was being so stupid about the Indian girl. Hadn't he learned anything from me? I rolled over, trying to get the sun out of my face.

"Well, look who's awake."

Sheriff Smith held a glass of water through the bars, and I stumbled out of bed to take it. When I was done drinking, I blinked at the sheriff.

"Your son is fine, if you care whether you killed him or not." His voice was hard.

I was confused. I hadn't hit him that hard, had I?

"It takes a great coward to hit his own son with a beer mug."

Suddenly I realized; I hadn't put my glass down before leaving the bar with Elijah. "I...I didn't realize..."

The sheriff chuckled humorlessly. "Of course you didn't." He walked away, leaving me alone with my thoughts.

Mia

Elijah was still asleep, and every few minutes he grabbed his head with a groan. I sat watching him, tears streaming down my face.

The door creaked open and the manager, Victoria, came in. "How is he?"

"Still asleep." I sniffled and wiped my face dry. "He keeps grabbing at his head."

Victoria put a hand on my shoulder. "He'll be okay. Why don't you go get some rest; I'll sit with him."

I smiled, but shook my head. "I don't think I can sleep. But I'd like to go down to the jail and talk with Mr. Bryant."

She nodded, sitting down beside Elijah's bed. I kissed his forehead and left the room.

The town had not quite woken up yet; it was still fairly early, and most of the men would be waking with hangovers. I couldn't understand why the white men acted so crazy. What was it about the games and the drinks that made the men fight and curse all through the night? Was it the sleazy women with far too much bosom showing who served them those drinks? Or were they just so caught up in the atmosphere that it was like an addictive drug? Whatever it was, I didn't know, but it was that drink that had almost killed Elijah the night before, and I was angry.

I walked into the jail house and smiled at Sheriff Smith. "Good morning."

The sheriff stood up. "Good morning, Miss Mia. How's Elijah?"

I sighed, wiping a tear from my cheek. "He's still asleep. Could I speak with Mr. Bryant, please?"

The sheriff nodded and led her to the back room that housed the damp, cold cells. Thomas stood up when he saw me, and glared. "What are you doing here?"

I gave him a stern stare back. I wasn't afraid of him anymore, and I was going to tell him so. "Why do you hate me, Mr. Bryant?"

I could tell he wasn't expecting that question, and he cleared his throat. "You're an Indian."

"So, because I'm not like you, because I don't have white skin, you hate me?" Thomas didn't answer, and I was getting angry with his lack of cooperation. "I can read, I can write, I can talk your language. I might even be smarter than you, Mr. Bryant." My face burned and I shook the cell's bars. "Those are trivial things, Mr. Bryant! What's important is that I love your son, and he loves me, and there's NOTHING anyone can do about it!"

I growled at him, my anger welling up inside of me like a hungry tiger. The knuckles on my brown fingers were growing whiter the madder I got, and I took in a deep breath. "You have the NERVE to hit your own son with a glass! Do you even know he almost died?!! And yet you call ME a savage?! I have done nothing but show you respect, but you?! I'm going to call you a savage! It was the white man who stole the land from my ancestors! YOUR people invaded our land, but I'M the one taking the initiative to try to show my people that interacting with white man is good, even after growing up to hate white man! I'm sorry you don't like the color of my skin, but there's nothing you or anyone else can do about it—so learn to live with it!"

He blinked at me, a little taken aback by my outburst. I shook the bars one last time and left the jailhouse, heart racing. I wasn't sure if I had gotten through to him, but at least I had tried. My head was throbbing; I needed to lie down.

It had been a week since my outburst. Thomas had been let out of the jail, and he went with his head hanging as low as he could get it. It would take him another week to get back home, and I was glad he was leaving. Elijah had been awake only for a few short hours, and he told me about the purchase of the house on the hill. I was working hard to clean it and make it fit for living. No one had been in it for nearly five years, and I couldn't wait to make it my own.

I had finally sent a letter to the chief, telling him where I was and how I was doing. Despite my weeklong abuse, something had told me that my pa hadn't known about it. I had received a letter back, but I was too nervous to read it. When Elijah came into the house, tired but healthy, he found the letter and encouraged me to open it. He wouldn't be able to read it himself, as it was written in my native tongue. I sighed, finally peeling open the envelope, and unfolded the letter. I read it aloud to him carefully, hoping it was good news:

Miakoda,

Me and mother were very happy to hear from you. Those who abused you have received punishment. You are always welcome to visit here. Do not forget your family. We wish the best to you and the white man who has taken your heart. Let us know when the baby arrives.

It was short, but thoughtful, and I was glad to hear from them. I folded the letter and smiled at him. "I wish your pa was like mine."

We both laughed, and he pulled me into a hug, kissing me on the cheek. "We should get married before the baby comes."

I nodded. "Yes, but please write your sister. I want her to know. And your ma."

Elijah smiled and kissed the top of my head, heading off for the desk to write the letters.

Hope

I was in the middle of a very good book when there was a knock on the door. I cursed and put a scrap piece of paper inside to mark my page.

"Come in." I made sure my dress was straight before the door was opened.

"Sorry to bother you, Hope, but you've got a letter."

I grinned at Jenny's words. It was either from my brother or Joshua. I held out my hand, and Jenny sat on the bed, putting the letter in my grasp.

147

I tore into the envelope and unfolded the dotted paper inside. Sliding my fingers across the page, I read it aloud to my teacher and friend:

My dearest sister,

I hope all is well at the school. I was angry when I found out what your housemother had done. Tell Miss Jenny thank you for scaring her ma off for me, otherwise I might have had to come and beat the woman myself.

Jenny and I shared a laugh at this, and I read on.

Spring is almost over, and I've got a surprise for you. First of all, Pa was here and we had a fight. I was unconscious for about three days, and once I woke up I slept for another five days. He spent a week in jail, but he's gone home now, and I haven't heard from him since.

The reason we fought is another story...I hope this gets to you in time, but at the end of June (on the 30th) Mia and I are getting married. I sent a letter to Ma, hoping she can come with the baby. I've also invited Mr. and Mrs. Tandra and Joshua. Mia and I both want you to come, but we understand if you can't make the trip.

Jenny stopped me to ask how old my brother and Mia were. I told her they were fourteen, and Jenny was surprised that they were so young. I nodded, but explained to her about the reservation. Jenny urged me on then, and my fingers ran along the paper again.

We were going to wait until we were
older to get married, but we found out that Mia
is going to have a baby (I gasped) in August,
so we thought we should be married before it
gets here. Please try to come.
We love you and hope to see you soon.

Love, Elijah

I folded the letter carefully, sliding it inside the book I had been reading. I wanted to be there for the wedding, but it was already the first of June. How was I ever going to get there in time?

Jenny was being quiet, and I wondered what she was doing,

"Jenny?"

She put a hand on my arm. "Just a minute, I'm calculating."

I tipped my head, wishing I could look over Jenny's shoulder to find out what was going on. After a few silent moments, Jenny jumped off of the bed. "Pack your bags; we're going to Virginia City."

My eyes widened. This wasn't happening, was it? "Jenny, we couldn't possibly afford that, and we don't have the time to get there, do we?"

Jenny pulled me off of the bed. "Don't be silly. I've got money saved, and I couldn't think of a better way to spend it. It won't take us more than ten days on the train."

I thought about this for a moment, and then shook my head. "What about the other children?" Jenny was going crazy!

"They'll be taken care of. I trust everyone here.

Let's go, Hope!"

I smiled. I was going to see my brother again for the first time in a year and a half! And I might even see Ma again! I hugged Jenny, and set out to packing a bag. I couldn't wait to get on that train!

The train ride to Virginia City didn't take long at all once we left. Actually, the ten days on the train seemed to fly by. Perhaps it was just my excitement over seeing my brother for the first time in sixteen months.

As the train whistle blew at midnight on June 20th, I jumped and shook Jenny awake. "Jenny! Jenny, wake up! We're here!"

Jenny groaned and took my hand. "Okay, I'm up."

I could hardly contain my excitement. We hadn't told Elijah we were coming; I'd wanted to surprise him.

The sleepy Jenny led me off of the train, and I breathed in the fresh, cool night air.

"Excuse us." Jenny had stopped someone to ask for directions. "We're looking for the Silver Queen Hotel. Could you direct us in the right direction?"

The man laughed as the train pulled away from the station. "The Silver Queen's a thirty minute train ride from here, way up in the mountains."

My stomach dropped. We still weren't there.

"Stay here, Hope." Jenny pushed me onto a bench and then there was silence...cold, dark silence. Not just silence for a moment, but silence for several moments.

I was so scared of that bench. It was a strange place, and I knew it was late at night. The train station was not the place to be alone in the dark, especially for someone not able to see.

My heart sped up when footsteps approached me. "It's just me, Hope." I breathed a sigh of relief, my heart returning to its normal pace. "The main train doesn't go into Virginia City; we've got to take the Virginia-Truckee. The last one leaves in five minutes."

I hugged her when we boarded the small train. Its whistle blew to announce its departure, and I sighed. "I was so afraid something was going to keep me away from my brother."

Jenny let go of me and moved to the other side. There were only a few others on the train.

She yawned. "No worries now. Why don't you lie down and take a nap. It'll be a strenuous trip up the mountain."

I nodded, remembering what the ride was like from the first time I had taken the trip, though this train might have been a little different. I slid over and fell onto the cushioned seat, drifting off into a light sleep.

Jenny

I climbed out of the train when it stopped at the station. I picked up Hope, who was sound asleep, and put her in the coach that would take us into town.

Virginia City was a nice little town, and very different from the city of St. Paul. I tried my best not to wake her when the coach stopped at the Silver Queen Hotel, and carried her inside.

"Can we get a room, please?"

The hotel manager led me down the hall and allowed us to stay in the only first-floor room available.

I set Hope down on the bed, and finding sleep a long way away, decided to explore the town a little bit. I paid for the room and left the hotel, wondering where to go first.

I wandered aimlessly through the town until I came to a sign, warning walkers about the mines that lay ahead. So I turned right and walked up the hill to the next street. There were fewer houses here, and I set my eyes on a smaller three-story mansion about halfway down the block.

"Wow, what a gorgeous place."

"Thank you."

I jumped and turned to see who had spoken to me. A small, pretty Indian girl smiled at me. She couldn't have been more than fifteen, if she was even that.

"My fiancé just bought it for me a few months ago." She held out her hand to me. "I'm Mia."

I took the girl's hand and shook it. "I'm Jenny." Something about Mia seemed familiar; it wasn't her face, but her name. "Mia, do you happen to know Elijah Bryant?"

Mia smiled. "Yeah, he's my fiancé."

I grinned. "Thank goodness I found you! I'm Hope's teacher!"

Chapter 14

Together

Elijah

I shivered. It was surprisingly cold in that big house for June, but that was probably due to the emptiness of a house that had not been lived in for so long. I took in the scent of the dusty wood, hardly believing that it was really my house. In ten days I would be married, and a father in a short two months. I just wished that my ma and pa would have been here, as angry as I was at my pa.

I settled onto the old love seat that had been left in the house. Mia had gone for a walk, and I was waiting until she got home to go to bed.

The front door came open and Mia, a small hand on her stomach, walked inside, followed by an older girl I didn't know. "Elijah, I didn't know you were waiting up for me."

I stood and kissed her on the cheek. "Of course I did. I can't have my girl go missing ten days before I marry her."

"Do I know you?" I was curious about her. Who

was she? What was she doing here at 2 o'clock in the morning?

Jenny smiled at me. "Well, not formally until now. I'm from the blind school in St. Paul."

My eyes widened and I grabbed Jenny by the arms. "Is it Hope? What's the matter?" Why else would she be here?

Jenny chuckled. Was she crazy? "No, honey, everything's fine. Your sister is fine."

I breathed a sigh of relief and let go of the blonde-haired girl. "Don't scare me like that!"

Jenny and Mia smiled at each other. "Actually, I wasn't planning on coming to find you until the sun was up at least, but I wasn't sleepy and I ran into young Mia down the road. So here I am."

I was glad that everything was okay. "Please, sit down."

Jenny took the invitation.

"Would you like something to drink?"

"No, I'm fine, thank you."

"So where is Hope?" Mia fell into my lap, and I wrapped my arms around her.

Jenny smiled at the two of us, and I blushed. "She fell asleep on the train coming up here. I didn't want to wake her. She's at the hotel."

"Good." I shifted under Mia so I could see Jenny better, and smiled. "We're so glad you're here, but you should go get some sleep. When you both wake, will you bring Hope here?"

Jenny nodded. "Of course."

I smiled. "Good, and we insist you stay here in this house."

"Oh, Elijah, that's too much. We couldn't impose on you."

Mia reached over and put a hand on Jenny's shoulder. "We insist. We have plenty of room, and it will be good for Elijah and Hope." She and Jenny shared a silent smile.

What was it with girls? Could they read each other's minds? I shook the thoughts away, and after Mia convinced Jenny to stay in the house the next night, we said our goodbyes. Jenny wouldn't let me walk her back, so Mia and I went to bed.

"Are you excited?" I hugged Mia before falling onto my pillow. The idea that Hope was so close felt really good. My wedding day would be almost perfect, now that she was here.

Joshua

The sun broke through the horizon like a knife. I been awake for a while an' was waitin' for my parents to wake. I wasn' sure why I had decided to come on dis trip; there was plenty to do on the farm an' for the lumber mill, but somethin' inside me kept tellin' me to go. We was about three hours from Virginia City when we decided to make camp. It seeme' pointless to try to climb the mountains in the dark.

I kep' lookin' up into the mountains. What was it abou' them that kep' callin' to me? They were pretty, sure, but it was like I was in a trance jus' from lookin' at dem. Hope tol' me about Virginia City in the las' letter I had gotten from her. She had describe' dem so well it was almos' as if she could see it again. I shook my head, tearin' my eyes away from the mountains, an' started making our breakfas'.

It was two hours before we were ready to leave. Finally, abou' mid-mornin', we set out up the mountains. The road that had been made near the train seemed to climb endlessly. It woun' aroun' an' aroun' the surroundin' trees an' through the crevices in the mountains. Jus' when I though' we was never goin' to reach the town, I caught sight of a sign that was warnin' visitors that they needed to watch out for holes that coul' be part of the undergroun' silver mines.

We continued into town an' found it already full of life. The saloons were busy, an' men were disappearing into the ground.

I looked aroun'. Where did the people live? There were two hotels in sight, one on each end of town, an' between them saloons, stores, a sheriff's office, a law office, an' a restauran' or two. There didn' seem to be more than ten homes on the main street. Lookin' aroun' further, I noticed all of the houses. There were hundreds, an' it seemed endless as the hills kep' goin'. Still, I foun' the town simple, but great.

Pa stopped the wagon at the Silver Queen Hotel, an' was headed inside to ask where to fin' Elijah, when I spotted Hope in one of the firs' floor windows. "Ma! Ma, look, it's Hope!" A smile spread across my face an' I jumpe' out of the wagon, headin' for the window.

"Jay, no! You be scarin' da girl to her deaf if you go knockin' on da window!"

I stopped just before makin' contact with the window. I had momentarily forgotten that she was blind, an' I lowered my hand in disappointment. I certainly didn't wan' to scare her.

Jenny

I yawned, finally waking late in the morning. The sun was shining brightly into the window, and I jumped off of the bed in alarm. "Oh no, I've overslept!"

Hope giggled. "It's okay, Jenny. I've just been sitting here reading."

I got out of bed and stretched. "I hope you haven't unpacked too much."

Hope shook her head. "Nope, I just got my book out."

I gathered our things and led Hope out of the room.

"Where are we going?"

I giggled and set the bags down. "You'll see."

"Miss Hope? Be dat you?" Hope tipped her head at the voice. I could tell she was trying to recognize the voice. "I be Joseph Tandra!"

Realization spread over her face and her eyes lit up. "Oh! Hi!"

I pulled on her sleeve, wanting to be introduced. "Oh, Mr. Tandra, this is Jenny. She's been my teacher at the school."

"Good to meet you."

I released Hope's arm to shake Joseph's hand, and then returned to her.

"An' you." Joseph shuffled on the boardwalk. "Uh, you be seein' your brother?"

Hope shook her head. "Not yet, and Jenny's dragging me somewhere, but I don't know where."

I giggled. "I met your brother and Mia last night."

Hope dropped her jaw in surprise.

"Now, Hope. You were asleep and I wasn't ready

to go to bed, so I went for a walk. I ran into Mia, and she took me back to her beautiful, not to mention huge, house, and insisted we stay with them."

"Oh, Jenny!" Hope pulled me into a strong hug, nearly knocking me over. "Oh, I'm sorry!"

Joseph chuckled. "Uh, Miss Jenny, we be like' to see Elijah an' Mia before we be getting' settle'. You come an' jump in our wagon an' we be drivin' you two up."

"Thank you, Mr. Tandra; that will be wonderful."

Elijah

Mia set lunch on the table and I sighed. "Mia, I wish you'd rest. You're going to wear yourself out."

She shook her head. "Don't start telling me what to do. I'm doing fine." We both jumped when someone knocked on the door. "Good lord; that must be Hope."

I smiled and stood up from the table. I passed through the dining room and into the sitting room to the front door. When I opened it and found Jenny standing with Hope at her arm; a tear rolled down my cheek.

"Hope." I hugged her and then pulled her back to look at her. "You look absolutely wonderful."

"Are you going to stand there and gape all day, or are you going to let them in?"

I chuckled at Mia, and let Hope and her companions inside. Then I greeted Jenny and the Tandras with smiles before taking Hope back into my arms.

"I've missed you so much."

Hope smiled a genuine smile, her green eyes

sparkling, and sniffled. "I've missed you, too."

Mia, who had gone to heat up food for the extra guests, came in, and I put Hope's hand on Mia's stomach. Hope grinned when the baby kicked. "Oh, Mia! It's so exciting!"

They hugged each other before we all finally went into the other room to eat.

I looked around the table. This was such a wonderful surprise! The only thing missing was my parents and new baby sister. Mia took my hand under the table and squeezed it.

"Maybe they didn't have the money, Elijah."

I smiled, considering this carefully. It was a definite possibility. They hadn't had a whole lot of money when I was still living there, and the trip to take Hope to the blind school had probably drained every last penny. I decided that this was the reason they hadn't come, rather than my pa's anger, and joined the rest of my friends and family in eating.

Georgia

I couldn't sleep. My coach had been delayed by three days already, and now, on the 29th of June, I was afraid I wouldn't make it to my son's wedding. Baby Cassandra was asleep in a blanket on the seat beside me, and I envied her.

The sky was turning dark when the coach came to a stop. I let out a great sigh of relief. "Oh, thank goodness."

I stepped out of the coach and looked around,

somehow managing to keep Cass asleep. We were at a train station. The station sign overhead read "Reno."

I panicked.

The conductor, seeing my face, stopped in front of me and smiled. "Everything okay, Ma'am?"

I shook my head and pulled my shawl tighter around my shoulders. "No, I wondered how far we were from Virginia City."

The conductor frowned.

"I'm afraid we're a bit behind. You'll have to take the train from here to Carson City, and then on to Virginia City."

The conductor walked away, leaving me with my thoughts. The baby was stirring, and I tried to feed her while figuring out where I needed to be. The train to Carson City didn't leave for several hours, nearly first light, and then who knows how far to Virginia City.

I spent most of the night nervously cat-napping in the station, and grew extra nervous as the train headed east towards Virginia City, with only a short two hours to make it to the wedding.

The train ride was hot and humid. The sun bore down on me and I wished I could make it go away.

Finally, the train reached Virginia City at the top of the mountain, and I stumbled out. The town was just starting to wake up, and I hurried towards the hotel with the baby in one arm and bag in the other. Once inside, I set my bag down and took a deep breath.

I still had time to make it to the church. "Excuse me, could you tell me where I can find St. Mary in the Mountains Church?"

The hotel manager pointed me in the right direction, and, sending my thanks, I headed down the hill.

People were piling into the church, but I hadn't found Elijah yet. Where was he?

Turning around, I ran right into someone. "Oh, dear, I'm so sorry."

"Mrs. Bryan'?"

I looked up into the face of Esther May, and breathed a sigh of relief. "Oh, Esther May! I thought I was going to miss it!"

She clicked her tongue at me, shaking her head and trying to straighten the collar on my blouse. "When you be gettin' in?"

"Just now."

"You slep'?"

I shook my head. "Just a touch on the train."

Esther May tsked. "Give me da baby." I was skeptical at first, but handed baby Cassandra to her. "Your son be in dat back room right there." She pointed to the small door at the back of the church. "Go see him. Da weddin's goin' to start shortly."

I smiled at the woman I'd always appreciated and, kissing the baby on the forehead, headed for the room.

Inside, I found a girl I didn't know, and Elijah talking just inside the door.

"Elijah!"

Elijah

I jumped and turned to see who had called my name. The heat in my face left, and I'm sure the color, when I realized who it was, and my eyes filled with tears. "Ma?"

She nodded, her eyes watering with tears of joy, and she held out her arms. I ran to her and she took me into her arms, kissing me on the cheek.

"Ma, I didn't think you were going to come."

Ma pulled me away and looked me straight in the eyes. The tears were pouring from my eyes and she wiped them dry. "I'm not going to lie to you, son. Your pa was too upset and ashamed from his last visit, and he refused to come."

I nodded in understanding before hugging her again.

"Now, let's get you married." She started to leave, but I held her back.

"Wait!"

She turned back, and I pulled her around the corner and into the main room. I pointed to the front, where Mia stood, a hand on her tummy, speaking to Hope, who was sitting in a chair. "She arrived last week."

Ma couldn't hold the tears back anymore. She watched Hope reading to Mia for a long time, a look of shock and surprise on her face. Finally, she stumbled towards the front of the room, trying not to cry out loud.

Mia had finally noticed her and smiled, nodding at Ma. Hope tipped her head, trying to hear the footsteps. "Who is it, Mia?"

Mia grinned as Ma covered her mouth to retain her cries. "It's your ma."

Chapter 15

Enter Days of Togetherness

Hope

I fell into Ma's arms. I'm sure my face looked like someone had thrown a soaking wet towel on me, but the tears didn't stop coming down. It had been fifteen months since I had been with her, and I gripped the silk blouse as tight as I could. Ma stroked my hair, trying to calm me down.

"Hope, darling, I'm here and I love you."

I smiled, rubbing my wet face with the apron on my dress. I shivered; it was a weird feeling to know that my ma was there. Mia had told me about everything that had happened between them and Pa. "I love you, Ma."

She kissed my cheek and took me by the arm. "Take a deep breath, this is supposed to be your brother's day. Let's go find our seats."

I nodded, letting Ma lead me out of the room. "Ma, where's the baby?"

She led me up the steps of the church. "She's with Esther May."

We went inside, finding it already filled with several people from town, and walked to the front row, smiles on our faces. Ma sat me down just in time for the wedding march on the organ to begin. I desperately wished I could see this, but being here was enough.

As the organ music stopped, Ma squeezed my hand. This, I knew, was my ma's way of smiling at me, and I leaned over and put my head on her shoulder.

Reverend Thornton, who I had met the other day, cleared his throat. "We are gathered here today to take part in the most time-honored celebration of the human family, uniting a woman and a man in marriage. Elijah and Mia have come to witness before us, telling of their love for each other. We remember, theirs is a love whose source is the affection of those who loved them into being.

"We remind them that they are performing an act of complete faith, each in the other; that the heart of their marriage will be the relationship they create. In a world where faith often falls short of expectation, it is a tribute to these two who now join hands and hearts in perfect faith."

I was listening to the short moments of silence, wishing I could see what was happening. I was about to ask Ma when Reverend Thornton spoke again.

"Elijah, will you receive Mia as your wife? Will you pledge to her your love, faith, and tenderness, cherishing her with a husband's loyalty and devotion?"

There was a sniffle from Ma, and I squeezed her hand.

"I will."

I smiled, hearing my brother's voice for the first

time. I was fighting back tears, both out of happiness for my brother, and for the small hint of jealousy I had. I wondered when and who I'd marry.

"Mia, will you receive Elijah as your husband? Will you pledge to him your love, faith, and tenderness, cherishing him with a wife's loyalty and devotion?"

"I will."

"Elijah and Mia, receive each other from your mothers, who give you into each other's keeping, by saying now, each to the other, words which will tell of your love."

I was confused, and I pulled on Ma's sleeve. "Ma? Is Mia's ma here?" I tried not to whisper too loudly so as not to interrupt.

"I'm not sure. We'll find out for sure after the wedding, okay?"

I nodded and returned my head to her shoulder.

Elijah cleared his throat: "I, Elijah, take you, Mia to be no other than yourself, in all the ways life may find us, tending you in sickness and rejoicing with you in health, as long as we both shall live to love."

I heard Mia sniff before speaking. "I, Mia, take you, Elijah to be no other than yourself, in all the ways life may find us, tending you in sickness and rejoicing with you in health, as long as we both shall live to love."

Reverend Thornton spoke again. "Will you now give and receive a ring?"

There was a quick moment of silence before both Elijah and Mia spoke. "We will."

"This circlet of precious metal is justly regarded as a fitting emblem of the purity and perpetuity of the Marriage and State. The ancients were reminded by the circle of eternity, as it is so fashioned as to have neither beginning nor end; while gold is so incorruptible that it cannot be tarnished by use or time. So may the union, at this time solemnized, be incorruptible in its purity and more lasting than time itself."

"Wear this ring forever, Mia, as a symbol of love and peace and of all that is unending."

Ma squeezed my hand again. "Your brother just put a ring on Mia's finger, and now she's doing the same."

"Wear this ring forever, Elijah, as a symbol of love and peace and of all that is unending."

"We speak to Elijah and Mia of love, in which the trust and freedom of the other person becomes as significant as the trust and freedom of one's self. We speak to them of generosity, which gathers the beauty of earth for riches, and the kindness which turns away the wrath of foolish men and women. We speak of each of our hopes for their continued growth through patience, one for the other. We speak of our confidence that new levels of understanding, discovered by them in experiences of sorrow and tribulation, shall bring ever new surprises of strength and fortitude they do not now know.

"In the years which shall bring Elijah and Mia into greater age and wisdom, we pray that their love shall be ever young; that they shall be able always to recover from moments of despair the lithesome ways of buoyant youth. In this hope may they keep the vows made on this day, in freedom, teaching each other who they are, what they yet shall be, enabling them to know that in the fullness of being, they are more than themselves and more than each other; that they are all of us, and that together we share joyously the fruits of life.

"Inasmuch as Elijah and Mia have declared their love and devotion to each other before family and friends,

I now greet them with you as husband and wife.

"Now you will feel no rain, for each of you will be sanctuary to the other. Now you will feel no cold, for each of you will be warmth to the other. Now there is no isolation for you. Now there is no more loneliness. Now you are two, but there is only one life in front of you.

"Go now and enter into the days of your togetherness."

The people around me burst into applause, and I finally let a tear slide down my cheek. My brother was no longer the boy I looked up to and admired. He was a man, who had taught me more than I ever could have learned from anyone else. He had taught me that the line between whites and persons of color could in fact be broken. It was possible to break that line and learn to love where it was least expected.

Going back to what was supposed to be normal life was hard for everyone. Christmas of 1877 was cold, and much too short for anyone's liking. I spent my eleventh birthday wishing I could see my new nephew. Elijah had sent a telegram announcing the arrival of the little boy. They had named him Elijah James Bryant Jr.—a name that Mia had chosen.

I spent most of my days in my classes, wishing I could leave and be with Ma. She had written several letters of concern about Pa. Since Ma's return to Linkville, he had distanced himself from everyone, including her. He was no longer the friendly, outgoing man he once was. He spent most of his time tending the fields. Working late into the night, he returning only when Ma was already asleep. Although he did stay in the house long enough to get through breakfast, he never spoke. However, he would kiss Ma and my sister on the cheek before leaving the house.

I found this unusual, even for Pa. I had never known him to isolate himself so much. I wanted to get home and talk to him, to find out what was wrong. But would he speak to me? And if he did, would he tell me what I wanted to hear or would he tell me the truth?

The questions and thoughts slowly faded as the summer of 1878 arrived. I was now the oldest student in the blind school, and was even teaching some of the younger and new students. Jenny and I had become very close friends since I had come to the school, and we often stayed up far into the night talking about nothing in particular.

July third was Jenny's birthday. She was turning nineteen, and I—who had had a hard time keeping the secret—was helping Jenny's beau, Edward, wrap up a small ring.

He kissed me on the cheek. "Thank you, Green Eyes."

I blushed as I stood from the table. "You better tell her soon. I'm going crazy trying to keep this a secret." Edward laughed, and the two of us returned to the sitting room.

"Jenny?"

"I'm here." Jenny pulled me into a hug, and then kissed Edward. "What have you two been up to? You've been sharing an awful lot of secrets lately."

Edward cleared his throat as I sat on the small sofa. "Have the children gone to bed?"

"Yes, they're all asleep."

"Good, because I've got a surprise for you."

I still had the small package in my pocket. Edward

touched my hand and I pulled it out, handing it over.

"Thanks, love."

He was nervous and cleared his throat again. There was some silence as, I assumed, Jenny opened the small package. Soon I heard a gasp.

"Jenny Ann Brinks, since the day I laid my eyes on you, I knew you were the only one for me. Will you marry me?"

Jenny sniffled and let out a sigh. "Oh, Edward, yes!"

I smiled, knowing my friends had fallen into each other's arms and were probably kissing.

I reached into my pocket and pulled out the letter I had received earlier in the day but hadn't had a chance to read. Leaving them alone in the sitting room, I returned to my room to read the letter.

Dear Hope,

This is Jay. I hadn' heard from you in a while so I thought I write and make sure you were okay. It hot in Oregon, and we had pretty hard winter. I was worried I wasn't going to make a crop, but I did.

Wheat seems to be worth a lot this year, so I decided to try my hand at that. Not sure if I'll get as much as my last crop, but I'll make do.

I spoke with your ma yesterday. She and Baby Cassandra say hello. It's hard to believe that little girl is already a year old!

Your pa left Linkville. We haven't seen him for nearly a month. No one seems to know where he gone, or when he be back. We don't even know why he's gone for that matter. Perhaps he just needed some time alone.

I better get to sleep. It won't be long before morning comes. Give Jenny and Edward my best.

Yours, Jay

I smiled, folding up the letter carefully and placing it in my bedside table drawer.

The drawer was becoming quite full. I received a letter from Joshua nearly every week. He had become a very good friend of mine, and I was glad. I couldn't imagine what I would do without Joshua's help in paying for my schooling.

I blew out the lamp and fell into my bed, falling into a peaceful sleep.

"My dearest daughter,

"It's hard to believe that twelve years ago your ma put you in my arms for the first time. I couldn't believe how small you were; how tiny; how helpless. You depended on us for every one of your needs.

"When you were born it seemed as though your brother was jealous of how much I loved you. I loved your brother too, of course, but we were never as close as you and I.

"The day you were sick and I was told I couldn't be with you, I was devastated. I think a little piece of me left that house that night, never to return. When I had found out about your sight, I blamed myself. I blamed myself for moving you to a new home, one that was much colder. I wondered what would have happened if we hadn't come to Linkville. Would you still have your sight?

"These questions died the day your brother left home. It would be an understatement to say that I was angry and hurt. It was much more than that, though I have no way to explain the emotions I had.

"This letter has taken me three months to write. I am in Virginia City, trying to make amends with Elijah. My grandson is a beautiful little baby, and he looks just like his ma. I have written your ma a letter to tell her where I am, and I will not return until you come back. I need the time with my son, not only for him, but so I can hopefully find myself.

"Enjoy your birthday and have a wonderful Christmas. I send my love to you.

"Love, Pa."

Jenny finished the letter and slid it into my hand. I caressed the letter as if it was Pa in person. I sniffled, trying to remember every word Jenny had read to me.

I wiped my face on my blanket, and Jenny pulled me into a hug. "Hope, do you need to go home?"

She paused. "You don't have to stay here anymore."

I looked up at her, shocked.

"I was going to tell you after the New Year, but I think now is the time."

I tried to rid the hitch in my breath, and rubbed

my face. I shook my head, sliding the letter into the book I had been reading. "No, not now. Your wedding is in February. I want to be here for that."

"Are you sure?"

I nodded.

"Okay". Jenny kissed me on the forehead and patted my leg. "Get some rest."

I nodded and sank into my blankets, visions of my family rushing through my mind.

Chapter 16

Homecoming

I yawned as the sun broke through the train's window. I could feel it on my face, and I wondered how close to San Francisco I was.

I was a little worried about traveling alone, but Jenny had sent telegrams, alerting all of the train stations I would stop at that I was coming and that I would need help. So far, everyone had been very friendly and helpful, and I wondered what it would be like in San Francisco. New passengers had entered the train on each stop, talking excitedly as it left whatever train station it was in.

"This is going to be so exciting." A woman sat down across from me. "I can't believe we're on our way to see the Thomas Edison."

I cleared my throat, curiosity getting the better of me. "Excuse me, but who are you talking about?" Just the excitement in the stranger's voice was enough to make me want to know more.

Another woman laughed. "Who are we talking about?! Goodness, child; don't tell me you've never heard of Thomas Edison!"

I shook my head.

"He's only one of the greatest inventors ever, save for Mr. Bell of course. Why, two years ago he invented the phonograph. You do know what that is?"

I nodded. Jenny had gotten one from Edward last Christmas. We spent many hours listening to the phonograph.

"He's speaking in San Francisco about his new experiments. He's working on something called a light bulb."

"A what?"

The first woman spoke this time. "A light bulb. It's a little bulb you put into a bulb socket and it emits light. It's like a lantern you never have to light! Wouldn't that be absolutely wonderful? It could light up the world and make everything easier to see!"

I shook my head. Hadn't these women noticed that I had not once looked them in the eyes?

"Sorry, ma'am, but it really wouldn't mean anything at all to me." I was hungry, and slightly angry. I stood up from my seat and, holding my hands out a little more than usual, left the train compartment.

The next morning came, and the train was pulling into the train station in San Francisco. The two women apologized to me; I accepted and agreed to go to lunch with them. They spent their time telling me about the latest inventions. Not surprisingly, I hadn't heard of any of them.

The newest invention was the cash register, created by James Ritty. I found this interesting, but personally I could see no use in it for it myself. There was also the new invention of saccharin. I didn't know for sure what it was, and the ladies had only read about it in the papers.

The invention that had interested me the most had actually been out for the last three years. Alexander Graham Bell had invented what was called the "telephone." I found this invention clever, and couldn't wait to try one. However, that would still be impossible for some time, as the phone lines had not reached the West Coast yet.

Eventually, I said my goodbyes to my new friends and settled into my coach seat.

It was a long week before I arrived in Linkville. It had been a little over three years since I had left and I wondered how much, if at all, it had grown.

When the coach stopped, the driver jumped down and, setting my bag on the porch of the mercantile, helped me out of the coach.

"I don't leave for a while, Miss. Do you need me to get someone to help you?"

I nodded. "Do you know the Tandra Bakery?"

"Yes! It's the best place to buy doughnuts." Obviously he didn't have a problem with the skin color of the owners.

I smiled and patted the man's arm. "Please get Mrs. Tandra. I don't want my ma to know I'm here just yet."

Suddenly I heard a familiar voice.

"Hope? Hope, is that you?"

My eyes widened at the sound of Joshua's voice. I smiled as I felt him pull me into a big hug.

"Thank you, driver, I take her now."

The coach clattered away.

Joshua pulled me up onto the porch of the mercantile. "Why didn' you write an' tell me you was comin' home?"

I took hold of Joshua's arms thankfully. My legs were a little tired from sitting so long. "I wanted to surprise Ma."

Joshua chuckled. "Well, she definitely will be, but she not here."

I let my smile fade. Where was she? Why wasn't she here? My panic must have shown.

"Not to worry, Freckles. She foun' out where your pa was an' she gone to talk him into comin' home."

I smiled. "That's good."

I suddenly noticed all of the voices coming from behind me. "What's with all the people?"

"Well, this town been goin' through some mighty big changes since you lef'. You remember that tinsmith who owne' that little tin shop by the river?"

I nodded.

"Well, now he buildin' this big hardware store."

"Really?"

"Mmm, an' they buildin' a new church an' school because the others was too small. There's about twice as many people as there use' to be, maybe more."

I was speechless. The Linkville I could still see in my mind was gone. How was I ever going to find my way around? I felt like going to my old house and hiding in the corner like I did before I left for St. Paul.

It took me nearly two weeks to learn the new layout of Linkville. Most of the people who had moved there lived on farms outside of town. There were about three more wood mills now, and the mercantile was busier than ever. Joshua, who made deliveries for the mercantile, checked in on me at home every day, so when he stopped on the first day of summer, I was ready for him.

There was a knock, and the door creaked open. I finished tying my bonnet, a grin on my face. "Good, you're here. Take me into town?"

Joshua kissed me on the cheek. "You in a good mood today." He put a heavy bag in my hands. "There the flour you wanted."

I set it on the table to put away later and turned back.

"Alrigh', I see you not goin' to change the subject. I take you into town."

He helped me into the wagon and we set off.

"Now, why all the excitement?"

"I've decided to take that job your ma offered me."

"Really?"

I smiled at his surprise. "To be honest, I've nearly run out of money, and I need the job. I have no idea when Ma's coming home, so I figured I have to take care of myself."

"Ma will be so happy."

The rest of the trip into town was quiet, until we crossed the river. I jumped when a man off to my right yelled at us.

"Slow down there, Tandra! I have a job for you!"

Joshua stopped the wagon. "What can I do for you, Mr. Baldwin?"

I finally recognized the voice, and I smiled.

"Who is this lovely lady you have here, Jay?"

"Oh, you remember Hope, don' you? She use' to bring you your ice on the way home from school."

"Oh! I remember you, now. My, how you've grown!"

I felt the heat rise to my cheeks as I shook the man's hand. "Thank you, Mr. Baldwin."

"How abou' that job?"

Baldwin had always been a bubbly man, and his enthusiasm showed in his voice. He clapped his hands. "Right! Now listen, when you take your next delivery north, I want you to pick me up two buckets of this paint." I assumed he had a paint bucket in his hands. "No substitutes. It has to be that exact one! I'm afraid the mercantile here is all out."

Joshua cleared his throat. "I'm sorry, Mr. Baldwin, but I been aks not to make deliveries there no more."

"No! A nice young man like you! They've got the wrong idear about you, young man. They don't know what they're missing. Have a good day, then!"

Joshua and I laughed when I heard Mr. Baldwin's door shut, and Joshua continued the wagon down the road.

He helped me down and led me inside the bakery. I didn't really need that much help anymore, but it made him feel important, so I usually let him.

"Ma? Where you at?"

Esther May's footsteps entered the room, and I smiled in her direction.

"Good morning, Mrs. Tandra."

"Hope! What a wonderful s'prise! Please, come in."

"Hope's decided to take that job you offere' her, Ma!"

"Really?"

I nodded, taking off my shawl and bonnet.

"Well, I'm-a give you da gran' tour."

Joshua bid his goodbyes, and Esther May taught me what I needed to do. It really was simpler than I thought.

"I'm-a glad you came for da job. Wha' wif all da new people in town an' more be comin' every day, I have a har' time keepin' up wif da store an' doin' all da bakin'!"

I smiled. "Thank you, Mrs. Tandra, for giving me the chance. Not many people would."

Esther May patted me on the shoulder. "You don' have to than' me. I be havin' sperience with dat myself, as you probably knowed."

I nodded, suddenly realizing that I now had something in common with the Tandras that I had never expected to have: I was discriminated against for something I had no control over.

"Hope! I jus' got a letter from your brother!"

I had been adding the fresh-baked doughnuts to the shelf, and hit my head on the top of the counter.

"Ow!" I rubbed it and stood the rest of the way up. "Don't scare me like that, Jay!"

Joshua chuckled. "Sorry, Freckles."

I wiped my hands on my apron and walked to the window, sitting down at one of the café tables. Joshua sat across from me, but didn't say anything.

"Well, are you going to read it to me, or do I have to force it out of you?"

"No, sorry." I heard him unfold the letter and he cleared his throat.

"Dear Jay,

"Just a quick letter to tell you that Ma and Pa should be arrivin' back in Linkville about the time you get this letter. They've spen' a lot of time with us an' each other the las' few

months, an' I think Pa's finally ready to accep' that times are changin'.

"Mia sends her love an' I hope all is well. The three of us will probably come that way for Christmas, so we might see you then. Have a good rest of the summer.

"Elijah."

I wiped a tear from my face. I was going to see my parents again, and I couldn't be happier.

I sniffled. "Has the mail stage left yet?"

Joshua moved his chair across the floor.

"No, not yet."

I smiled. "Good. Run down there and ask him not to leave yet. I want to send a letter to my brother."

Joshua got up as I grabbed paper and a pencil from behind the counter. I wrote quickly:

Dear Elijah, Mia, and baby Elijah,

Guess where I am? I've graduated from my blind school and I've been in Linkville since the end of April. You will not believe how much this place has changed! Jay read me the letter you sent him and I'm so excited! I can't wait to see Ma and Pa again after all this time! I was glad to hear you are all doing well. I'll write more later on. All my love.

Love, Hope

I sealed the letter and scribbled Elijah's name on the envelope, just in time for Joshua to return and take the letter to the postman.

The bell on the door jingled as I returned to

my usual seat behind the counter. "Good afternoon. Welcome to Tandra Bakery."

"Hope?"

1879 seemed to go by fast for me. November was significant; it was the month I turned thirteen, and though I still relied very much on my parents for some things, it was a very important year of personal growth for me. I had survived the fever that took my sight, and I had become so much more since then.

I was certainly closer to my parents, and I loved being there to help take care of my baby sister. Cassandra liked asking me questions, like "why is the sky blue?" because I usually came up with ridiculous answers like, "The sky is blue because someone tried to find a quick way to paint a house and accidentally exploded a blue paint can all over the sky." We would share laughs before she left for school to share these stories with her schoolmates, and it left a smile on my face all day at the bakery.

It was a good crop year for Linkville farmers, and everyone seemed to be celebrating. There was a small festival at the big red barn outside of town that Christmas, and I was escorted by my brother. Little Elijah had gotten sick, and Mia stayed with the children so the rest of us could have a good time.

January of 1880 rolled around, and we shared tearful goodbyes before seeing Elijah and his family off on the stage back to Virginia City. I promised to visit soon.

When winter left Linkville, I was ready to make that trip.

"I'd like to stay for a while if I can." I was finishing up my work at the bakery before catching the evening stage.

Esther May took the plates and wet rag out of my hand. "You be out of here an' have a good dinner wif your family before you leave. I be finishin' up here."

I sighed. "It's my job, Mrs. Tandra."

"If you don' get your little pale arse out of dis store, I'm-a fire you."

I grinned and headed for the door. "Tell Jay I'll write."

I left the bakery and headed for the restaurant next door, where my parents and Cassandra were waiting. We ate dinner together, and Cassandra fell into my arms when we were finished.

"I don't want you to go! Stay here!"

I kissed the top of my sister's head. "I won't be gone forever, Cass, and I promise I'll write to you."

Cassandra hugged me again, and after saying goodbye to Ma and Pa, I climbed onto the stage. I didn't know how long I was going to stay in Virginia City, or what the real reason was for going, but something was urging me to go.

As the stage pulled away from Linkville, I reached out of the side and waved, unaware that the person who had seen me wave would change my life in just a few short years...

Chapter 17

Fears and Dreams

Joshua

Dear Jay,

I hope all is well in Linkville. It's hard to believe I've been in Virginia City for nine months. Elijah, Mia, and E.J. are all well and they send their best.

I got a new student today. Her name is Marie, and she reminds me a lot of myself, except she's older than I am. She too was blinded by the fever, and she refuses to let me help her. I remember it wasn't until Elijah sent me a letter in Braille that I finally agreed to learn. Whether it would work on her or not, I don't know.

I better get back to my own studies. I take my teaching exam in two weeks. Wish me luck!

Yours, Hope

I folded the letter carefully an' place' it in the small box I kept all of her letters in. It seeme' odd that I had only seen'd her for a short time before she went on her holiday to visit her brother, an' she had not come back.

Hope been in Virginia City for two weeks when she was 'pproached by the school teacher. There was a blind chil' at the school who would fail without her help. She had agreed, an' before she knew it, she had three other blin' children from the state. The prospec' of her comin' back turne' to just a thought, knowin' that there were children who needed her. That was six months back.

Though it had been nearly six years since that fateful day when Hope knocke' on my door, I still blame' myself sometimes. It hardly seeme' fair that she had spen' so little of her life seein'. I always wishe' there was somethin' I could do to help her, but as far as I knew there was absolutely nothin' I could do.

The snow was comin' down lightly, an' it was getting' cold in the house. I started a fire an' sat to write a couple of letters. The firs' went to Hope, an' the secon' to my uncle in Minneapolis.

Hope

I sighed. "Listen, Marie. You can't go through the rest of your life expecting everyone else to take care of you. You are fourteen years old. You should be out in the world, reading and working and having a family of your own. Instead, you are stuck here because of your stubborn pride! Pull yourself together, Marie!"

I slammed the Braille book shut and headed up the stairs, where I threw myself onto the couch next to my sister in-law and sighed.

"Still not getting through to her?"

I shook my head, rubbing my face out of frustration. "I just don't get it. She's so smart, but she won't touch that book. She barely eats because she refuses to learn how the clock system works. She shuns the younger children because they're passing their tests and she's not, obviously because she can't read them. Am I doing something wrong?"

Mia chuckled. "No, darling. It's not you. You've just got to find a way to reach her. It was your brother who finally got to you. Maybe she needs her special someone, whoever it is."

I sighed, and Mia patted me on the head. "Use the time to get some rest. E.J.'s asleep and I'm going to take a nap myself."

I nodded, laying my heavy head on the couch; maybe just a short nap would help me regain my energy so I could try to find a way to help Marie.

Joshua

I yawne'. It been a very long day out in the fields. Summer was gone an' Christmas of '80 was slowly creepin' up on me. A bad hailstorm had obliterate' most of my crop, an' what I did manage to salvage wasn' worth much. After spendin' almos' a whole year needin' to supplemen' my pay from my crop wif another job, I was disappointed to learn I wouldn' make it through the winter wifout one; not that I had a problem findin' somethin'.

I spent mos' of my days makin' deliveries for the mercantile. I didn' wan' to take a job at the mill. I wanted my strength for the farm. Still, somethin' kept naggin' at me. Was I makin' the right decisions? Why, even though I was livin' my dream, did I feel empty? After everythin' good that had happene', could there possibly be somethin' missin'?

The thoughts fade' away when Alice, the pos' woman, came out of the post office. "Joshua! Now don't run off too fast. I've got a telegram for you!"

I nodde', paid her, an' then read through the words carefully:

Jay. All is well. After second attempt, passed teaching exam. Now have teaching license. Will write soon. Hope.

I smile', avertin' my paf instead to the bak'ry. "Ma? Where you at?"

Ma entere' the room, wipin' flour off of her hands. "Jay! How you be?"

I hande' her the telegram an' she read it over. "I wonder if she tol' her parents."

I shook my head. "I don' know. I jus' thought I'd show you. I know you grew attache' to her when you cared for her an' then when she worke' here."

Ma nodded, handin' the telegram back. "Yes, I did. Now get yourself to da mercantile. Don' get fire' on your firs' day back."

I kissed her on the cheek and lef', headin' for the mercantile, though my min' would not be anywhere near my work. I somehow manage' to get through it though, an' when I returne' home I returne' to my desk. I picke' up my Braille-writer, debatin' on what to write. Finally, I set the writer on the paper:

Dear Hope,

I was so glad to get your telegram. I'm very happy for you. I hope you have not left your parents out of this news. They will be very disappointed if they have been.

I wasn't going to say anything until I saw you again in person, but who knows when that will be? I have an uncle who lives in Minneapolis. He works in the kitchens of the hospital and has made friends with an eye surgeon there. The last time I heard from my uncle, he was telling me about an experimental surgery they've been looking into to fix the eyes. If it works, it could correct a completely blind eye and it would see again!

Please consider being one of their patients if they decide to try it. You'd be one of the first, so they might do it for free. Otherwise, I'll think of some way to get it paid for.

Hope to hear from you soon.

Jay

Hope

I folded the letter and put it in my pocket, thinking

about what Jay had written. Could it be possible that I might see again one day? What if I got my hopes up and the surgery failed? What if they told me I wasn't a good candidate for the surgery?

"Who's that letter from?"

I had forgotten that Marie was still in the room. She was my only student currently, which was good because I needed the time alone with her. "Um...it's from a good friend back home."

"But you're blind, too, right?"

"Yes, I am."

Marie was silent for a moment or two before speaking again. "How do you know what they write, then?"

I smiled. "Is this a sign of wanting to learn?" I would be so excited if something had finally gotten through to her.

The blind girl cleared her throat. "Maybe. I don't know...I mean, how...how do you know what your friend writes? And Mia says you like to read, but I don't understand how it's possible."

I returned to my seat across from Marie and took her hand. "Did you like to read before you got sick?"

"Yes, especially history."

I grinned. "I'm glad. That's what I like to read too. It's fascinating, and I get new history books all the time." I paused. "Oh! And I love Mark Twain. Brilliant man!"

Marie gasped. "I've heard horrible things about that man!"

I chuckled. "Oh, those are just rumors. I met him myself about two months before you came to live here. He gave me every one of his books. And they're all written in Braille."

"In what?"

I grinned. This was it! Finally something had gotten through to the girl, and she was going to learn how to read! I got up from the table and crossed the room to the bookshelf. I ran my fingers across the bindings before settling on two books. The first was a Braille copy of *Adventures of Huckleberry Finn,* and the second was the book that was used to teach me how to read. Jenny had sent it to me after learning of my teaching.

I returned to the table and put the Twain book in front of Marie. "I want you to put your hands on the book in front of you and tell me what you feel."

Marie was silent. I heard the book scrape across the table. "It's just a cover with a bunch of dots on it."

"Good." I sat beside Marie this time, shoving the Twain book aside and placing the Braille-reader book in front of my student. "Those dots are called Braille. They were invented by Louis Braille as a way for those of us who are blind to be able to read. Open the book in front of you." Marie followed my orders and I took her hand, placing it on the first page. "What do you feel here?"

Marie ran her hand up and down the book. "It's… it feels like someone carved an 'A' in the paper."

I grinned, remembering the last time I had heard those words. "Right." I moved Marie's hand away from the book and turned the page. I put her fingers on a six-dot cell. "This is the Braille cell. It consists of six dots. You read by learning a combination of these six dots which represent a letter in the alphabet. The next cell is the letter 'a'."

Marie ran her fingers across the next cell. "Oh!"

I grinned. It was going to be a very successful day!

Dear Hope,

I received a letter back from my uncle. The doctor should be responding back to me soon. He says you might be the perfect candidate for this surgery, and he'd like to talk to you about becoming his first patient when the operation is approved.

I hope all is well in Virginia City. Sorry this is so short, but Ma's making me serve Christmas supper! Well, at least we won't starve! Have a wonderful holiday!

Jay

I had re-read the letter about a million times since the day I received it. It was 1881, and I no longer had any students to teach. I was starting to feel a little homesick, and nervous about the possible operation.

I shook the thoughts away and ventured into the kitchen for lunch.

"There's my bestest sister!" Elijah kissed me on the cheek, and I shook my head.

"You shouldn't leave Cassandra out, bone-head."

"Hey, no calling names, Aunt Hope."

I grinned at my nephew. "I'm sorry, you're right."

I retreated to my room early, wanting to read the letter over again. However, I was interrupted by a knock at the door.

"Come in."

Mia's footsteps came across the floor. "We're thinking of paying Ma and Pa a visit. There won't be much work down in the mines for Elijah until they dig more out anyway, and we'd all like to see how much bigger Linkville is. What do you say?"

The thought of returning to the home I hardly knew anymore wasn't that thrilling, but I decided to go anyway. I was fourteen, and I wanted to find some more students to teach. "Maybe I can find someone else to teach over there."

Mia hugged me. "That's a wonderful idea! We'll leave in a couple days, how's that?"

I nodded, pulling out a piece of paper and a pencil. I stared into the darkness for a few moments after Mia left, and then began to write.

Dear Jay,

I've been thinking a lot about the surgery idea, and I'm not sure I like it. What if something goes wrong? What if it works, but then it quits working after a short time? What if once I get to Minneapolis they tell me I'm not good enough for their surgery? I can't help but ask these, because it's scary.

To have my eyesight taken so rapidly hurt a lot. I felt cheated and betrayed, not by you, but by God. I thought, how could he let such a thing happen to me, a child? I was angry, and I didn't want to trust anyone again, but those feelings went away, and I'm a better person for having gone through that challenge. I don't want to be disappointed by something that might not work again.

Keep me updated anyway, and I'll think about it.

Yours, Hope

P.S. All four of us are coming for a holiday.

I wished I could have reread the letter, but knowing that was impossible and that I didn't want anyone else to read it, I folded it carefully and stuffed it into an envelope to be mailed. I sighed and set it on the bedside stand.

Something was missing from my life, and it wasn't just from the lack of children to teach. What it was I couldn't put my finger on, but I hoped this sinking feeling would go away.

I left the house for a moment to go to the outhouse, and returned to my room. Yawning, I blew out the lamp I didn't really need and fell onto my pillow.

My dreams were filled with a face I couldn't quite pinpoint, but must have been important and fun, because I even had a smile on my face—something that was rare lately.

Who was that man?

Chapter 18

Tandra School for the Blind

Elijah

Spring of 1881 was cold in Linkville, but still the children spent most of their time playing outside. Everyone seemed to be on edge from the previous year, worrying about another bad crop-year, which would mean no more money and the loss of their farms.

Linkville had grown since the last time I had been here. I really hadn't seen much of it since the night I left it—not even on my last visit. As the wagon came closer, I smiled at the children playing.

The sun was starting to go down as the wagon pulled up to the Linkville hotel. We climbed out of the wagon, and Hope led us through the new part of town. Thankfully, most of it hadn't changed since the last time she had been here, and when we reached the closed Tandra Bakery, she sighed. "I guess we missed them."

"That's okay. It's getting late and we're hungry.

Let's just go back to the hotel and we'll go out to Ma and Pa's house tomorrow." Hope nodded to agree with me, and we turned to leave.

"Hope? Mia? Elijah?" I turned around and found Esther May poking her head out of the bakery door. "It be you! You comin' in!" She nearly bounced with excitement.

The four of us entered the quiet and warmth of the bakery and greeted Esther May. "We not be spectin' you til tomorrow."

I nodded, taking off my coat and handing it to her. She led us up the stairs and into the dining room. "We got an early start so we got here early. We were surprised to see the bakery closed already. Is everything okay?"

Esther May seated us all around the table and put bowls in front of us. "Yes, but we not be doin' da bak'ry no more. It be too much for us to be keepin' up wif. We be doin' alright for now. We got some money save' back an' Joe be workin' at da new Timber Mill out on da big lake."

Mia shook her head. "I know there's a lot of trees, but it still hurts to see the trees being cut down."

I kissed her on the cheek. "Don't worry, the forests are plentiful, and we need the lumber or you wouldn't have that beautiful house you live in." Mia smiled and kissed me back.

We ate the hot stew and then stood to leave. "We'll come and visit tomorrow."

Esther May gasped. "You do no such thin'. You be stayin' right here. We got plenty of room for all of you."

I smiled and agreed, and Esther May showed us where we would stay. I turned to Mia as Esther May started to leave.

Mia cleared her throat to get their attention. "Um, before we all go to bed, I have an announcement to make."

Esther May came back, and Hope took my arm. My heart started pounding. I had a hunch I knew what was coming.

"I'm going to have a baby."

Hope

"Miss Hope! I heard you were in town! How are you?" Reverend Hunt took me by the arm and walked with me down the front of the shops.

I smiled politely. "I'm okay. I miss teaching, but there are no students left for me in Virginia City."

Reverend Hunt stopped and turned me to face him. "Actually, that's one of the reasons I've been most anxious to talk to you." I tipped my head, curious as to what the reverend was going to tell or ask me. "I've just received a post from a reverend way down in California. It seems that there are about fifteen children in a blind school down south. Their teacher passed away, and they need a new home. It's a boarding school. The children come from poor families, so they can't pay a lot of tuition, but the church community helps. They were very excited when I told them about you."

"So you're asking me to take these children in?" I wasn't sure I'd be able to handle them all, and where would we live? "I don't know, Reverend."

Reverend Hunt patted me on the arm. "Well, just think about it and let me know, child."

195

I nodded and headed for the Tandra's.

The thought of taking in fifteen children was exciting, yet scary. The only place I knew that had capacity enough for that was the building that the Tandras lived in, but surely I couldn't ask them to turn their home into a blind school.

The thoughts were swept away when I suddenly walked into someone. "Oh! I'm so sorry!"

The next thing I knew, I was taken into a tight hug. "It so good to see you, Freckles!"

I felt the heat in my face rush, and pulled away from Joshua.

"What the matter?"

I shook my head. "Nothing, just embarrassed about running into you."

He squeezed my arm. "Don' worry, Freckles, but I know there somethin' on your min'. What is it?"

I'm not sure what made me so nervous that day about running into Joshua. I mean, we were great friends; there was nothing for me to be embarrassed over. Still, with everything going on around me I couldn't help but think about it.

Six months had gone by since then. I had spent the rest of that day with my family, discussing the situation and what I should do. Elijah's house in Virginia City was brought up several times, but finally it was decided that, as big as the house was, it was not big enough for all of the children and us. It had finally been decided that we would find a place we could use in town.

Overhearing the conversation, Esther May had hurried into the ground-floor room of the bakery, clapping her hands. "I insist you be movin' right here wif us," she had said. "We got enough room for thirty people here, an' da main floor be perfec' for a classroom. An' you can' do it all alone. I help wif da children, an' I not take no for no answer."

I loved the idea, and had gone to the church to tell Reverend Hunt.

November 20, my 15th birthday, came quickly, and the Tandra Blind School was finally ready. The children would be arriving any time on the stage, and I couldn't wait to meet them all.

I was sitting out on the porch of the Tandra house, listening for the stage. "Hope! I jus' been out to deliver some supplies to the lumber mill. The stage is less than a mile out!"

I smiled at the sound of Joshua's voice and I rushed inside to get Esther May. We emerged onto the porch just in time for the stage to pull up in front of us, thirteen children clutching ropes behind it. "Mrs. Tandra and Miss Bryant?"

I nodded. "Yes, I'm Miss Bryant." I extended my hand and shook the hand that grasped mine. "How was the trip?"

"Long, but we're here. I'm Julie."

The children were led up the steps by Joshua, passing me and Esther May as they went. "This is Meghan, Jeremy B., Tyler, Jessica, Cassandra, Beau, Andrew, Jacob, Alyssa, Kevin, Jeremy C., Charles, Caroline, Grace, and finally Jenny."

I shook my head. The children had gone by so fast that there was no way I would remember the sound of their footsteps or their names. All the same, a smile formed on my face, and I led Julie inside. The children were waiting just beyond the door.

"They've all got their night clothes on the tops of their bags. All they need to do is be shown to their rooms, and they'll be ready for bed."

Esther May sighed. "Now, Miss Julie, I not be sendin' these beautiful childr'n to bed wif empty tummies. They be havin' a decen' supper. Come along childr'n. Take hands an' we be goin' to da dinin' room."

I smiled as the children were led away into the next room. Julie sighed in protest, but followed. I, however, stayed.

"Everythin' alright, Freckles?"

My cheeks went hot again, and I wasn't sure exactly why. "Yes, I'm fine. Just trying to remember all their names."

Joshua chuckled. "Is there anythin' you need before I head home?"

"No, I think we're okay."

He kissed my cheek, and a shiver raced through my veins. "'Nigh', Miss Hope."

I cleared my throat. "Good night."

Chapter 19

A New Light

I rolled over in my bed. My stomach was flopping, and I was finding it hard to breathe.

It was 1885, and I was about to leave on the stage for San Francisco. I was eighteen, and the Tandra House blind school was growing. There were twenty children in the school, and the thought of leaving them all behind worried me. Not that I thought Esther May couldn't handle the children, but I had grown very much attached to them all.

The winter weather was gone, and as spring approached Linkville, I was packing my bags. There was a knock on the door and it creaked slowly open, and I knew instantly who it was. I stopped packing long enough to greet her "Hi, Ma."

"Do you need help packing?"

I shook my head.

"You look sick. Are you okay?"

I fell onto the bed, rubbing my face. I felt like I was going to be sick, but shook the feelings away. "I'm just nervous, I suppose. I wish you were going with me."

Ma took me into her arms and stroked my black curls. "You are strong, and you're beautiful. The worst that could happen is that the surgery doesn't work. It won't change anything, right?"

I shook my head. I didn't want to think about the surgery failing. I would be devastated and disappointed.

A tear fell down my face before I could stop it, and I blinked it away. "Did Pa come?"

Ma squeezed me and sighed. "No; he's still upset that you're going away with Joshua. You know how he feels about him."

I wanted to scream and yell. How could my pa be so stubborn and unwilling to change his views? Especially after everything that had happened between Mia and Elijah? Hadn't he changed at all in the presence of his grandson and granddaughter? I shook my head, a tear falling down my cheek. "Why does Pa have to be so stubborn about the Tandras? They've been nothing but wonderful to all of us, including Pa—and he doesn't even deserve it."

"I don't know, Hope. That's just the way your father is."

I pulled away and sat back down on the bed. Ma sat beside me, taking my hand. "Do you want to know the truth?"

I nodded.

"Ever since the moment your brother left home with Mia, he's been afraid that someone would take you away from him."

This was news to me, and I contemplated it for a moment. How could he have been so selfish? "Ma, the only thing that kept me away was having to go to school, and then teaching."

"I know."

I sighed and returned to packing. Ma helped me finish up and walked me to the front room downstairs where everyone was waiting to say goodbye. I hugged all twenty children and the Tandras before Joshua took my arm, leading me to the waiting stagecoach. My heart thumped and I thought it would jump right out of my chest. He helped me into the stage and climbed in after me.

It lurched forward and I shivered. This was going to be the scariest trip of my life.

The stage arrived in San Francisco a week later, and we boarded the train. As every day passed, I became more and more nervous. I didn't know what to expect when we reached Minneapolis. Joshua continued to try to cheer me up, and it usually worked—at least until the moment when I thought about my upcoming surgery again.

We spent a night in Virginia City visiting my brother before setting off on the train again. It would take two weeks to get to Minneapolis, and I spent a lot of that time reading.

Joshua had been asked to leave when we reached one of the stations. This was something that I hadn't experienced before, and I didn't like it at all. I had taken the train conductor by the shirt collar, and though I couldn't see him, I pulled his face to mine, furious at the unfairness of it all.

"He is here to escort me. He will be allowed on, or you will refund our tickets AND pay for us to ride the stage to Minneapolis."

The conductor backed off and set us inside the

caboose. It wasn't as comfortable as our previous spots, but it was the only place Joshua would be allowed.

"Thank you for that, Freckles." I smiled at him and he kissed me on the cheek. "You didn' really have to do it."

I nodded, re-opening my book. "Yes I did. He was rude, and taking advantage of us both."

The rest of the trip was silent for the most part, and after another week we arrived at the Minneapolis train station. Joshua led me through the town, explaining it to me. It sounded lovely, but I didn't want to get my hopes up that I would see it any time soon.

Finally we arrived at a small cabin just outside of town. Joshua knocked on the door.

"Joshua, m'boy!" We were both pulled inside, and I was taken into a hug. "This must be Miss Hope."

I nodded, pulling away from the strange man. "Hello."

"Uh, this be my Uncle Ben, Hope. He's the uncle I told you about."

We shook hands, and Ben set us down to drink some tea. "Now, m'boy. We must discuss you for a minute."

His hand touched mine. "You don't mind, do you?" I shook my head, sipping my tea and curious about what was going to commence in the conversation.

"When you gonna get yourself hitched, son?"

Joshua choked on his tea, and clanged his cup down. "Well, I...to be perfectly honest I haven' even thought about it."

Ben clicked his tongue. "You not getting' any younger, an' neither am I. I want a niece in-law to spoil."

Joshua chuckled. "Maybe soon."

Ben clicked his tongue again. "Thought you

woulda been married by now. You be twenty-seven."

Joshua cleared his throat nervously, and I tried to stifle my laughter. "Come on, Uncle Ben. Leave me about it."

We spent the rest of the evening getting to know one another. The next day was my pre-surgery appointment, and I felt like throwing up.

"Yesterday's exam was perfect. Your eyes are very healthy, and I think the surgery will produce perfect results, though I wish I could give you a 100-percent guarantee. The only thing left is for you to go to sleep."

I had no response. I was far too nervous, and even though I was older, I wanted to go home and crawl into Ma's arms and sleep there, but home was halfway across the country; there was no turning back.

"I just need to sign some papers and get the rest of my associates ready. I'll be back in a few minutes."

The door closed behind the doctor, and then it opened again. Joshua's familiar footsteps crossed the wooden floor, and all the heat from my face drained away. I felt sick.

"'Lo, Freckles."

I shook my head, fighting back the tears. "I can't do this. Take me home, Jay."

Joshua took up my hand and kissed the back of it. "I never seen you afrai' of anythin'."

I couldn't hold the tears back anymore. They rushed out of my eyes as if they had just broken through a dam that had been holding them back for years. I let out a sob and he took me in his arms.

"Everythin' will be fine. I be here the momen' you

wake, an' God is wif you always."

I gasped in my sobs, and Joshua climbed onto the bed. He pulled me closer and stroked my head. I was glad for it. I felt safe in his arms. He would never let anything happen to me, and would see that I returned home unharmed. I started to calm, and felt so comfortable in the man's arms that I didn't even realize the doctor had returned until a needle poked me.

I winced, and every inch of me turned warm and relaxed. Joshua let go, climbing off the bed. He stroked my head and I smiled. His free hand came to rest above my shoulder, and I tipped as his knee pushed down on the bed.

His lips were soft and warm as they found mine, and I had barely realized what had happened when he pulled away. It startled me, and I wanted to know what it was about, but before I had the chance my dark world went silent.

Joshua

I was pacin' the floors. I had spen' the las' few hours pullin' out my pocket-watch to see what time it was an' how long I been waitin' for some news. Four hours gone by an' I still hadn' heard anythin'. After five hours I decide' my legs was tire' an' collapse' in a chair.

"Jay!" A familiar girl was runnin' down the hall towards me. As she came closer, I recognize' Jenny. She was older, an' expectin'.

She hugge' me, wipin' a tear off her cheek. "I tried to get here sooner, but the stage never came and Ed is out of town, otherwise he would've driven me here! How is she?"

I fell back into my chair wif a sigh. Frustrated, I threw my hands into the air. "I don' know. These people won' tell me a thin'! They obviously bothere' that I'm here because not one of them will look at me. Not one!"

Jenny squeezed my hands. "Calm down, Jay. How long has she been in surgery?"

"Five hours."

She got up to talk to the nurse, an' I was clenchin' an' unclenchin' my fis's. I was thinkin' about the momen' in the room jus' before Hope fell asleep. I kisse' her, but why? I never thought no more than friendship for her. There couldn' be no more; there was no way it woul' work. So why had I kisse' her?

Jenny came back an' sat beside me. "The nurse says they weren't ignoring you, they just haven't heard from the doctors yet. She said we'll know as soon as they do."

I nodded. This helpe', but it wasn't good enough. "Jenny, I think I made a mistake..."

"What are you talking about, Jay?"

I looke' into Jenny's blue eyes. "Hope, before she wen' to sleep." Jenny waited patiently. "Jenny, I kisse' her."

Her eyes widened. "You mean on the cheek like you always do?" I shook my head. "On the lips?" I nodded, and she smiled at me.

Hope

I screamed. I felt like a thousand knives were stabbing

at my face. What had I agreed to do this for? The pain was unbearable, but I couldn't cry. I was too scared to let the tears come. The salty water would definitely hurt. I clutched at the side of the bed. "Help me!!! Somebody, please!!!"

I felt a hand take mine, but it wasn't Joshua's. It was smaller and softer, less worked and smooth. He was supposed to be there. Where was he?

"Hope? Hope, this is Jenny."

"Jenny, it hurts! Make it stop hurting!" I gasped for breath; I wanted to curl up and die. I was glad that Jenny was there, but where was Joshua? He had promised he'd be there when I woke. "Where is he?"

Jenny chuckled. "Don't worry; he's just gone to the water closet. I had to force him because he was worried he wouldn't be in the room when you woke."

I wanted to laugh, but it hurt too much. I never wanted to feel this pain again. What would happen after the bandages came off? Would it all be worth it?

After a few moments, the door opened and Joshua walked in. He took my hand, not wanting to go near my head, and squeezed it. "I thought you...I thought you left."

"I promised you I'd be here."

It had been six weeks since the surgery. I had been told not to do much, and we needed a way to make money. Jenny made me return to St. Paul with her for the summer, and Joshua went to work in Minneapolis.

The coming visit to the doctor could possibly change my life. It was time for the bandages to be removed, and I found my stomach spinning for the third time since I left Linkville.

The door opened and I swallowed the lump in my throat.

"I see you've got an extra one with you this time." I nodded, and Jenny introduced herself. "Pleased to meet you, Jenny."

The doctor slid a chair across the floor. "Alright, Hope. I'm going to remove the bandages off your right eye first. It's going to be sore, but I don't want you to open your eye until I tell you. If you can see out of your right eye, then we'll assume that the surgery will have worked in both. Are you ready?"

I took in a deep breath, and Joshua took my hand. I smiled, squeezed his hand, and then nodded.

Slowly the bandages were cut through, and I felt my muscles flinch away from the scissors with every cut. Finally, the bandages broke loose and were pulled away.

"Okay, Hope. When you're ready, I want you to slowly open your eye."

I took another deep breath and tightened my grip on Joshua's hand. The success of the whole surgery rested with the fate of this eye.

It hurt, but slowly I opened it. The light burst through the crack in my lid as if it had been blown away, and I wanted to close it immediately. I had never seen anything so bright, nor had I seen anything so wonderful. The window shade was pulled down, and I risked opening my eye again.

Slowly the light turned into shapes and colors, and I stared into the doctor's eyes. I sniffled, afraid to cry. "I can see you."

Joshua laughed out loud, dropped my hand and took Jenny into a flying hug.

The doctor spent the next few minutes removing the remaining bandages and cleaning my face. "She'll be in pain, but I'll send home some medicine, and it must be strictly monitored. We don't want her to get dependent on it."

The doctor put his tools down and clapped his hands. "Okay, Hope. Open both eyes."

The tears flooded out of my eyes before I could stop them. It stung, but it was a beautiful feeling. I could see everything, and even the floor was beautiful to me. I stumbled out of my chair and walked over to Joshua. I looked up into his chocolate eyes. His face was different than I remembered it, but something was familiar.

Suddenly it hit me, and I hugged him tightly. "The dream…"

Chapter 20

Realizing the Truth

I let go of Joshua and met his eyes. He was looking at me as though I was crazy. I smiled at him, and then remembered Jenny was in the room.

I looked at her round face for the first time, and then hugged her. "Oh, Jenny! After everything you've done for me, and now I don't even need it!"

Jenny pulled me back and took me by the shoulders. "What about your children at the school?"

I blushed. How could I have forgotten my children, waiting for me to return? "You're right." I turned to the doctor. "Do I need to stay longer or can I go home?"

The doctor smiled at me. "I want you to stay in town one more night. We'll check and see how things are in the morning, and then you can go home."

I nodded, and the three of us left the hospital. For the first time in nearly ten years, I walked out into the light.

I squinted. The sun certainly was brighter than I remembered, and I felt like a little kid again. I turned and took Joshua by the arm. "Take me on a horse ride, Jay!"

Joshua shook his head. "I don' think we should do that jus' now, Hope."

I was disappointed, but I knew he was right. I didn't want to risk damaging my eyes so soon. Instead, he treated me and Jenny to a grand dinner.

I had never enjoyed the sight of food more. Finally, when the sun was setting (the sky was the nicest shade of purple), we headed for the stagecoach. It was time for Jenny to go.

My beautiful former teacher hugged me.

"I wish you didn't have to go, Jenny."

"I know, but I do have a husband to get home to, and children to teach." Jenny bid her goodbyes and climbed onto the stage.

As the horses started moving, I looked around the darkening city. There was a fountain down the street in front of the city hall.

I pointed toward the water. "Let's just sit and talk for a while."

Joshua smiled. "Da night is yours, Freckles."

I blushed, and we walked in silence to the fountain, sitting on its edge. "Can I aks you somethin', Freckles?"

I nodded, putting my hand in the cool water.

"Earlier when you hugge' me, you mentione' a dream."

I nodded again. "Can I ask you something before I answer your question?" He nodded back.

I didn't say anything at first. I had wanted to ask this question for the last six weeks, but hadn't seen him enough. I wondered how exactly to word the question without making him uncomfortable.

Finally, I cleared my throat. "When they were taking me into surgery, right before I went to sleep, you…"

"I kisse' you."

I nodded, my heart racing.

"Hope, we knowed each other for eleven years. You was always kin' to me when others weren'; even when your pa forbade you." I lowered my eyes to the ground. I hadn't wanted my pa brought up, but somehow, when it came to Joshua, he always managed to creep into the conversation.

"We nearly ten years apart in age, so you never been more than jus' a frien' to me, but somewhere, an' don' aks me where because I don' know, I suppose I might have started seein' more."

I met his eyes, a little shocked at what I was hearing.

"Freckles…Hope, I care for you. I don' know what that kiss mean', maybe it didn' mean anythin' at all."

I felt a tear slide down my cheek. It was hard to believe this man, whom I had been forbidden to befriend, was now sitting here saying these things. What was happening?

It was my turn. "I've been having a dream about a man I could never see well. The dream was too dark." I paused, waiting for a reaction, but he just blinked. "He was putting a ring on my finger…and then he kissed me."

Joshua

I blink at the young girl in front of me. I stare' deeply

into her green eyes. My heart was racin', an' I didn' understand it. What was it about this girl that made me feel like I could fly?

I watched her carefully as she looked aroun' the darknin' city an' then she looke' back to me. "Let's just sit and talk for a while."

I smile'. "The night is yours, Freckles."

Hope blushe' an' we walke' in silence to the fountain down the road, sittin' on its edge. I looked aroun'. It seeme' dat we was the only two left outside tonight. It was now or never.

"Can I aks you somethin', Freckles?" The black-haired girl nodded, puttin' her han' in the water. "This mornin' when you hugge' me, you mention a dream."

Hope nodded. "Can I ask you something before I answer your question?" I nodded back, watchin' her. She seeme' to be stallin' to aks me the question.

Finally she cleare' her throat. Was she nervous? "When they were taking me into surgery, right before I went to sleep, you…"

My heart leap'. I been hopin' the whole time that she was already asleep when I done it. She hadn' mentione' it to me, an' now…now…

I sighe'. "I kisse' you."

Hope nodded. I shook the nervous feelin' away. I just neede' to tell her what I been feelin' "Hope, we knowed each other for eleven years. You was always kin' to me when others weren'; even when your pa forbade you." She lowere' her eyes to the groun' an' I wondere' whether I had made her uncomfortable, but still I continue'. "We nearly ten years apart in age, so you never been more than jus' a frien' to me, but somewhere—an' don' aks me where because I don' know—I suppose I might have started seein' more."

She met my eyes, an' my heart skippe' again. She looke' as though she migh' be mad. I had said too much an' curse' to myself.

"Freckles...Hope, I care for you. I don' know what that kiss mean', maybe it didn' mean anythin' at all."

A tear fell down her cheek an' she took a deep breaf. "I've been having a dream about a man I could never see well. The dream was too dark. He was putting a ring on my finger...and then he kissed me."

A secon' tear fell down her cheek, an' I raise' my han' to wipe it away. Her face fell into my han' an' I stroke' her face wif my thumb. Her white skin was sof' an' almos' glowe' against my brown han'. She shivere' wif the light breeze an' I immediately took my coat off, wrappin' it aroun' her shoulders.

"Thank you."

I smile', lookin' into her eyes. It felt strange that I could look an' she was seein' me back, but I was happy for her. Even after all the years she had live' blin' I still foun' myself feelin' responsible for her catchin' the fever.

I took her han' in mine an' took in a deep breaf. "Hope, could I...may I kiss...kiss you again?"

Her green eyes widene' an' my heart sunk. I had finally said too much, an' she was goin' to run away. I knew the prospec' of bein' wif her was too farfetche'. It wasn' possible for us to be together. We were from two differen' worlds.

I droppe' my head an' sighed. "I sorry; I was out of line to aks. I shouldn' have..."

Hope placed a long soft finger over my lips an' I met her eyes again. "Yes, you may."

I smile' an' slowly I leane' forward. I pause' briefly, my heart racin'. I leane' a little farther, an' our lips met. I took in the scent of her hair. It smelle' of lavender, an' her lips were sof'. I took her into my arms an' ran my fingers through her black curls. I was tryin' desperately to ignore the chills runnin' down my spine.

She pulle' back then, an' our eyes met again. She smile' at me an' fell into my arm, her head on my shoulder. I looke' up into the sky an' hugge' the young girl in my arms.

How on God's green earf would I survive Thomas' wrath?

Hope

I rolled over in my cot. The sun was shining through the window, and a pot on the stove was whistling. I carefully wiped my sore eyes and opened them up.

We were still at Uncle Ben's house, and I stood up to get dressed while the two men were outside. I pulled my skirt up just as they walked in the door.

"Oh! I'm so sorry, Freckles." Joshua's brown face turned a bright red-brown and he turned away.

I laughed. "Don't worry, I was done." I met his eyes when he turned back, and we smiled at each other. Uncle Ben looked between the two of us, and when I noticed, I tore my eyes away and sat down to tie my shoes. "What time are we supposed to be at the hospital?"

Uncle Ben chuckled. "Oh boy! Oh my! Joshua, you big black liar! How dare you keep somethin' like dat from me?!"

I looked up, confused. "Excuse me?"

Joshua shrugged, pouring a cup of coffee from

the pot on the stove. "I don' know what he talkin' 'bout."

The old man laughed, and Joshua and I looked at him curiously. "You love her, you ol' fool!"

Joshua's eyes widened and I shook my head. Joshua set his coffee down before he dropped it and chuckled. "Uncle Ben, I think you losin' your min' again."

"Alrigh', if you say so."

Joshua laughed and pulled out his pocket-watch. "We best be goin'."

I nodded, finished my packing, and handed my bag to Joshua.

I turned to Uncle Ben. "Thank you so much for letting us stay here."

He gave me a strong, tight hug. "You come back any time, an' you write me, ya hear?"

"I will."

Joshua bid his goodbyes to his uncle, and we walked side by side into town and to the hospital. He stopped me before going in and set the bags down. "Hope, what my uncle said back there. He overdoes it sometimes."

I smiled. "I know you don't...well, not like that."

"Well, I didn' say that either. I jus'...not yet."

I chuckled. "I know. Can we go in now?"

Joshua nodded and picked up the bags again. I was smiling all the way down the hall, and when I walked through the exam room doors, the doctor was already waiting for us. "Good morning."

"Ah! Miss Bryant. How are you feeling?"

"I feel wonderful."

The doctor proceeded with his exam, and when he finished, he smiled. "Everything looks great! You're going to go down in history, Miss Bryant. You are the first successful corrective eye-surgery."

I smiled back. I felt wonderful.

"Now, your eyes will probably get tired. The muscles have not been used in a very long time and they need to regain their strength. If they do get tired, I want you to find a place to rest and keep them closed for about fifteen minutes. After some time the need for rest will diminish."

I stood and shook the doctor's hand. "Thank you so much."

The doctor shook his head. "No, thank you. This is a breakthrough in medical history. Thank you for being my first patient."

Chapter 21

Homecoming

I took a deep breath. Joshua was standing at the end of the road, waiting for me. We were in Virginia City to surprise Elijah and Mia. Joshua had sent on a telegram to both them and my parents to let them know I was safely out of surgery, but we hadn't reported on the results.

I turned and looked down the street, and he smiled at me. I smiled back and knocked on the door.

After a few moments the door creaked open, and I met my brother's eyes. I smiled a big smile as the color in Elijah's face drained.

"Hope?" I hadn't broken eye contact with him and he smiled as wide as the sky. "It worked! Mia! Oh, Hope!" He took me into a hug and twirled me around. "You look absolutely wonderful!"

I dropped out of his grasp and turned as Mia came down the stairs. "Hope?"

I nodded, winking at my sister in-law. "Hope!" She ran into my arms, and we hugged so tight I choked.

Mia pulled away instantly. "Oh! I'm so sorry!"

I laughed. "You're fine."

Mia hugged me again. "I can't believe it worked! Can you see everything?"

I nodded, smiling at them both. "Yes, as good as new."

I looked around the quiet house. It really was much bigger than I remembered, but perhaps that was because I had never seen it before. It was also quiet.

"Where are the children?"

Elijah shut the door. "E.J. is at school and Jenny is sleeping."

I was disappointed. I was going to miss seeing the children. We had to catch the next train back down the mountain in order to get on the evening train, or we would have to wait three days for the next one. "I guess I'll have to come back for a visit to see them then. Jay and I have to catch the train in about fifteen minutes."

Elijah opened the door again. "Jay's here? Where is he?"

"He's waiting down the road so we don't miss the train."

"Are you sure you can't stay?"

I shook my head. I wanted to, but I was anxious to get home. "Ma and Pa don't know my surgery worked yet, and I want to get back to the school."

We bid our goodbyes and, wiping a tear from my face, I headed back down the hill where Joshua was waiting. He slid his arm around my waist and kissed me on the cheek. "How are they?"

I hugged him, taking his arm as we headed down the hill to wait for the train. "They're fine. I didn't get to see the children, but I will soon."

Joshua kissed the top of my head before we reached the sight of people. "Are you hungry? We could grab sandwiches before we get on the train."

I nodded, and slid out of Joshua's arms.

He shook his head. "I don' think so; you not getting' out of it that easy." He laced his fingers between mine and I smiled.

We went into the delicatessen and bought some sandwiches, just in time for the train to pull up across the street. He paid quickly and I nodded my thanks to the worker, handing Joshua his sandwich.

As we walked across the street hand-in-hand, I couldn't help but notice the people on the boardwalks whispering and pointing our way. This was something I had already anticipated, and I shrugged it off. I didn't care what other people thought; I only cared that I was happy and loved, and that was exactly how I felt.

The train groaned to a halt. We were about twelve hours behind schedule, and the sun had already gone down. I rubbed my still-bruised eyes and looked out of the window. The sign hanging from the station read 'San Francisco' and I sighed. This was the end of our comfortable train ride.

"Jay, honey. Wake up." I slowly shook him awake and he moaned.

"I don' wanna get up."

I shoved him playfully. "Get up, old man. We're in San Francisco."

"Who you callin' ol', woman?!"

We laughed all the way off of the train and into the station. We were given several disgusted looks and scoffs, at which Joshua shrugged. "Don' worry 'bout dem, Freckles. They wouldn' knowed a good time if it hit them in the arse!"

Everyone gasped and hurried out of the train station. I shook my head, smiling. He winked at me and laced his fingers through mine. When we reached the counter, he gave my hand a squeeze.

"When's the next stage to Linkville?"

The man behind the counter shook his head. "T'ain't another 'til tomorrow, sir."

Joshua paid the man for two tickets and we left the station. "Where to, m'lady?"

I looked around the dark city hills. I knew exactly where I wanted to go, but how to get there was another question, and one I didn't know the answer to. I closed my eyes and took a deep breath.

I could smell it and hear it. I opened my eyes and met his. "I want to see the ocean."

Joshua smiled and kissed my cheek. He took my hand and led me up and down the hills before coming to wooden steps that led down the hill off to the right. I smiled. I remembered these steps!

I grabbed his arm to steady myself and leaned over to take off my shoes. Setting them aside, I kicked at his boots with my bare feet. "Take yours off, too. Walk in the sand with me!"

He shook his head, but obeyed. I took his hand, and together we went down the wooden steps, flying into the sand. I pulled him further through the soft, cool shore. The water was getting closer and closer, and it was the most beautiful thing I had ever seen. In that moment I understood why it sounded the way it did, and I ran into the flowing water.

"Hope! Don' go too far!"

I let go and spun around, the water splashing over my knees. "Isn't it beautiful?" I stopped and took in the scent of the salty air. "I could stay here forever."

Joshua shook his head, trying his best to avoid the waves. "No you won'."

"Oh? And what makes you say that?"

He reached out and grabbed my hand. He pulled me closer and wrapped his arms around me. "Well, your childr'n woul' never forgive you for not comin' home." I nodded in agreement. "And, I'm in Linkville."

I smiled. "But I could live without you."

Joshua dropped his jaw and threw me out of his arms. I laughed as he walked away.

"I was only joking!"

I ran after him, but was rewarded with a face full of water. He had splashed at me, and I was not going to take it. I ran after him and jumped, knocking him over in the sand.

It was no use trying to stay dry now; we were both consumed by a wave, and as the water was sliding back over us, Joshua took me into a passionate kiss. I fell into it, my heart skipping. I felt like I could float away. The water washing over us was cool, but the heat emanating from his kiss kept me warm. My emotions got higher, and I forced myself to pull away.

"I'm sorry." I gave him a small smile.

Joshua shook his head and ran his fingers through my wet hair. "Don't worry, Freckles."

We smiled at each other as another wave consumed us. We needed to get out of the water before we caught cold. I stood up, pulling him up after me, and we left the beach for the hotel we had seen on the way. I smiled, thinking about the kiss in the ocean, and for the first time in my life my heart felt full.

Three months after my departure, I stepped back onto the Linkville soil, but this time I could see it. It was much bigger than I ever remembered it, but it was the most beautiful place I had ever seen, except the ocean, of course. I breathed in the warm fall air and smiled at Joshua.

"Thank you, for everything. It means the world to me."

He shook his head. "You mean the world to me, Freckles." I blushed as the stage pulled away. "Listen, I don' think we should tell anyone about our relationship jus' now."

We headed for the blind school, and I nodded. "I agree. I'm not ready for you to die yet."

We laughed and stepped inside the house.

"Ma, Pa, we home!" Joshua set our bags down just in time for Esther May to run into his arms. "Hello, Ma."

"Oh, I miss you so much!" I watched as she examined her son carefully. "You be lookin' diff'rent."

I chuckled as his cheeks turned reddish-brown. He cleared his throat. "I don't know what you talkin' 'bout."

I smiled when Esther May turned to me. "Hello."

A tear fell down her black cheek as she pulled me into a hug. "It work, didn' it?" I grinned and nodded. "Oh, honey. I be so happy for you."

Joshua blew me a kiss and set off to put the bags away. I pulled out of Esther May's grasp and looked towards the other room. "How are the children?"

"They be missin' you." She led me into the classroom, where they were all sitting and listening to Joseph read Tom Sawyer. "I was jus' 'bout to set dem down to lunch."

She left for the kitchen, and I looked into each of their faces. They were beautiful, and I wiped a tear from my face.

"I should take a picture of all your beautiful faces."

The children jumped out of their seats and surrounded me so fast it was hard to believe they were blind. I let the tears fall as I hugged them all. I don't know why I loved the children so much, but I did.

As they filtered away to the table, I dried my face. Joseph put a strong hand on my shoulder and I smiled.

"Welcome home, darlin'."

I looked around at the new buildings in Linkville. Everything looked so different since the last time I had seen it all. It was bigger and busier. It reminded me of Virginia City: small but busy. The biggest difference was the large hardware store owned by Mr. Baldwin and partner, and the Lakeside Hotel near the Link River. I smiled and crossed the bridge that would take me to my parents' house.

After twenty minutes, I looked up and saw Cassandra playing with a dog outside the house. I smiled; she was a beautiful child, though I was probably biased about her.

The child stopped and met my eyes. I smiled at her and she smiled back, her eyes wide with excitement.

"Ma! Pa! It's Hope! She's back!" Cassandra ran down the street and jumped into my arms. I picked her up and swung her around in a big hug. "We missed you, Hope!"

"Oh, I missed you too, Cass." I set my sister down and looked up into my parents' faces.

"It worked. It really worked." Ma and Pa scooped me up and kissed my face. I hugged them back and pulled away.

"Sorry, I couldn't breathe."

We all laughed and headed for the house. Pa put his arm around me and rubbed my arm, kissing the top of my head. "Welcome home, sweetheart."

Chapter 22

Special Delivery

Esther May

"Da childr'n be sleepin', an' your pa be puttin' a pot of coffee on da stove."

I sat in da chair an' wipe' my face on my apr'n. I be getting' no response, an' looke' at my son. He be starin' into da orange flames of da fire. He be deep in thought an' barely blinkin'.

"Jay?" No response. "Joshua?"

He blinke' an' turn to look at me. "Sorry, Ma. I didn' hear you come in. Da childr'n asleep?"

I nodded, worried. "An' your pa puttin' coffee on da stove." He nodded an' turn back to stare into da flames.

Somethin' be both'rin' him. He been actin' funny since he come back, but why? I sighe'. "Jay, what be wrong?"

Joshua shrug his shoulders. "Nothin', Ma. I suppose I jus' tired. From da trip, you know."

I watch him silently. Somethin' be goin' on, an' I knowe' he not be tire'. He looke' as though he was thinkin' deeply 'bout somethin' or someone. I coul' see it in his eyes.

I sigh again an' kneel on da floor in front of him. I place' my han' on his cold one. "Jay, look at mama."

Joshua smiled. "Ma, I'm not ten anymore."

I smile' back. "Jus' tryin' to brin' you back to life, son. Tell me what be wron'. I'm a not aksin', I'm-a tellin'."

He stare into my eyes for a lon' time, an' then he sighe'. "Alright, but can we keep it 'tween us for now? There is a few people who don' need to know right now."

I be quiet, squeezin' his han'.

"Ma, I met someone, an' I in love wif her, but I worried it's not goin' to work."

I widene' my eyes. My son be in love! "Who it be? Tell me!"

Joshua look to da floor, not wantin' to say no more. He open' his mouf, but close it again.

Da fron' door creak open, an' Hope come in da room. "I'm back, are the children asleep?"

His face turn red, an' I cover my mouf.

Joshua

I stare' into the fire. I couldn' help but turn red the momen' she walk in the door. I wanted to jump up into her arms, but I couldn' because I didn' wan' to get her into trouble wif her parents. Ma had gone to bid Hope g'night, an' any momen' she would be back in fron' of me, interrogatin' 'bout what I said.

I wishe' it was an easier sitiation, but the fac' was we would mos' likely be kep' apart by her parents. How were they ever goin' to 'ccept me into their fam'ly? They had barely 'ccepted me as a frien'. I knew Mr. Bryant was angry at Hope for goin' wif me to Minnesota, but she had, an' she had confided in me as we lef' that she didn' wan' to go wif anyone else. That had to coun' for somethin' didn' it?

I shook the thoughts away. I needed to get out of the house before Ma come back. I rushe' to the door an' grabbed my hat.

"Joshua, you bes' not go out that door! You come talk wif me!" I sighed disappoint'dly an' turned to her.

She was starin' at me in the eyes like she was tryin' to read my thoughts. It made me uncomfortable. "Ma, please don' look at me like that."

Ma smiled at me. "You really be in love wif dat girl?" I nodded. "An' what 'bout her. You tell her how you feel?"

"Yes, we been together since the day Hope had the bandages off."

"You bes' been respectful, cause if you haven'..."

"Yes, Ma! Of course I have. How could you sugges' such a thin'?"

She took me into a tight hug. "Oh! I'm-a happy for you!"

Hope

I was on my way to the mercantile. We had run out

of pencils at the school, and I needed to grade the children's work. The stage pulled up as I got there, and I stopped to watch. Why, I didn't know.

"Hope!"

I turned to see who had whispered my name. Joshua was peeking around the back of the mercantile, waving for me to come. I smiled, shaking my head, and went to him.

"What are you doing?"

He wrapped his arms around me. "I had to see you. It been ages."

I chuckled. "It's only been two days, and you've been farming."

Joshua squeezed tighter. "It feel like three weeks."

I laughed and looked up into those warm brown eyes, and smiled as he leaned in to kiss me. I took it in, savoring every moment. My biggest fear was that Pa would keep us apart, and I had to make each second count.

I pulled back as Joshua tried to pull me in for more, and noticed the look on his face.

"Jay, what's the matter?"

A single tear fell from the corner of his eye, painting his cheek as it fell. I started to worry. "Ma knows. She been naggin' me to talk to your pa. She say if I don' do it, she will." He closed his eyes. "I can' lose you. I love you."

My heart skipped. Had I heard him right? Did he say those three words every girl dreams of?

I wiped the tears from his face, and he opened his eyes. I smiled at him and kissed him on his forehead. "I love you, too."

Joshua

It was nearly midnight an' I was pacin' the floor; I had to fin' a way to be wif her. Somehow I would make Thomas Bryant like me, but how? What had Mia done? She was part of their family now. My. Bryant 'ccepted her, but why? Finally, I droppe' into my chair an' punche' the table.

"Don't take it out on the table."

I leap' up again an' scoope' her into my arms, kissin' Hope's face an' neck repeatedly. "Calm down."

"Marry me, Hope." The words jus' come out the way 'I love you' had twelve hours afore. I kisse' her an' she pulle' away. I looke' into her beautiful green eyes an' smiled. She was lookin' at me like I was crazy. Maybe I was. "Marry me?"

She shook her head. "I want to say yes, but..."

"Please don' think 'bout your pa. I'm-a run away wif you like 'Lijah did if I have to, but I need you in my life, Hope, an' not jus' the frien'ship we had these las' years."

She pulle' out of my arms an' walke' across the room. I finally had said too much. She didn' turn to me or say nothin'. She jus' stood there. My heart pounded.

At las' she turn to face me. "We need to talk to Pa."

I looke' to the floor. He' never approve. Hope was his baby, even though there was Cassandra, an' he wouldn' let her go to someone like me. Her hand pulle' my face up an' I met her eyes.

"I love you." She kisse' me on the nose an' I pulled her into a hug.

"Tell me how to be 'ccepted. What do I need to

229

do?"

She ran her fingers through my rough hair. How I loved that feelin'. "Have you taken that delivery job for the lumber mill yet?"

"The one to Jacksonville?" Hope nodded on my shoulder. "No, not yet. Ma wanted me to fin' someone to go..."

Then it hit me. I pulle' back an' looked into her eyes an' she smiled. I smiled back, lettin' her know I understood, an' kissed her.

A trip like that woul' be difficult, potentially hazardous...an' possibly bondin'.

I climbe' the wagon carefully, watchin' over my shoulder to ensure I hadn' broken anythin'. I eased the horses forward an' headed for the Bryants' house. It was still hard to believe that Mr. Bryant had actually agree' to help me.

When I pulled up to their house twenty minutes later—it normally woulda only taken about five—I foun' Mr. Bryant waitin' for me outside.

"Thank you for the help, Mr. Bryant; 'specially on such short notice."

Mr. Bryant climbe' onto the wagon. "What's so special about this delivery?"

I ease' the wagon forward. "Have you ever been over the Topsy Grade, sir?" He shook his head. "You fin' out."

Da wagon ride out of Linkville was slow. We had to cover a lot of rough an' bumpy terr'tory in the nex' few days, an' we had to do it wifout breakin' the windows in the back of the wagon. So far we been on the curvy part of the trip for six hours, an' it was spent in total silence. I needed to fin' a way to get my companion to talk to me. I ease' the wagon to a halt. "Are you hungry, sir?"

My. Bryant sat silent for a momen', an' then sighe'. "I am, actually."

I smile' an' left the wagon. I might finally get somewhere with the man, an' that was the mos' important thin' about the trip. I pulle' the food bag out of the corner of the wagon as Mr. Bryant climbe' down. "Your daughter an' my ma are quite the cooks together. I'm 'fraid I been getting' spoilt."

He scoffed an' found a tree stump to sit on. "You're lucky my daughter is teaching, or she wouldn't be living in that house."

I wante' to defen' my parents but decided 'gainst it. Instead, I opened my pack an' pulled out a couple of san'wiches. "For lunch we got ham, turkey, or cheese. What would you like?"

He looked up as I sat down nex' to him. "Ham, I suppose."

I handed him one of the ham san'wiches an' set in on a turkey. When we was finishe', I stood up to stretch. "I reckon it will be night afore long. We could probably reach the bottom of the summit by nightfall. There's a little place off the road to park the wagon."

Mr. Bryant stood an' climbe' back into the wagon. I re-packe' the bag wif a sigh an' climbe' up nex' to him. This certainly was goin' to be a long trip.

Three days passe', an' I was startin' to get discourage'. We was about twenty minutes from da top of da summit an' Mr. Bryant hadn' said more than thirty words since we left. Words was runnin' like cougars through my min' of thin's to say, but so far I hadn't foun' any of them useful. Of course, I coulda jus' come right out an' told da man I was in love wif his daughter, but I didn' think that would help the sitiation at all.

Finally we hit the top of the summit an' Mr. Bryant widene' his eyes. "Good lord, look at the road down!"

I chuckled. "I tol' you this road was hell."

He jumpe' off the wagon, lookin' aroun' the groun'. It was almos' dark, an' we needed to set camp. He bent over an' pushe' some dirt into a hole. "Okay. Ease the wagon to the left and you should be fine. Let's get it off the road for the night."

I let a small smile creep onto my face. This was the mos' the man had said in a long time, an' the words weren' as cold as the last. Carefully I turne' the wagon an' guided it off the road.

"I'll start supper. I think we should unhitch the team an' give them a break. We can' lose the wagon here." I set the brake an' Mr. Bryant set to unhitchin' the wagon.

Twenty minutes later, I dished up a steamin' bowl of hot stew—made wif pork, potatoes, an' carrots, it was my favorite—an' passed it to Mr. Bryant.

"Who made this?"

I smiled as Hope's face flashe' across my mind. "Your daughter did."

He nodded an' took a taste. "This is good. Does she always cook like this?"

I nodded. "Yes, sir. An' she is quite the cook." I chuckle'. "Don' tell Ma, but Hope is turnin' out to be better than her."

Mr. Bryant chuckle' too, an' we sat in silence, eatin' the hot stew. I couldn' help but let the smile stay on my face. Finally we shared a laugh together, an' I couldn' a been happier.

Another three days went by, an' we only made it halfway down. The hard winter washe' out quite a few holes in the road, an' they had to be filled in before allowin' the wagon to go over them. One bump could break all the glass in the wagon, an' I woul' lose my hundred-dollar paymen'—which I was splittin' wif Mr. Bryant.

After makin' another 300 yards, he shook his head. "I think we better pull it off for the night, Jay."

I nodde', an' he directed me to a safe spot away from the cliff's edge. Rememberin' to set the brake, I jumped off the wagon. "Think we should try to fill in some of those holes afore nightfall?" He sighed, lookin' aroun', an' then nodded. We set out to fillin' in the holes, an' as night crep' on us we hiked back up the road to the wagon.

"I'm ready for some more of that stew." He smiled an' foun' a log to sit on.

When the stew was ready, I decided I wasn' hungry. I rather try to talk. "Could I aks you somethin', sir?"

"Mmm." Mr. Bryant took a bit of the stew an' turne' to listen.

"What...what kin' of...man would you like your daughter to marry?" My stomach turned.

He blinke' an' set his stew inside. "Why do you ask?"

"I was jus' wonderin'. We talk a lot, an' that topic came up once, so I was wonderin' what your opinion was."

He picked his stew back up an' ate. I sighe' an' ate mine too, an' when we was finishe', Mr. Bryant cleared his throat. "Well, I'd like someone who will take care of her, be respectful not just to her but to her family, and someone who knows the value of family."

I nodde'. I could fit those requirements. Actually, I already did.

Mr. Bryant stood an' grabbe' the bedrolls out of the wagon. He threw one at me. "Get some sleep. It's going to be a long day tomorrow."

I nodded an' set out to makin' my bed, makin' a poin' to talk to him about Hope the moment we hit Jacksonville.

Chapter 23

Proposal

The res' of the trip down the Topsy Grade was long an' strenuous. The road seeme' to get worse the farther we went, an' it took nearly three more days to reach the bottom. When we did, we set the wagon a good distance off the road, unhitched the team, an' went for a horse ride. Homemade fishin' poles in han', we foun' a spot an' caught our dinner. Mr. Bryant did the cookin' that night, an' I spent almost an hour praisin' it. Finally, about three hours after dark, we pulle' out the bedrolls an' went to sleep.

The road into Jacksonville was smooth an' nearly straight. We bof felt safe enough to pick up the pace, an' hit Jacksonville within five hours.

"Where do the windows need to go?"

I turne' the wagon into town. "Down to the mill on the other side of town. They should be waitin' for us. Today was the delivery day, so we made it jus' in time."

Mr. Bryant pulle' the reins from my hands, which I was grateful for, an' I spent the trip into town lookin' around. It been a lon' time since I been to Jacksonville, an' it grown almos' as much as Linkville. Whether it would grown morc I didn' know.

There didn' seem to be very many people aroun'. Mr. Bryant stoppe' the wagon in front of the mill an' I climbe' down. "Wait here an' I'll let them know we here." He nodded an' I went inside.

The mill was cold, dark, an' quiet. It seeme' as it hadn't been runnin' for quite a while, an' I was confused. Obviously there was nobody workin' today, an' I wondered if somethin' was goin' on. I shrugged; there was only one way to fin' out.

"Hello? Anyone here?"

A woman came out of the office, wipin' at her eyes. She sniffle' an' looke' up. "Can I help you?"

"Yes, ma'am. I brought Mr. Smith his windows he ordere' from Linkville."

The woman seeme' to been cryin' an' I tippe' my head. "Mr. Smith passed away last night. Doc says it was his heart. Everyone's gone to his funeral."

I felt like my stomach would drop to the floor. After all that work to get here...

"I'm sorry, ma'am. Is there anythin' I can do?"

The woman smile' an' looked into my eyes. "You're a sweet young man. Are you married?" I shook my head. "No? Some girl will be lucky to have you someday."

"Is there a problem, Jay?" Mr. Bryant had come in to see what was takin' so long.

"No. The man who ordered the windows passe' away las' night."

He nodded. "I see." He was obviously thinkin' the same thin' I was.

I turne' back to the woman. "Will the windows still be needed?" I tried to look an' soun' considerate—an' I was—but deep down I feare' we would have to return to

Linkville with the windows.

The woman nodded. "Oh yes. My son will be taking over for Mr. Smith. How much did he promise for them?"

I counted on my fingers. "He ordere' five windows at forty-dollars apiece. Two hundre' is right."

The woman nodde' an' went back into the office. She returne' a few moments later wif money in hand. "Two hundred, it's all there."

I took the money an' put it into my pocket. "Thank you, ma'am. Oh, an' the wagon belon'ed to Mr. Smith, but the horses is mine. Where do you want me to leave it?"

She looked out the window. "Oh, just leave it there. That way they can unload the windows from there."

I nodded. "Will do. Thank you for your business, ma'am, an' my regards to Mr. Smith's family."

"Such a sweet young man." The woman sniffle' an' returne' to the office.

I turne' to Mr. Bryant. "Now we know why dis place looks like a ghost town."

He nodded an' held out his hand. "It's been quite a trip, son."

I nodded an' shook his hand. I smile', realizin' that Mr. Bryant really had called me 'son,' a sign of respec' an' frien'ship in the Bryant family.

"Let go home."

Mr. Bryant an' I prepare' the horses to leave an' headed out of town. We made it about halfway back up Topsy Grade before nightfall an' pulle' out the stew. When it was ready, we sat to eat.

"Sir, could I talk to you about your daughter?"

He stopped mid-bite an' looke' at me. "About my daughter?" I nodde', tryin' to shake off my nerves. "What about my daughter?"

I cleared my throat, debatin' exactly how to word it. "Well, sir, I wondere'—there that fall church social comin' up in a couple week, an' I wondere' if I could...if I could escort your daughter."

Mr. Bryant wipe' his mouth from the stew an' set the bowl aside. He glare' into the flames, an' I shook my head. I already knew what the answer was goin' to be, an' then what would we do?

"Well, let me tell you something, Jay."

I looked up, a little surprise' at these words. "I listenin', sir."

"I've learned a few things from my children." He took a drink from his canteen an' laid back on his bed roll. "And I've learned a few things about you on this trip."

I was listenin' intently, wonderin' what was goin' to be said.

"You're a good man, Joshua; I'll admit that, but I'm not sure I like the idea of you escorting my daughter." My stomach drop an' I tried to protest. Mr. Bryant shook his head an' held up a han'. "Let me finish."

I nodded an' fell silent. "I will give it a chance, but if I find you've been less than honorable and respectful, I will be at your door with my shotgun, understand?"

I smile', fallin' back onto my own bedroll. He really had said yes. This man...this highly prejudice' man was givin' me, da son of a slave, a chance.

"Yes, sir."

I returned the spare horse to the barn an' set for town, my horse runnin'. We skidded to a halt outside my parents' house an' I jumpe' off. I race' for the door an' ran inside.

"Joshua! What be the meanin' of dis?"

Ma was glarin' at me from across the room, mop in hand. I grinne', slidin' to a halt on the wet floor. "Sorry, Ma."

"You actin' like a child!"

I chuckled an' spun her aroun'. "That's because I feel like a chil'! Nothin', an' I mean nothin', coul' dampen my spirits today!" I kisse' her on the cheek an' heade' for Hope's room. I had already seen the childr'n outside with Pa an' knew she would be somewhere inside.

I knocke' on the door. "Hope?"

"Come in."

I race' inside an' scoope' her out of her seat. "We can go! Your pa said he goin' to give me a chance!"

"What?!"

I spun her aroun' an' took her into a kiss. "I love you."

She kisse' me again. "I love you, too."

Hope

I smoothed out my dress. I was wearing my best—a pale blue with ruffles, and a blue bonnet on my head. Any moment Joshua would knock on my door and escort me to the church social.

I took a deep breath, but still jumped when the knock came. My stomach dropped, and I attempted to shake my nerves away. "Come in."

The door creaked open and Joshua walked in. He smiled at me and took me into his arms. "You look beautiful." I smiled as the blush warmed my cheeks.

He bent down and kissed me softly. His lips were warm and soft.

My heart skipped as he pulled back. "I got somethin' for you."

I smiled again, my heart racing. "You do?"

"Mm-hmm." He slipped his hand into his pocket and pulled out a small box.

My eyes widened. There was only one thing that came from a box like that. I was nervous. It couldn't really be happening, could it? My breath quickened, and a tear slid down my cheek. Joshua handed it to me and I could feel my heart beating in my throat.

I sniffled and opened the little box. Inside was a small gold ring with a single purplish stone.

"It not much. It belon'ed to my gran'mother. She gave it to me afore we move' to Linkville. I was only five an' didn' know what it mean', but she tol' me that I shoul' keep it an' woul' know what it for when I was older." I was speechless. I had never seen anything more beautiful. "I knew it was mean' for you when I fell in love wif you."

I blinked and tears fell down my face. "Joshua, it's beautiful."

He pulled the ring out and fell to his knee, taking my hand. "I know it will be difficul' getting' pas' your pa, but I ready to do what it takes if it means I get to keep you. Will you marry me?"

I sniffled and nodded. "Yes, I will."

He kissed my hand and slipped the ring on my finger. Then he stood up and kissed me. I fell into the kiss, slightly dazed.

It seemed hard to believe that only a few months ago I was blind and dependent upon my parents and everyone else. Now I could see, and the world around me shone bright with love and passion. I pulled away from him and smiled, my eyes meeting his. "I love you."

"I love you too, Hope."

I couldn't take my eyes off the ring. It had already been four months since he had given it to me, and the church social couldn't have gone better. Sure, everyone was surprised to see the two of us together, but by the time the night was through everyone was completely natural about it; everyone except Pa.

I still couldn't get him to realize how I felt. Surprisingly, Ma was fine with it all. Then again, Ma hadn't been nearly as prejudiced as Pa.

I shook my head as I sat on the edge of my bed. Somehow I would make him understand.

A soft knock on the door made me jump. "Come in."

The door gave a creak, and Joshua came into the room. "Hi, Hope."

I grinned and rushed into his arms, not seeing the anguished look on his face . "Oh, six weeks is far too long to be away from you!"

He and his parents had gone on a trip. Joshua's grandmother had passed away and they had gone to see her grave. He gave me a weak hug, and I looked into his eyes. They were red, even for him, and a tear slid down his cheek.

"What's the matter?"

"Ma an' Pa been thrown in jail by their ol' owner."

Chapter 24

Slaves Again

"What do you mean, they've been thrown in jail by their old owners?" I couldn't believe what I was hearing. Slavery was over now; they couldn't possibly have been forced back into it. The Tandras were sweet people...what could they have possibly done to be put in jail?

Joshua shook. "I hate those people! They cruel an' think of nothin' but themselves!" He slammed his fist into the wall, and I jumped. He fell to the wooden floor in tears. "I tol' them we shouldn' go back there!"

I fell to my knees and took his soft but worn hand. Farming really wasn't good for his hands. "Jay, what happened?" He shook his head, not wanting to talk about it. I stroked his face, wiping his tears away. "Tell me, please?"

He looked up into my eyes and sighed. "Everythin' was fine at firs'. We was goin' to see the grave an' then get out of there quickly, but they good at findin' us."

Joshua

I lef' the stage wif my parents feelin' wary. I didn' like bein' back here; somethin' fel' funny an' I could almos' feel eyes watchin' our every move. The stage driver had calle' us crazy when we aks to be let off three miles from town. We already passe' one plantation wif its thrivin' cotton fields, an' Ma an' Pa couldn' take their eyes off of them.

We campe' out, an' when mornin' broke we made our way into town to fin' the graveyard.

It was a startlin' place. I never seen more graves, but there was somethin' unusual about it.

"Pa, why does it look like this? There hardly any markers; nothin' but a stick stickin' out of the groun' at the head of each of them."

He pulled Ma close as she let out a cry, strokin' her shoulders an' kissin' the top of her head. "It be da slaves' graveyard. There be no single white man buried here. They all be slave, young an' ol'. They just die, or beaten to death, or execute' for tryin' to run away."

My heart raced. It was a disgustingly brutal place, an' I didn' like it at all. But I remember' my gran; she had given me the ring that now rested on Hope's finger, an' I wanted to thank her for it any way I could. We walke' silently through the yard until we came to a recently-dug grave an' a small stick pointin' out. The stick had the words Old Lady Yates carve' into it.

Ma fell to the groun'.

I trie' to be sympathetic, but she been cryin' very loudly. I trie' to ignore it, wonderin' what had been the cause of Gran's death. I wondered what it might been like if my parents hadn' escape'. Woul' I be workin' in those nearby cotton fields? I never woul' have met Hope; an' what would happene' to her? Would she still be helplessly blin', hidin' in the dark corner of her room? Would she even have gone blin' at all?

My thoughts were interrupte' when a man Ma's age ran into the graveyard. "Esther May! You got to get out of here! They know you here! They knowed since you got off da stage!"

Ma scrambled to her feet an' took the man in her arms. "I know, but I had to come say goodbye to Ma."

The man pulle' away. "An' now you have ta go! I won' see my sister force' back into a life hardly worf livin'. Get out now!"

Ma kissed his cheek an' took me an' Pa by our han's. Together we race' for the road. "I sorry, son. If anythin' happens, we fin' a way to get you back to Hope. Promise me you get home to her an' marry her." I was confused, an' scared, but I nodded an' squeezed her hand.

We hid in the woods overnight, waitin' to leave at firs' dawn. I didn' understan' why we was hidin'. Slavery was over an' it would be illegal for these plantation owners to try an' force us into slavery again. But still we hid, an' when firs' light hit, I felt a gentle hand shakin' me awake. "Get up, boy. We got to get goin'."

I pulled my boots on an' stretched. It looke' like it would rain afore lon', an' I followed my parents out of the trees into the open air.

I been watchin' my steps rather than where we was goin' an' hadn't noticed the white men waitin' for us. It was when Ma screame' that I finally looke' up, alarmed.

A man had her around the waist, pinnin' her arms to her sides.

"Get your hands off me!"

The white man struggled to hold on, but he smiled. "Now, calm down there, Esther. We're not going to hurt you. The boss just wants a word with you."

Pa put a free han' on Ma's shoulder. "Don't struggle. They can't force us to stay. Jus' remember dat."

Ma stopped the struggle reluctantly, an' allowed us to be led up the lon' drive to the plantation I barely remembere'. There was men workin' in the fields. They looked tired, hot, an' extremely thin.

My heart thumpe' loudly in my chest. What if I didn' make it home to Hope?

An ol' farmer stood waitin' for us on the white porch. He shook his head when we approache' an' sighe'. "My, my. It wasn't very smart coming back here after you ran away. You should've stayed away."

Ma glared at him. I admire' her spirits. "You has no rights over us no more, so let us go."

The white man shook his head an' gave a loud laugh. "See, we can't do that. You owe me services from when you ran away."

Pa shook his head this time. "We be owin' you nothin'. You can' keep us here no more."

"It's not you I want. You were never mine, but she is, and so is that boy of yours."

My heart sped up. We could not still be owne' by this cruel man.

"See, the problem is, when you left we realized some of our family heirlooms were missing. We searched for days. They were never found, and neither were you. One can only assume that it was you who took them."

Ma was angry an' shook her head. "We take nothin' from you! We lef' wif nothin' but the clothes on our backs an' a couple of trinkets given to us!"

The white man chuckled. "Right. Somehow I don't believe you, but I'm a fair man. I would wager three years of service would pay me back for those heirlooms. I suppose I'll have to pay you just enough to eat." He looke' at the three of us before sighin'. "I'll cut the time in half if all three of you work for me."

Ma let a tear fall down her cheek; she turne' to me an' Pa. "They not goin' to let us leave. They be havin' people statione' at the train to make sure we not be gettin' on."

Pa hugge' her, an' I thought of Hope again; my heart begun to ache. Woul' I ever see her again?

Finally, Pa spoke. "We give them the service they wan' if it be gettin' you home to Hope."

I nodded. I would do anythin' to get back home to her; she was everythin' to me. "What happens if we don' do it?"

The white man smirked. "You'll find yourselves sitting in jail for a very long time."

Pa glared at him. "You be gettin' your service, but not without payin' us."

The white man grinned. "I thought you might say that."

We worke' tirelessly for two weeks. I stood by an' watche' as Ma slowly got sicker. We was goin' broke. Our pay was too small, an' the mercantile owners charge' all of the black families twice what they charge' the white ones. It was injustice, but I couldn' think of what to do.

We had to eat, but how we woul' get home wif no money I didn't know.

Several times I had tried to send a letter to Hope, but every time the letter disappeared. The plantation owners didn't like their workers doin' anythin' but workin', an' it showed in all of us.

One night, I collapsed on my bedroll in the small cabin we was stayin' in, an' sighed.

"Jay, get up."

Pa was standin' over me, holdin' a travel sack an' a spare bedroll.

"What are you doin', Pa?"

He put a worn finger to his lips. "No talkin'. It be only a short time before they come checkin' on us all. Get out of here. There be money in da sack; it be all we had but it will get you home to Hope."

I shook my head. "I can't leave you behin' without money an' bein' so sick."

"No arguments, son. I promise' your ma I be gettin' you out of here. Jus' promise me you won' come back. We be breakin' contract."

I wanted to protest, but the sight of Ma layin' there so sick made me upset. I hugge' Pa goodbye an' left the small cabin.

It was a couple hours afore I heard a gunshot somewhere behin' me, an' then bayin' hounds. The dogs was getting' closer, but I had a promise to keep. I ran as the moon rose higher in the sky, an' collapse' two hours later, unable to run anymore. I could no longer hear the dogs behin' me, an' I let loose and cried. I didn't know where my parents was or what was goin' to happen to them now that we had broken the contract. I crawled under a row of bushes an' fell into a dreamless sleep, thinkin' 'bout Hope an' my promise to my parents to return to her side.

Hope

I ran down the street, out of breath and scared. I was at a loss for knowing what to do, so I was trying the first thing that came to mind. My parents' house came into view, and I saw Pa working the field behind the house.

I ran into his arms. "Pa! You've got to help!"

He stroked my head as the tears fell from my eyes. "What's the matter, darlin'? Is it one of the children?"

I shook my head. "No, the children are fine. It's Mr. and Mrs. Tandra. They're in trouble."

He led me off of the field and sat me down on an old log. "What do you mean?"

I couldn't think. Those two were like my second parents, and I loved them like parents. I knew that, after everything they had done for me, after all the bills and medical treatment they had paid for, I owed them to find some way to bring them home.

"They went back to the south because Jay's gran died, and they got caught by the people who had owned them. They were bullied into signing a service contract, but Jay ran away and broke it. He doesn't know if they're okay or not. Please, Pa...you've got to try to get them home!"

Pa stared off into the distance for a while, and my stomach dropped. For three long minutes I thought he was going to say no, and then he stood me up.

"Let's go tell your ma what's going on. I'll want your brother to come along."

I smiled and hugged him tightly. Then I ran to the house and, after explaining to Ma, Pa and I headed for the school.

I found Joshua reading a book to the children. I had almost forgotten it was their suppertime.

"Oh, dear."

I kissed Pa on the cheek and sped off to the kitchen.

Thomas

I was left alone in the front room of the school. Hope had gone off to make the children supper, and I cleared my throat uncomfortably. I made my way to the back room to make my presence known.

Joshua finished the chapter and sent the children off to finish their homework. I shook the young man's hand, removing my hat politely. "I'm sorry about your parents."

He nodded. "Thank you, sir." He looked around nervously at the children, and ushered me into the other room. "We not tol' the childr'n. We don' wan' to worry them. They already wonderin' why Ma and Pa not come back yet."

I nodded. "Listen, I think we should send a telegram to Elijah. I'll help you try to get them back because it means a lot to Hope, but I can't promise you anything."

Joshua smiled and shook his head. "I want no promises. Jus' the effort is enough."

He led me across the street to the post office.

"Hello, Mary. I need to send an urgent telegram."

"Hello, Mr. Tandra, Mr. Bryant." I nodded, and the woman behind the counter pulled out a piece of paper and a pencil. "Okay, what's the message?"

Joshua nudged at me; I cleared my throat uncomfortably. It was still new to me to be seen in this kind of...company, and it wasn't easy. What were people around Linkville saying about me?

"It's to my son, Elijah Bryant, in Virginia City, Nevada. Tell him to meet us at the Reno Train Station in a week and that we'll explain once we get there."

Mary nodded and scratched the message on her piece of paper. "And...who is 'we'?"

I shuffled nervously. "Me and Joshua."

She nodded and set off to send the telegram. Joshua and I returned to the school, and found Hope waiting in the front hall for us.

"What's going on?"

I smiled at her in an attempt to reassure her. "We're going to go to Nevada and meet up with your brother. We'll take the train from there."

Her eyes widened, and I shook my head. She was going to overreact and frighten the children if I knew her as well as I thought I did.

"Oh, Jay! You can't go back there!"

Joshua sighed and pulled her into a tight hug, at which I turned my head. Wretched idea, those two were.

"Listen to me, Hope. These are my parents. I have to go. Besides, I wouldn' think of askin' your Pa an' brother to go rescue my parents an' then stay behin'. It wouldn' be right. I promise you, I come home."

After a few silent moments, during which I wondered what they were doing, Hope left the room.

"I'll make you some sandwiches while you saddle

the horses."

Joshua and I left and saddled a couple of the livery horses. She arrived after a short time, and packed away the food and some blankets. "Promise me you'll be careful, both of you."

Joshua kissed her cheek (I looked away again), and then she hugged me. I kissed the top of her head and climbed on top of the horse. "I'll send a telegram when I can."

Hope wiped the tears from her face and backed away as we raced the horses past her. I led the way out of town, wondering what was going to happen on this trip.

I would have much rather left things alone. The Tandras did, after all, run away while enslaved, and owed the service. I would be a criminal for helping them escape, but I promised my daughter I would try to help. For her I would do anything, and that wasn't an exaggeration.

Chapter 25

The Carolinas

Elijah

It had been four weeks since Joshua and Pa left Linkville behind, and spring was upon us. The train ride to the Carolinas took longer than planned, and all three of us were tired and frustrated. Pa spoke mostly to me, and I tried my best to include Joshua in the conversations. It was as though we had come from different places and were going separate ways, but we weren't. Pa just wouldn't admit to anyone else that the three of us were traveling together.

The farther south we went, the better people reacted to seeing the black man with the two of us. Most folks seemed to think that Joshua worked for Pa and me, and Pa liked it that way. He didn't want to tip people off about what we were really going to do, so if they thought we had power over Joshua, they wouldn't find out we were headed to retrieve his parents, and that's how he wanted it.

When the train stopped at the station in the Carolinas, Joshua tried to stay on board. "I can't go back out there."

Pa glared at the man before us. "We've come all this way to get your parents. Get up or we'll leave them behind."

What Joshua hadn't mentioned was that he was scared that he might find his parents dead.

We chose to walk to where we needed to go. If we didn't get on the stage, it would be less likely that the wrong people would detect us. Joshua led the way the best he could, while I hoped he hadn't steered us in the wrong direction.

Pa was about to stop and give up when Joshua halted mid-step, a look of horror on his face.

We were here.

The plantations were in full operation. Men were cutting in the fields and didn't even stop when they were asked to take a drink by the bosses. White men patrolled the edges of the fields, making sure no one slacked off. The working men were thin, and bones were visible; many of them looked exhausted or sick.

Joshua forced his gaze away and seemed to be looking for a place to hide. Pa didn't want to keep going, but I, rolling my eyes, pushed him along.

"What's wrong, Jay?"

He shook his head. "I don't think it a good idea for me to be seen out in the open. I promise' Ma I wouldn' come back here. If she hears I come back to get her she'll have my head."

Pa snorted, not seeing what the loss would be. I threw him a cold stare, and turned back to Joshua.

"Tell me where to look. I'll..." I paused, trying to think of what to say next, "I'll pretend I've come to call, and go from there."

Joshua shook his head. "It too dangerous, Elijah. I don' want anythin' to happen to you."

I sighed. "Don't worry about me. I've come here on my own free will to help you, and that's what I'm going to do."

Joshua shook his head, but explained to me which house I needed to go to. I turned to Pa, and after some persuasion we headed for the second plantation.

I walked nervously up the driveway, Pa following behind me reluctantly. The black men stopped long enough to watch us walk up the dirt path, wondering what we were intruding about. The only one who didn't look up was trying to fix a wagon that was being used to carry weeds out of the fields. I ignored them, and was glad when we reached the door to the house.

There was a friendly-looking woman with red, curly hair sitting on a swing on the porch. She smiled and stood to greet us.

"Hello, sirs. How are you today?"

I tipped my hat to her and reached out to take her hand. "Ma'am, my name is..."

I paused, wondering if I should use our real names; we'd better not in case we needed to run. The last thing we needed was to be chased and tailed. "Jacob, ma'am. This is my pa, Harrold."

Pa, giving me a small glare for the fake names, also extended his hand. The woman shook it kindly and smiled at us both. "Julia. What brings you this way?"

I cleared my throat. "We're travelers, ma'am. We got thirsty and wondered if we could bother you for a cold drink?"

The woman looked at us skeptically. "Travelling with no packs?"

I shook my head quickly. "No ma'am, we left them at the end of the road."

"Mmm, well, please, come in."

I sighed with relief. She had, for the moment, believed my story, and led us inside the house. "I apologize for the mess, the maid is sick and I'm afraid she's going to have to get disciplined for not doing her cleaning."

I was a little surprised by this comment. Punished for being sick? These people were cruel and heartless, no matter how friendly she portrayed herself to us.

"We've got nice cold lemonade." Pa and I both nodded in agreement, and the woman led us into the sitting room.

"Esther....company! Get out of that room, wash your hands, and bring them some drinks!"

Julia settled herself in a fancy sitting chair with its pearl inlay, and shook her head. "I do apologize for my words. She really has been a bother. I'm afraid she's been horrible since her return. I won't tell you where she's been, but she's had far too much freedom. She and her husband are under contract for us, and so was her son, but he's run off. If we find him back here we'll throw him in jail for breaking it."

Pa and I shared a look of understanding. We were about to be face-to-face with Esther May again, and I was worried she'd give us away. Finally, the woman came into the room and set down a tray without looking up. I watched her carefully, and as she left the room, I cleared my throat.

"Excuse me, could you point me in the direction of the outhouse?"

Julia chuckled. "Outhouse, dear? Good heavens, we don't have one of those. You're welcome to the water closet. Just down the hall and the fifth door on the left."

I thanked the woman, and though I was curious to see this 'water closet', I turned instead to the right, making sure she wasn't looking, and followed Esther May into a small room that looked as though it were a food cellar. It was empty save for a few chairs across the room, and she was curled up in the farthest one in the corner.

"Esther May." I looked behind me, and knowing the coast was clear, made my way to the woman in the corner. She was small and looked nothing more than skin and bones, and it made me mad. Someday I would make these ignorant people pay for the treatment of these people.

"Esther May." I knelt down beside her, and she jumped, turning to look at me.

"Elijah?"

I nodded, a smile forming on my face. She stifled a cry and wrapped her arms around me. "What you be doin' here?"

"Joshua led us here. He's hiding in the thicket down the road. The next time you go outside, I'll be waiting to lead you out. Where's Joe?"

Esther May shook her head. "You not come back here." Her whispers were panic-stricken, but she seemed glad to see me. "Just leave us. We be really doin' okay."

I shook my head. "None doing. I promised your son and my sister I would bring you and Joe home safe. Promise me you'll come outside soon?"

Esther May looked scared, but she nodded. I kissed her cheek and left her, realizing I had been gone far too long. I made my way to the water closet quickly, figuring I should probably use it, which I did, and I stood there staring at it.

How did it work?

I jumped when there was a knock on the door.

"I wondered where you got to." It was Julia.

I cleared my throat. "Come in." The door opened, and Julia chuckled.

"I was trying to figure out how this worked."

She chuckled again. "You've got to pull the cord."

I obeyed, and jumped when the water began to swirl and was sucked down into a pipe.

"Now wash up, and I've got some biscuits for you and your pa."

She left in a hurry and I washed up. When I returned to the front room, Pa was finishing his biscuit, and I—not wanting to be rude—ate one. When I was finished, we said goodbye to Julia.

I took one last worried look down the hall before exiting the house. "Let's wait out by the horse barn."

Pa nodded, and we found a place to crouch out of sight.

It was some time before two figures headed our way in a hurry.

"Thank goodness." I was relieved to see them.

Joseph was shaking his head, wiping the dirt off of his hands. "I not believe it when Esther May tol' me." He looked furtively behind him. "You got to get out of here."

Pa stomped his foot, clearly frustrated. "We didn't come all this way to leave you here. If you don't want to pack anything, then let's get going."

After some protesting, Joseph and Esther May finally agreed to follow. We hurried quickly through the thick grasses, trying our best to stay out of sight. After reaching their cabin, we grabbed the few things they had, and headed to the site where Joshua was waiting.

After a short but happy reunion, we wondered what we should do next.

Joseph played with his suspenders. "It not be long afore they discover we be gone."

Esther May nodded. "I be surprised if they not knowed already."

We couldn't discuss it anymore. A gunshot had sounded through the air, and I poked my head out of our hiding place. Men were scrambling through the fields.

Esther May was right. They were out looking already.

I closed my eyes, trying to slow my heart rate. "What's the quickest way out?"

Esther May shrugged. "We not use da tunnel; they know about that."

Pa was growing angry. If we were caught, we'd be thrown in jail for helping them break the contract. I'm sure he was wondering what everyone back home would think of him if that happened.

We had run for so long that I didn't know where we were. The sounds of the hounds baying behind us slowly diminished, and the five of us collapsed on the cold, soothing grass. The trees above hid us in shadow and I tried desperately to catch my breath.

After a few moments of silence, Esther May fell into Joshua's arms.

"You brainless, Boy!"

Joshua looked slighted.

"I beg you not to come back here! What you be

doin' here?"

He pulled away from her and glared. "Hope." He turned away and shoved his hands into his pockets.

"Excuse me?" Pa had so far been silent, but I could tell his attempts to ignore them were overtaken by annoyance. "My daughter, the one you claim to care for so much, begged him and me to come here and find you, and now I'm sorry I came. I was right all along! You people think of nothing but yourselves! You're all the same, and I don't want anything to do with you!"

He grabbed me by the arm and started to walk away. Stopping abruptly, he turned back quickly and pointed his finger at Joshua. "And you! You stay away from my daughter and my family."

He tried to drag me with him, but I protested.

"Fine!" Pa left in a rage.

I watched helplessly as Joshua dropped to his knees, his head in his hands. Esther May wrapped her arms around him and he sobbed into her blouse. I met Joseph's eyes.

"I'm sorry. I didn't realize my Pa still felt that way, or I would have made him stay behind."

Esther May looked up, a single tear sliding down her face. "I 'presiate you risks in comin' to fin' us, an' we grateful, but I woul' take it all back for Jay to still be at home wif da one he loves."

I was a bit surprised to hear this. I certainly didn't know their friendship had gotten so far on. I looked in the direction Pa had gone and sighed. Hope was in deeper than he knew, and I worried that her heart was going to be broken.

I had to do something. Just what I didn't know yet, but I had to do it for my sister's sake.

I put a caring hand on Joshua's shoulder. "Meet me at the station for the morning train. I saw an old abandoned house about twenty miles up the road when we were walking down here. You should stay there tonight." I met Joseph's eyes again. "I will get you all home to Hope. I know how much you care for her, and how much it means to her."

He gave me a weak smile before I turned and left the way Pa had gone.

I didn't like the Carolinas very much, and I was becoming homesick very quickly. I just wanted to go home, but I had made a promise and I intended to keep it.

I spotted Pa going into a hotel down the road and ran to catch up. A saloon brawl landed in the street in front of me, but I was used to this by now; it happened all the time in Virginia City. I jumped over the men and went into the hotel.

At the registration desk, Pa put money back into his pocket without looking at me. I sighed and followed him up the stairs.

"I didn't pay for you, boy."

I followed him in and slammed the door shut behind me. "I don't care. I'm not here to sleep."

Pa pulled his suspenders off of his shoulders and threw his hat on the bed. "Get out if you're going to associate yourself with those niggers. I'm okay with Mia, but I'm not okay with that!"

I grabbed Pa by the collar of his shirt. "You are a selfish, prejudiced man and I am ashamed to be your son!"

Pa just glared back, so I went on. "Like it or not, Hope is in love with that man, and he with her! I am going to go to her and stand beside her if they get married and if you ever want to see any of your grandchildren again, you better change your attitude!"

I threw him back and left the room.

I had a bad feeling about the Tandras. I shouldn't have left them alone.

It was dark by the time I found them, hiding in a large burrow hidden by a few berry bushes a bit before the old cabin. I crawled inside and lay near them without a word.

The sun came through the branches, shining on my closed eyelids, and I growled in frustration. I hadn't gotten much sleep.

Esther May put her hand on my shoulder. "Morning."

She nodded to greet me. "We best be gettin' goin' or we be missin' da mornin' train."

I crawled out of the hole and stretched. It was a chilly morning, and a group of black clouds was headed our way. "Looks like rain. We better hurry."

The four of us headed for the train station. We walked against the wind for twenty minutes and, just as we got to our destination, Joseph held his arms out to stop us at the edge of the trees.

"Hell, they gots da guards waitin' there."

I looked up to examine the scene. There were guards questioning everyone before they were allowed to buy tickets.

"Follow me." If I had learned anything from sneaking out, it was hiding from people, and talking myself out of trouble. "Esther May, they don't have pictures of you, do they?" I was double-checking my plan before moving.

Esther May shook her head. "No."

I grinned. "Good, come on."

Before they could stop me, I left the safety of the trees. The Tandras followed me reluctantly. I made my way towards the station as the train whistle warned of its departure.

The guard stopped me at the door, eyeing Esther May, Joshua, and Joseph suspiciously.

"What's your name?" He clutched his gun tightly.

"Name's Elijah. What's with the guard?"

The guard's lip twitched. "Got a couple of plantation workers trying to break contract. They disappeared after a couple of white men called at the house. We've been asked to arrest them."

I chuckled. "Well, it's certainly not us. We're just passing through. And besides, you said 'a couple of workers.' I've got three. You also said a couple of white men, and there's just me, so you've got the wrong ones."

The train whistle blew again, and I stepped past the guard. "If you'll excuse us, we have a train to catch."

I winked at Esther May as they passed the guard, making my way to the counter.

"You got a lot of spunk to be scarin' us like that." She was glaring at me.

I just smiled and pulled my money pouch out of my pocket. "I need four tickets to Reno, Nevada please."

The man behind the counter shook his head. "They can't ride."

I cleared my throat; this was a set-back I hadn't

been expecting. "And why is that, sir?"

The man chuckled. "Are you blind? They're niggers!"

My good mood left me. I thought these people were idiots, and this agent needed a big slap in the face. I made to grab the man by the collar, but Joseph pulled me back by the arm.

I shrugged him off and we left the station. We would have to find another way to get home.

Chapter 26

The Last Straw

Hope

*F*all of 1886 was cold, and it seemed winter would fall on the Oregon territory early that year. I spent a lot of time with the children, in hopes of keeping my mind off of the absence of the Tandras and Pa. Ma and Cassandra had pretty much moved into the blind school, and the three of us kept the school running.

Ma came down the hall from the kitchen, wiping her brow. "I've never seen so many dishes in my life!" She fell into a chair beside me.

I gave her a weak smile and stared into the flames of the fire.

"I guess that's what comes from having all the parents visit."

I nodded half-heartedly. The parents of all twenty blind children had come for a visit. It had been Esther May's idea, and we had sent out the invitations a year ago. The children had been looking forward to it for so long that I hadn't had the heart to cancel it just because the Tandras hadn't been here.

Overall, it had gone well. The children had a wonderful time entertaining their parents, and the parents seemed proud that their children were doing so well. I hadn't felt much like celebrating, so I spent a lot of time away from the parents. I was starting to get worried about Pa, Elijah, and Joshua. I just wanted them all to come home soon, or at least send word that they were alright.

Mia had sent several letters of worry; she hadn't heard any word on them either. I had to talk her out of getting on the train several times. There was no need for us all to be here just to worry together.

The days were long and the nights were short, and I couldn't stand it anymore. I shook my head.

"I think I'm going to go up to bed, Ma." I stood up, kissed her on the cheek, and headed for my room.

It was dark and I didn't bother to light the lamp. I pulled my clothes off and slipped my nightdress over my head. Then I fell onto the bed and into the pillows. I hadn't realized how tired I was, and the bed was cool and comfortable. A single tear fell down my cheek before I finally drifted off to sleep.

Joshua

I rolle' over in my bedroll. Four months ago, I been sound asleep havin' dreams about Hope, warm in my own bed. Four months ago seeme' more like four years, but we was all safe an' only a few hours from Linkville. I wanted to keep goin', but there was safety in numbers an' my parents an' Elijah was tired.

We made camp an' the others fell asleep right away. I was awake, waitin' for dawn to break. I coul' think of nothin' but runnin' into Hope's arms.

We come across Mr. Bryant a week earlier. He was angry an' he ignore' even Elijah. Elijah didn' seem to care. He wen' about takin' care of the camp, an' I felt grateful. I been very lucky, growin' up in an area where the color of the skin didn' bother mos' people. Goin' back to the Car'linas proved that to me.

I took for granted how much Linkville an' its people mean' to me. I wanted to throw them all a party jus' to show 'em how much I 'presiated the kin'ness. But the thin' that mean' the mos' to me right then was getting' home to Hope. The longer I was away, the more I realized how much I felt for her.

I coughed an' wipe' the tear from my cheek. The sky above was black save for the moon shinin' on me. The wind rustled the trees, an' I thought I shoul' at leas' try to get some res'. A gus' of wind race' across our camp as sleep finally foun' its way to me an' I fell into a res'less slumber.

Elijah

I woke to the sun bearing down on our camp. Esther May was already up and heating up last night's stew for breakfast, and she smiled as I pulled myself out of bed.

"Mornin'."

I nodded, not intentionally being rude. My mind was fully aware of the morning sensation as I disappeared into the trees. I found a spot a few feet away, and returned a short time later. Feeling much better, I smiled at her.

"Feel better?"

"Much. That smells wonderful. I'm hungry."

She scooped some stew into a cup and passed it across the fire. I took it thankfully. "The others still asleep?"

"I not want to wake them jus' now." She scooped her own cupful and sat beside me. "I hear Jay up in da middle of da night. He not sleepin' well. He stir a lot." She looked at Joshua sadly, and I gave her a small smile.

I understood exactly how she felt. My children were everything to me, and their happiness meant the world. I missed them dearly and couldn't wait to hold them in my arms again. It would be at least a week before I would be able to see them, if not more. Now, however, my concern lay with my sister, and bringing Joshua home to her.

It was another hour before Joshua and Joseph finally roused, and they ate and packed the travel bags quickly.

I knew these woods well, and led the way towards Linkville, stopping only for outhouse breaks and drinks at the riverbeds. I knew Joshua was anxious to get into town and, perhaps a bit selfishly, I knew the sooner the Tandras were home the sooner I could return to Virginia City.

Six hours we carried on through the woods, and the wind was starting to pick up. It was a harsh, cold wind, and it seemed an early winter storm was headed our way. Still, I didn't stop, trudging on until finally a familiar sight came into view.

Linkville was quiet, and I wondered what was going on. Surely people wouldn't be home so early in the evening? The sun hadn't even reached the horizon yet.

Then I saw them. A group of children all dressed in costumes were headed into the hotel, which cast an eerie glow over the street below.

"I didn't realize it was Halloween."

Joshua shook his head. "Neither did I."

I wondered if the blind children would be going to this party at the hotel. I shrugged and headed for the school anyway, and sighed when I came upon the dark building.

Joshua pushed past me and tugged on the doorknob. It didn't turn, and he turned around with a quick move of his heel. "They mus' be at the party. Do you have your key, Pa?"

Joseph nodded and slipped a key into the door. We put our travel packs inside, and Joshua headed quickly towards the hotel. I smiled at his retreating back, easily seeing how much he cared for my sister.

I stopped the Tandras about fifteen feet from the front of the hotel. Hope was emerging onto the step, looking exhausted.

"Hope!"

She looked up, startled, at the sound of Joshua's voice. I watched her green eyes and face light up with joy.

"Jay!" They ran into each other's arms; Joshua picked her up and spun her around.

I was thinking of Mia. I missed her terribly, and watching my sister so happy made me miss her even more.

Esther May fell into Joseph's arms, and I couldn't help but wish it would all stop.

The feeling escalated when Pa made his way into the street. My stomach dropped as he stopped mid-step, staring angrily at the scene before him. He threw his travel pack into the dirt beside him and ran towards Joshua and Hope.

Angrily, and perhaps a little too strong for my liking, Pa ripped the two of them apart and threw a burly fist into Joshua's jaw.

The color drained from Hope's face as he fell, unconscious and limp, to the dirt road.

"PA! What on EARTH was that for?! How dare you!"

I ran forward and took Hope into my arms, if not for anything else but to restrain her from hitting him. "Pa, that was unnecessary."

"Stay out of this, Elijah! This is between me and your sister!"

Hope opened her mouth to speak, but Pa stopped her. "No! I've had about enough of this! I was tolerant because I thought it wouldn't last long, but I'm not going to be tolerant anymore! Hope, you are a bright young woman! You don't need this riff-raff, and you certainly aren't going to live the rest of your life with them. Now go to the school and get your things. You're coming home with me."

Hope gave a look that could kill, and I tightened my grip on her.

"Who do you think you are?! You don't own me, and you certainly aren't going to tell me how to live my life! If you haven't noticed, I like where I am and there's nothing you can do to take me away from it!"

"Don't you dare raise your voice at me, child!"

"THOMAS!"

We all looked up to the crowd that I hadn't realized had formed around us. All of the children from the hotel had come out, dressed up in their costumes. They certainly didn't need to be a witness to this madness.

Ma moved into the middle of the circle. "Don't raise your voice at your daughter! And don't you dare try to tell her what to do! It is not your place anymore." She put a caring hand on Hope's shoulder and kissed me on the cheek.

"I won't have her marrying that nigger!"

I had never seen Ma looking so angry. "She is a woman! In case you've forgotten, she spent most of her life blind! Color of skin means nothing to her! Learn to live with it, or you don't belong in this family anymore!"

My stomach dropped again. I had never heard Ma say any such thing. I certainly didn't want them to divorce over something so insignificant. "Ma, why don't we go into the school house and talk this out?"

Ma shook her head. "I'm done with talking, Elijah. As far as I'm concerned, your pa has no right in this family anymore." She quickly wiped a tear from her cheek before turning to Joshua lying behind us. "Let's get him up and inside. He'll need ice on that jaw."

Hope

I placed the ice softly on Joshua's jaw and took his hand into mine. "I'm so sorry he hit you, Jay."

Joshua just shrugged, and I grinned. He flinched,

but held the ice himself. I let go and let my hand fall to his shoulder.

"No harm done. Bruises don' las' forever. I jus' glad to be home." He looked up at Elijah, who was sitting across the table with Ma and the Tandras. "Thank you, Elijah. I know you risked a lot doin' that."

I met Elijah's eyes, and we shared a silent understanding; he would've done it all over again. It was something we had been able to do for a while now, even though we didn't see each other very much. Our bond had grown so much during the time we were only able to correspond through letters that we were almost able to communicate just by looking at each other when we were together. He smiled at me and turned his gaze to Joshua. "I did it for my sister. All that I want in return is for you to take care of her."

Joshua nodded, leaning over to whisper in my ear. "Have you told them about the ring yet?"

My heart skipped. I shook my head, trying to ignore the tingling in my veins from the closeness of him. "Can I tell them?" I smiled, butterflies swimming in my stomach.

He snuck a kiss to the side of my face, sending shivers down my spine, and turned to the others. I felt my cheeks turn warm, and was sure that my face was pinker than usual.

"Hope an' I have an announcement to make."

Chapter 27

The Copper King

*N*ews had spread quickly through Linkville and nearby areas about our engagement. Most had accepted our relationship immediately. Perhaps it was because the people had known Joshua longer than me. Perhaps they were just more accepting of things out of the ordinary. Whatever it was, I didn't care.

I would've felt a lot better about the whole thing had Pa been around. Ma and Cassandra had chosen to stay with me at the blind school. Pa was back at the farm, reportedly sitting alone with his thoughts. This news only made me feel worse about him, and I often found myself wondering if it was all worth it.

My mind quickly changed every time Joshua walked through the front door of the school, dirt on his clothes and the look of exhaustion on his face. I always greeted him with a peck on the cheek and sent him into the washroom for a clean-up before supper. We spent hours just talking before the fire, and my heart broke every time we had to say goodnight. It meant I would not see him again until the next day's supper.

However, I was kept busy by Ma and Esther May. Just choosing when we would marry was a horrible adventure.

"You must pick the perfect day and month, Hope," was always what Ma said, with Esther May nodding behind her. I had wanted to talk to Joshua about it, but he had usually been too tired for the discussion. But time was ticking, and the people of Linkville were anxious to know when the wedding was going to be.

I made the decision to talk to him about it when he came in after finally finishing the plowing. I sat him down with his favorite ham and cheese sandwich, cookies, and a glass of milk. "Jay, we really need to discuss the wedding."

Joshua took a bit of his sandwich and a drink before looking up at me. "Thank you, Hope. This is my favorite." We smiled at each other. "Okay, what do you wan' to talk about?"

I sat down beside him. "Ma and Esther May want us to pick a day, for starters."

He took another bite and swallowed. "Okay, how about May?"

I shook my head. "'Marry in May and rue the day'." He looked at me as if I were crazy. I laughed. "Don't look at me like that. I brought it up to Ma too, and that's what she told me."

"Hmm." He kept eating his sandwich. "Well, you pick then. It makes no difference, does it?"

I stood up. "But don't you see? It makes all the difference. If we marry in June it means prosperity and happiness. If we pick April, November, or December we won't interrupt anyone's farming. If we choose October it means a bountiful harvest. If we choose May it's unlucky. 'Marry in September's shine, your living will be rich and fine.' Don't you see? It makes all the difference."

Joshua laughed and stood up. He took my hands in his and kissed the tip of my nose. "Let's choose April. The jasmines down by the lake will be in bloom, an' I know you love those."

I took a deep breath and smiled. "Okay, so April then. Now we just have to pick the day."

He sat me in my chair and returned to his seat. "Let me guess. There are proverbs for the days of the week, too?"

I nodded. "'Marry on Monday for health, Tuesday for wealth, Wednesday the best day of all, Thursday for crosses, Friday for losses, and Saturday for no luck at all'."

Joshua chuckled. "Well, we don' want to pick Saturday then, do we?"

I smiled. "No, we don't."

He finished his sandwich and cookies and I stood up, putting his dishes in the wash bowl. "I was thinking about Wednesday."

Joshua stood up behind me and wrapped his arms around me. "Wednesday sounds wonderful to me."

I turned and we kissed, our arms wrapped tightly around each other.

We settled on the third Wednesday the coming April, 1889, which gave me ten months to plan everything. When the news reached the ears of Linkville's residents, the town was bouncy and happy. It was the talk of the area, but still I couldn't enjoy it like I should have.

After three months, I still hadn't heard from Pa.

I met him at the mercantile one August night. He had come in to buy some food, and I was there to choose a cake topper. It was as though nobody dared to talk. The silence in the store could have been cut with a knife.

Pa and I stared at each other for an agonizingly long minute. I wanted to say something, but I was afraid. Afraid of rejection, again. Finally, he turned and left without his food.

The hurt deep inside me burst through, and I fell to my knees, sobbing into my hands. I felt abandoned and betrayed, and as an arm fell across my shoulders for comfort, I stood and ran out, leaving the mercantile behind.

I found myself on the stage that night. It was the last one out of Linkville, and nobody saw me go. I left a note on my pillow, sealed for Joshua, and as the stage made its way to Northern Oregon, I wondered when I might see anyone again.

Joshua

I woke before dawn, a sinkin' feelin' in my stomach that somethin' was wrong. Panickin', I pulled my pants on an' raced for my horse. The town was quiet an' dark, but all I wanted to do was get to Hope.

I didn' wait to be let into the school. I went to her room as quickly an' quietly as I could, an' my stomach droppe' when I realize' the room was empty. Her bed never been slep' in, an' the lantern long since burnt out. I foun' the sealed envelope jus' as Ma came into the room. After relighting the lamp, she sat on the bed nex' to me without sayin' a word. I slowly opened the letter an' we both read it silently:

My Dearest Jay,

I'm so sorry I left without telling you. I have some thinking to do after what happened this afternoon at the mercantile. I just had to get out, and I left on the last stage out of town. I haven't decided exactly where I'm going yet, but I'll let you know where I am as soon as I can.

Tell Ma and Cass that I love them and tell the children I'll miss them while I'm away. Please know this has nothing to do with my feelings for you. I love you still, more than ever, and I always will.

All my love, Hope

A tear slid down my cheek while I read the letter. When I finishe', I folded it an' looked at Ma. I was numb. "What happen at the mercantile, Ma?"

She sighed. "Hope was there to pick da decorations for da cake an' her Pa come in. They never spoke to each other, an' he lef' wif nothin'."

I stared out the window. The mornin' sun was jus' startin' to break over the horizon, an' I wipe' the second tear to fall.

"Take care of the childr'n, an' Mrs. Bryan' an' Cassandra." I stood, headin' for the door, an' Ma followe'.

"What you goin' to do?"

I trudged on quietly through the school, pullin' open the front door. I mounted my horse, Ma pullin' the reins to keep me from leavin'.

"I'm goin' to fin' the stage an' go wif her. It not me she has to think about, it her pa, an' I'm goin' to have a little chat wif him 'afore I go."

Ma shook her head. "Jay, jus' come off that horse an' leave it alone."

I clenche' my fists.

"Of course it not you she be thinkin' 'bout, honey. She love you, an' she don' has to prove that to you. But she be hurt by what her pa done, an' she be needin' time to heal before she can move on wif you."

I looked towards the window that was her room. I sighe' an' reluctantly slid off the horse. She was right.

"I don't like this."

Ma pulle' me into a hug. "I know you don', son. Come in an' have some breakfas' an' we talk it over wif Mrs. Bryant. She be knowin' her husban' better than we do."

We sat at the table for what seeme' like hours, discussin' where Hope might have gone. I didn' say a whole lot. My heart ached; I fel' abandone' an' wanted more than anythin' to go after her. It been nearly twelve hours since the stage lef' Linkville, an' nobody seeme' to know where it was goin' for sure.

The sun broke all the way over the horizon as I walke' back to my house. Another tear slid down my face. Why had Mr. Bryant been this way to his own daughter? I been lucky. I knowed a life where I been cared about, an' only when new folk arrive' was I reminded that my skin was different. But Mr. Bryant was the wors'. Everyone a'justed 'cept him, an' I wondered why.

Da sound of footsteps on gravel brough' me out of my thoughts. Mr. Bryant was approachin'. With all the emotions I was feelin', I had to keep myself from throwin' a punch.

278

"What you doin' here?"

He gave me a cold glare. "You drew away my family."

"I did nothin', sir."

He pointed at his empty house.

I looked, surprised, I hadn' realized I come this way.

"My daughter won't speak to me, my son won't either, my wife and child left, and Georgia wants a divorce! All because you came along and made nice with my Hope!"

It was like a fire been lit inside my stomach. I groun' my teef together an' made a fist. How dare this man blame me for all that? Didn' he realize that it be his prejudices that pushe' his family away?

"If I was the kin' of man you are, I' beat you, but I be better than that!" I'm sure my face was rather pale. A night of anger an' no sleep was burstin' through.

Mr. Bryant pointed his finger at me. "Don't you dare blame this on me!"

I let another tear slide down my cheek. I was too angry to stop it. "Hope lef' 'cause of you!"

All the color draine' from his face. "What do you mean?"

I couldn' stop it. The tears broke their barrier an' I droppe' to my knees. I know I mus' have looke' silly, a grown man of twenty-seven cryin', my face burie' in my knees that now rested on the hard dirt beneath me. I tried several times to make it stop, but the pain was too fresh, too much for me to bear. When I coul' fin'lly catch my breath, I looke' up.

"Hope left. We don' know where she is, but she said she lef' 'cause of you in her letter."

Wif that, I got up and raced for my farm. I couldn'

look at that man any longer. I needed sleep, but whether it would come, I didn' know.

I bolted through the front door and into my room. My head hit the pillow, an' I sobbed. I sobbed 'til exhaustion took over an' I fell into a dreamless sleep.

Hope

It was four weeks before I stopped my travels. I hadn't eaten for two days, and my funds had run out. I would have to find work before I could return home.

I had found myself in Butte, Montana. It was a small but growing city nestled in the Rocky Mountains. I found it interesting that most of the buildings were built of brick or stone. I had never seen anything like it. However, it reminded me a lot of Virginia City, only they were mining for copper instead of silver.

As I walked away from the station, I spied a large mansion near the top of the hill. I couldn't take my eyes off of it. It was three floors tall and had a white front porch. The closer I got to it, the larger it seemed to become.

"Gorgeous, isn't it?"

I jumped at the sound of the voice and turned around. A small woman stood nearby. She wore an old, beat-up hat, and the bottom of her skirt was torn in several places. She looked as if she hadn't eaten in several days.

"Yes, it is." I turned back. "Who lives there?"

"Man by the name of Clark. He's the owner of most of the mines and pretty much the reason Butte's here." The woman shook her head. "Wish I could get close enough just to peek inside. They've been buildin' it for four years. Just got it finished last week."

I was about to reply when the front door opened and a woman stepped onto the porch, followed by a man. "I wish you wouldn't leave. I hope it wasn't anything bad that's making you go."

"No, sir. Just making a choice to move on. Thanks for everything, Mr. Clark."

"You're very welcome. We enjoyed your cooking while it lasted. Just wish we had more time to find a replacement."

They shook hands, and the woman left.

My face lit up, and I ran up the front steps, holding my skirt so I didn't trip. "Sir, could I speak to you?"

Mr. Clark had almost closed the door, but opened it again. "Can I help you?"

I smiled warmly. "I'm sorry. I was admiring your house and I couldn't help overhearing you." He nodded. "Sir, you'll need someone to cook for you until you find a replacement, won't you?"

Mr. Clark smiled. "I suppose you're right. Do you have any experience?"

I nodded. "Yes, sir. Back home I run a blind school. We feed twenty-five children at every meal."

He offered me entrance. "Come inside and we'll talk."

I nodded my appreciation and followed him inside.

The house was incredible. The staircase was carpeted and had hand-carved railings. When I looked closer, I realized each carving was a different picture. The oil lamps and chandelier in the entry-way, every one of them lit, made the walls dance.

To the right was an octagon-shaped room with a

wood floor and a hand-painted ceiling. The dining room was beautiful, as was the sitting room and billiard room. He led me past the staircase into the dining room and offered me a chair. I accepted it, and he sat across the table from me. "Back home is...where, exactly?"

I smiled. "Linkville, Oregon, sir."

"Oregon?" I nodded. "You're a long way from home."

My smile shrank. "Yes, sir. I can't tell you the reason I left. I just needed some time to myself. But, I've no money to return, sir."

Mr. Clark nodded. "I see."

He stood and crossed to the window. I sat in nervous silence, waiting. My heart pounded as the man in the suit turned around. "Very well. I'll pay you nineteen dollars a day for two weeks. I'm having a dance party here on Saturday night, and I expect about thirty guests. You'll get twenty-five dollars for that, and Sundays off. That should be enough time for me to find a replacement."

I couldn't believe my ears. He was promising me two-hundred and fifty-three dollars for two weeks? It was more money than I had ever seen. "Yes, sir. Thank you so much. I promise you won't be disappointed."

Mr. Clark smiled at me. "And what is your name?"

"Hope, sir. Hope Bryant."

He extended his hand. "Mr. Clark."

I accepted his hand, and we shook. "Follow me. I'll show you the kitchens."

I stood and followed him through the next room and into the stone kitchen. It was beautiful, with an ice box that had a cold-water spout, and two quick-meal stoves. On the wall was a box with bells.

"This is our call system. If someone needs you

from another room, you will look at this box to see what room we're in. If you have any questions, let me know, okay?"

I nodded, and he tipped his hat. "If you need a place to sleep, there's a place behind the house. Don't worry about expenses." With that, Mr. Clark went on with his business outside and left me alone.

I sat in the silence, devouring what had just happened. I began my work later that day, and was glad that I had some time to myself.

I decided to take a walk. The air was cold outside, but surprisingly there was no wind. I had never been to the Rocky Mountains before. They looked as though the giant boulders had been designed and hand-placed. It really was beautiful country, and if I hadn't loved Linkville so much I might have chosen to stay.

After a week, I realized how much I missed home. I thought about the children and Mr. and Mrs. Tandra. I thought about Ma and my sister, and my brother and his family. But the one person I missed the most was Joshua, and the way I felt when we were together.

Three nights before I would head back home, I sat down and stared into the darkness. I wanted to write a letter, but to whom I didn't know. Joshua perhaps? I put my pen to the paper, but no words came. I sighed, and as sleep pushed its way closer to me, I began to write.

Chapter 28

The War

Thomas

Dear Pa,

I can't tell you how much I miss talking to you. I've been in Montana for two weeks, but this is the first time I've thought of you. It seems forever ago that we hugged goodbye and you left me at the blind school. I guess a part of me has always felt abandoned.

But, you see, our whole world changed that day I woke blind. My world changed. I began to see things so differently. We had always lived in a world of black and white. You taught us white was better. When I was blind, my world became all black. I was the same as Joshua, and so was everyone else.

Pa, I love you so much, but I want happiness. I live in a world where color doesn't

matter to me anymore. Joshua makes me
happy. I choose him, even if I risk losing you
as my pa.
    I miss you.

Love, Hope

I folded the letter carefully, and slid it in my shirt pocket.
I had received the letter two weeks ago, and Hope had
not yet returned. Just yesterday, I had heard that she
was returning on the evening stage, and I would be
there to greet her.

I hadn't been paying much attention to how far I
had walked until I heard Joshua's voice up ahead.

"I know, an' I want to be here, Mrs. Bryant. I just
so afraid she goin' to tell me she callin' off the weddin'."
Joshua scuffed the ground with his boot.

Georgia placed a hand on his shoulder. "Joshua,
you love my daughter, right?" He nodded. "Then have
faith in that love. If I know my daughter like I think I do,
she'll choose you."

I didn't like that she was saying this without
knowing the truth. I stayed back, hidden in the shadows,
and sighed.

I probably should have told them all years ago
what had made my heart so cold towards colored folk.
There was a time when I might've been okay with them,
but not after what had happened. It hurt too much.

The stage pulled up, and the door opened. I was
watching Joshua carefully. He quickly wiped a tear from
his face as Hope stepped out of the coach. I saw him as
he placed a hand on her face and stroked her cheek.

"I missed you." It was a soft, pained whisper; it
was exactly how I had spoken to Georgia when I returned

from the war. Finally I saw just how much he loved her.

Hope smiled. "I'm so sorry I left like I did."

Joshua shook his head. "It only matters that you come back."

He kissed her softly on the lips before turning her over to Georgia. They hugged, and as the three started to walk away, I stepped out of my hiding place.

They stared at me uneasily.

I cleared my throat. "Could I talk to you; all of you?" I looked up at the school as Mr. and Mrs. Tandra came to greet them. "That includes you."

They looked surprised, but Hope nodded. She didn't say a word as she went on to the kitchen inside the school.

We all sat around the table. I didn't quite know where to begin.

Finally, after many painful thoughts, I sighed and looked up at my wife. "I should have told you this years ago, but I didn't. I was hurt and angry."

Georgia looked as though she finally understood. "Does this have to do with your brother?"

I swallowed a lump in my throat and nodded. "Yes."

It was June 15, 1863, and my brother and I stepped off of the train, our travel bags over one shoulder. We didn't have time to talk to each other before being ushered off to our bunkhouse. We spent our first night in the camp scrubbing dishes before going to bed, to be woken at dawn by bugles.

There were many weeks of dodging gunfire and shooting back before we were finally told to take a breather. My brother John and I spent our first night off in the nearby saloon. We were applauded when we walked in, dressed in our uniforms. I had never felt anything like it, to be honored for fighting other American citizens. I hadn't really thought about it before, and it made me a bit sick to my stomach.

John patted my shoulder. "Aw, come on, brother! We're fighting to keep this country ours. Those... people...if you can call them that, are trying to take over our country; we're trying to push them out, remember?"

I nodded, not completely convinced. Sure, I had been a bully when I was in school, but everything changed when I met Georgia. The thought of killing fellow human beings hadn't totally sunk in until this moment.

Still, I fought on for the next several months.

Word reached me at the end of January 1863 that my wife had birthed a son. It bothered me that I hadn't been there with her, but I celebrated with my troops anyway. John and I both went to bed that night drunk.

It had only been three hours when we were awoken by yells and gunshots.

Our camp had been attacked in the middle of the night. Gunfire came from every direction. The end of the bunkhouse was burning with blue flames. John didn't think twice before leaping out of bed and shouldering his rifle. I panicked and fell out of bed, my heart instantly racing. I grabbed my rifle and stumbled after my twin.

We dodged bullets and flames before finding a place to duck behind. John laughed and punched me on the shoulder.

"What could possibly be funny?"

John pointed down and took a deep breath. "You forgot something."

I blushed instantly when I realized I was only in my long-johns. "Shut up. I panicked."

He nodded. "I know. You always act without thinking. Stop and smell the flowers once in a while."

I opened my mouth to retort, but stopped when the color drained from my brother's face.

"John?"

He slumped over, a hand on his chest and blood oozing over it. I rushed to his side and held his other hand. He squeezed it and smiled.

"I love you."

John swallowed painfully and nodded. It was a pained whisper that came from his lips instead of his usually happy voice. "Get home to your wife and baby. I've always loved her."

I ignored the tears dripping from my eyes and nodded.

"I love you, brother." He took one final breath and closed his eyes. His hand went limp as the breath left his lungs, and John Bryant was dead.

I wiped my eyes. I was angry, but I wouldn't show it. I slung the rifle over my shoulder, stood, and turned around.

A young black man stood not too far away. A look of fear rested on his face and a rifle at his feet. "I be not meanin' to do it, sir. I jus' be...I be sorry."

I felt the heat rise in my face as I looked in the chocolate eyes staring back at me. "What do you mean, you didn't mean to? You're on the enemy's side. You're wearing one of their jackets! Of course you meant to!"

The black boy shook his head. "It be not mine. I only pick it up! I be not meanin' to pull da trigger!"

I ran and took him by the collar of his jacket. "What do you mean it's not yours?"

Tears slid down the young man's face. "My uncle, it be his. He be da one doin' da fightin'!"

"What be goin' on here?" An older black man came around the corner. He wore a jacket similar to the boy's, but it had a name sewn on it. The name "Tandra" stared back at me. It was a name I would never forget; it was the name that had killed my twin brother.

"Get this boy out of my face before I kill the both of you!"

It didn't take long for the boy to run.

The older man shook his head. "I be sorry."

I stared at him, anger spread across my face. He left quickly, seeing my rage.

Suddenly it was silent and cold. I was alone, standing next to my brother's body, and all I could do was cry.

Joshua

We was quiet. Nobody knew what to say when Mr. Bryant finishe' tellin' the story about the brother we not known about. Mrs. Bryant later tol' us that even she not known what happene' that day. It was a great shock to us to learn about the killin'.

The young boy was Pa's cousin. He known his cousin done somethin' terrible, an' soon after he hung hisself in the plantation barn, but Pa never known what it was.

I was upset to learn this, but now felt I understood why Mr. Bryant always treated us the way he did. Finally, Pa cleared his throat. "Mr. Bryant, dat be my

Pa's rifle that kille' your brother. I not be proud of my pa, but he was fightin' to free us."

There was a moment of silence before he spoke again. "If I thought I be repayin' you somehow I woul'. I only hope it be helpin' to tell you my cousin hung hisself after he come back. He not be alive wif what he done."

Mr. Bryant wiped the tears from his face wif a nod. "I was colder to you because of the name. It's not a common name."

He turne' then to Mrs. Bryant, Hope, an' me. "I blamed them for what had happened, but I see now I was wrong. You're a good man, Joshua. My daughter is lucky to have you."

Hope grinned. "Does this mean we have your blessing?"

Chapter 29

Love Everlasting

Hope

hree months had gone by since Pa revealed the story of his brother and his horrible death, but despite the sadness, the wedding plans were taking off, and it would only be a few weeks before the big day. Still, Pa distanced himself. Part of him didn't want the wedding, but I knew he would get used to it.

It seemed like everyone was going out of their way to help with the wedding. Everyone insisted on a grand Victorian event, even though I wanted something small and quiet. Nevertheless, I felt the wedding was for the town just as much as it was for me. It was a rarity to marry outside race, and ours would be one of the few in Linkville.

It was cold the morning Ma and Esther May rushed me to the Linkville dry goods store.

"Now listen, Hope. You have to pick just the right color."

I shivered, but followed them inside. "Does it really make a difference, Ma?"

"'Course it does, honey. Even I knowed that." Esther May went to a rack of fabric. "White be you choosed right. Blue, love be true; yellow ashame' of her fellow; red, wish herself dead; black, wish herself back; grey, travel away; pink, of you he always think; an' green, ashame' to be seen. See?"

I sighed. "Why does it have to be so complicated? I just want this to be simple."

Esther May patted my shoulder. "You no worry. You jus' pick a color an' we be doin' da res'."

I nodded, trying to remember what all the colors meant.

Finally I saw it. It was already made, and on a display in the far corner. The dress was the most beautiful thing I had seen. It was made of fine cashmere, with a fitted bodice and a full skirt. The sleeves were made of lace and were wrist-length. The train was made of silk tulle, and the veil was the same length as the train, with a crown of orange blossoms attached to it.

I pointed excitedly. "That's the one."

Ma moaned. "It looks awful expensive; I don't know if we'll be able to afford it."

I touched the sleeve, imagining how it would feel to wear it. Fearing the worst, I turned the price tag over. It read "$200 w/ accessories."

"How much were you putting in on it?" Truth was, I still had money left over from Mr. Clark. If Ma and Esther May put in enough, I'd have my dress and still have money left over for the other wedding necessities.

"I save' up twenty-five." Esther May pulled the money out of her pouch. "That is, I got twenty-five for each of you."

I smiled and turned to Ma.

"I've got the same."

"Good. It's mine."

Thankfully, they didn't ask questions. I went around the store gathering everything I needed. By the time I was finished, I left with my dress, embroidered white gloves, embroidered silk stockings, and white slippers. I went home, guarding my packages carefully.

That afternoon it was Joshua's turn. He walked into the store with an uneasy look on his face, accompanied by Joseph.

The man behind the counter smiled. "Hello, Jay. Miss Hope was here this morning." Joshua nodded. "She went for the Victorian elegance of the year. A used one, of course."

"Did she?"

The man nodded. "Yes, sir. She set her eyes on the Victorian dress we got in and there was no changing her mind."

"Oh." Joshua turned to his pa. "I suppose I has to do the same, won' I?"

Joseph nodded. "Come on. I got some money to be helpin'."

Joshua turned back to the man and tried to act excited. "Okay, what do I need?"

The man smiled and stepped out into the store. "You shall need a white waistcoat." He pulled out three different waistcoats made of organdy. "Choose your size. After that you will need a blue frock coat for the ceremony." He pulled out three of those. "Now, you will need a vest. It has to be black."

Joshua was overwhelmed, but still he nodded as he pulled aside the two coats. "That be fine."

"Very well; the next thing will be lovely, dark-grey

trousers. Again, you'll have to figure out your size. You'll also need patent-leather button boots, a black top hat, and a folded cravat of medium color. Oh!"

He rushed off to the corner and then back. "We can't forget these."

Joshua took the pearl-colored gloves embroidered with black and tried to put them on. He couldn't even pull them onto his fingers.

"If I have to wear gloves, you has to give me bigger ones."

Twenty minutes later, he was walking out of the store with his arms full. He still owed for the new shoes, but he really had no choice.

That night, we were all sitting around the table without a lot to say. I was getting more nervous with every hour, but I tried to hide it.

Finally, our families decided to go to bed, leaving Joshua and me alone in the room. After a few moments of silence, I finally yawned.

I moved over and sat down next to him, kissing him softly. "I think we were set up."

He chuckled. "Why you say that?"

"It's just that you and I wanted something simple, but our mothers took me to that store so I'd fall in love with that dress. I did, and now I feel a little obligated to keep going with the whole Victorian theme."

Joshua nodded. "Yes, but it be all worf it. We enjoy it in the end. Let them have their fun."

We said our goodnights and went our separate ways.

The next few weeks were spent on the rest of the

wedding plans. Mia would be in the wedding, wearing a light rose-colored dress with an orange-blossom headpiece. Elijah would be there too, wearing a suit similar to Joshua, but wearing a subtle brown waistcoat.

Cassandra was classified as a junior bridesmaid because she was too old to be a flower girl. It was her job to help Elijah and Mia's daughter, Jenny, in her role as flower girl. Both of their dresses were made of white muslin tied with a ribbon sash, matching shoes, and stockings. Elijah Junior's job was to hold my train as I walked down the aisle, and he would be dressed in a blue velvet jacket, short trousers, and a round linen collar. The collar was fastened by large bows of white crepe de chine. He had black shoes with buckles on them, and though he protested, he wore white silk hose.

It seemed like everyone was looking forward to the day, after seeing all the fancy costumes. There had been an article in the newspaper about the wedding. It was touted as "one of the grandest events of the year."

Two days before the wedding, Joshua and I had been banished from seeing each other or venturing near the lake where the wedding was to be held.

"You not be seein' anythin' until you there," was the only thing Esther May said as Joshua tried to leave the house one day. She turned and left quickly.

She spent a lot of time working on the cake, making sure there was enough to feed everyone that was coming. It seemed as though the whole town, and possibly the county, would be there. It made me nervous, especially when it was time to transfer the cake to the town center where the reception would take place. Under normal circumstances, the reception would have taken place at my home, but as there would be too many people, everything had to be outside.

Finally, the time came when everyone was dressed and prepared to leave for the lake.

It was a beautiful morning on April 23, 1889, when I turned and greeted my pa. I took in a deep breath and pushed the veil out of my face. "I can't tell you how much it means to me that you are here."

Pa took me into a hug and kissed my forehead. "I want to apologize for the years we've missed together."

A tear slid down my cheek and I shook my head. "It's okay, Pa. It's over now."

He hugged me again before pulling the veil back over my head. We left the house together and entered a wedding coach decorated with orange blossoms and lavender.

The ride to the lake was quiet and surprisingly short. My nervousness grew with every step the four white horses took. The sun was just coming up over the horizon, casting an orange glow over the water as the lake came into view.

"Pa, I love you."

He was silent but squeezed my hand, just like he used to.

Orange blossoms and white chairs decorated the lakeshore banks. I had never seen so many chairs. Surely there wouldn't be that many people there? The more I looked, the more I realized the seats were filled with nearly two hundred people, some of them being Mia's relatives.

A church-type bell sounded as the ushers helped me out of the coach behind the many chairs. Pa stepped down next to me, and shook Joshua's hand. Then he hugged me, and put my hand in Joshua's. The bell continued to ring as we walked down the aisle between the chairs, across a white carpet covered by rose petals set out by little Jenny.

Reverend Hunt stood waiting for us at the end, along with Mia, Elijah, Cassandra, and Jenny. He smiled at us as we took our place in front of him, then looked around at the people of Linkville.

"We, who have gathered in this circle, are now privileged to witness and to participate in a ceremony, celebrating the public acknowledgement of a love which Joshua and Hope have for each other, knowing that by our presence here with them, we are saying that they, together, are loved by many others. We have come to surround them as they stand before us in this center, where Joshua and Hope in essence say, 'Welcome to our marriage! Welcome to the celebration!'"

My heart skipped as Reverend Hunt smiled at me. Part of me still couldn't believe it was happening, but still, I smiled back, and the reverend continued.

"Marriage is too for children! For them it is, or can be, more than just witnessing. There is an opportunity for them to bring themselves into the new family and, in a symbolic sense, to give themselves to this new venture, as they bring a 'Gift of love' which they will present now to Joshua and Hope."

All of the children in the seats came forward and handed us red roses. After quick hugs and their return to their seats, Joshua and I turned back to Reverend Hunt.

"When you love someone, you do not love them all the time, in exactly the same way, from moment to moment. That is impossible. Yet that is what most of us demand. We have such little faith in the ebb and flow of life and of love and of relationships.

"We leap forward at the flow of the tide and resist in the terror its ebb, for we are afraid it will never return.

We insist on permanence, on duration, on continuity. But the only continuity possible in life, as in love, is in growth, in fluidity, and in freedom, as dancers are free, barely touching as they pass, but partners in creating the same pattern.

"I speak now to Joshua and Hope of love, in which, the trust and freedom of the other person becomes as significant as the trust and freedom of one's self. I speak to them of generosity, which gathers the beauty of earth for riches and the kindness which turns away the wrath of foolish men and women. I speak of all our hopes for their continued growth through patience, one for the other. May Joshua and Hope keep the vows made on this day, in freedom, teaching each other who they are, what they yet shall be, enabling them to know that, in the fullness of being, they are more than themselves and more than each other, that they are all of us and that together we share joyously the fruits of life on this Earth, our home."

He paused and looked at us. "Do you have some words you wish to speak to each other?"

Joshua turned to me then, and kissed my gloved hand. I couldn't breathe.

"There was a darkness for a long time an' then there was light, an' that light was you. Your love has given me wings, an' our journey begins today. I pledge afore this assemble' comp'ny to be your husban' from this day forwar'. Let us make of our two lives one life. I wan' you for today, tomorrow, an' forever."

I ignored the tear sliding down my cheek and swallowed the lump in my throat. I had to get through my part...

"I have dreamed my whole life of having someone as wonderful as you love me the way you do. I give myself to you as your wife, and I promise here to treasure for all of my days the love we celebrate today. Let us bring together our lives and find ourselves anew each day."

Joshua pulled a ring out of his pocket and slid it onto my finger. It was simple, and fit perfectly next to his grandma's ring and its small purple stone. "May this ring forever be to you the symbol of my growin' love."

I had almost forgotten that I had a task to do, and I shook my head slightly.

Little Jenny came forward and handed me a gold band. I kissed her head and put the ring on his finger. "May this ring forever be to you the symbol of my growing love."

It was at this point that Esther May stood, a wrinkled piece of paper in her hand.

"I like to read somethin'. I fin' this in a ol' book of my mama's an' it be a poem that be read at many weddin' ceremonies. It be by Kahlil Gibran." She turned then to me and Joshua. "I do hope you can fin' truf in these words." She wiped a tear from her face and cleared her throat.

"'You were born together, an' together you shall be forever more. You shall be together even in your silent memory. But let there be spaces in your togetherness. An' let da win's of heaven dance between you. Love one another, but make not a bondage of love. Let it rather be a movin' sea between da shores of your souls. Fill each other's cup, but drink not from one cup. Give one another of your bread, but eat not of da same loaf. Sing an' dance together an' be joyous, but let each of you be alone, Even as da strings of a lute are alone, though* *they quiver wif da same music. Give your hearts, but not into each other's keepin', For only da han' of life can contain your hearts. An' stan' together, yet not too near together, For da pillars of da temple stan' apart, An' da oak tree an' da cypress grow not in shadow.'"*

I wiped the tears from my face as Esther May sat down. Joshua squeezed my hand, and we turned back.

Reverend Hunt turned to the audience. "May these two find happiness in their union. May they live faithfully together, executing the vows they have made between them; and may they ever remain compassionate and encouraging, that their years may be rich with the joys of life, and their days be long upon the Earth."

He smiled at us. "I now pronounce you husband and wife."

Joshua and I smiled at each other before turning to walk past our friends and family. We didn't look at anyone as we left; this was a true Victorian wedding, and it was in bad taste to kiss and acknowledge anyone as we left. Our parents followed us out, watching us get into the carriage I arrived in. As it turned and headed back for the center of town, Joshua turned and lifted my veil.

"You are the mos' beautiful bride I ever seen."

Though I was married now, I blushed. I felt like a child again, and in love for the first time. I smiled and leaned forward, kissing my husband for the first time. "I will never forget this day."

He placed a soft hand on my face and stroked my cheek with his thumb. "Neither will I." He kissed me again as the coach pulled around the last corner of the lake, and I took in the smell of the cool morning air.

I wanted to remember this moment forever. I wanted to let it consume me. He was a part of me now; we had beaten all of the prejudices and obstacles standing between us. It was this day that we would be starting new, and there was nothing in this world that mattered more than the man sitting beside me.

Epilogue

Etched in History

*V*irginia left the museum and took a deep breath. She looked up at the old brick building, a tear contrasting with the smile on her face, and clutched the old book next to her chest.

She'd been searching for so long, and the only people who could give her answers were dead. Her father's face flashed in her mind, and she let a tear fall. He was so weak, so scared, so helpless. She had been the one to make the horrible decision to pull his life support, and as he took a last breath, he had whispered two things.

"I love you" was the last, and the first was "Nana's journal's in Oregon."

Virginia had asked her mother what he had meant, and that's when she had handed her another old photograph, of the same black man, with her great-great-great grandmother holding a baby in her arms.

Since her father's death, and then Nana's, she'd searched for her family history. Now she was holding Nana's journal in her hand, and she stroked the binding as she closed it.

It only took her forty minutes to read the story on the yellowed pages in the journal, and she left with the musty, wrinkled old book in her hand. Its pages held the story she desperately needed. It was the story of her family, and she would never let it go.

Most people didn't know of her heritage just by looking at her. The color had since run out, and there hadn't been anymore interracial marriages. Her Nana had been the last one in the family to know of the story, but the truth lay in the journal and other articles and papers and such in the museums in the old Linkville museum.

The curator, after they finished reading the journal, told Virginia the rest of the story.

Three children were the outcome of Hope's and Joshua's love for each other: Austen, Sarah, and Marie. They stayed in Linkville until 1926, when Hope and Joshua decided it was time to move on, and they made their final home in Butte, Montana. Their children followed, and their first great-grandchild arrived in 1945, Hailey Brown.

It was only a short time before Joshua passed away, asleep in Hope's arms. She grieved for him only a short time before following him.

It was a sad time for the folks still alive to remember Miss Hope and her love, Joshua. There had been a large gathering at the Baldwin that year, and that gathering had continued every year since then, celebrating Joshua and Hope. It was Hailey, Virginia's grandmother, who had brought the wedding dress and suit to the museum, along with the journal.

Virginia took in the smell of the cool summer's night air as she walked across the road to the bench in front of the lake. The sun was going down, and as the water slowly turned a deep shade of purple, Virginia opened the old book, flipping through the pages. The intricate way their handwriting fell on the page impressed her.

If only people today wrote like this.

She would read the book again, over and over until she had it memorized.

It wasn't until just before dark that she spotted it for the first time. There was one final note on the back inside cover.

> I don't know who will read this letter first. I write this last page on a very sad day. The date is November 20, 1945, and my 79th birthday. Today my love, Joshua Joseph Tandra, has moved on to a better life and left me to grieve alone. I don't blame him; he has spent most of his life being besmirched purely for the color of his skin. My only wish is that people learn that we are all the same. I found that out for myself. Hailey, you are only a month old as I write this letter—the end to this story lies with you. I trust that you will read this and share the story with your children and grandchildren and great-grandchildren should you be so lucky to see them as I have seen you. I love you child, and though you may not know me, remember that there is no black and white, just those too weak to realize that we are all the same. ~ Your great-grandmother, Hope

Hailey could no longer share the story of her great-grandmother. There would be no one left to do it if Virginia didn't do it herself.

It was at that moment that she decided she would travel the country and share the story, and she would continue to do it as long as God would allow her to.

She closed the old book and rubbed it affectionately. The sun was down now, and the lake's water fountain shot up in colors of red, blue, and green. Oregon really was a beautiful place.

She took in a deep breath of the cool summer air and stood up. She would go home for a time, and then she would begin her work on sharing her story.

Turning around to leave, she bumped into someone tying his shoe, dropping the journal on the ground. "Oh, excuse me."

The person stood up, and Virginia met his eyes. His face was dark, especially in the moonlight. His arms were strong, the muscles showing through the small windbreaker jacket he wore. He smiled at her, and his chocolate eyes lit up in the moonlight.

"It's okay." He picked up the old book and handed it to her. "That's quite an old book."

She let a tear slide down her face. "Yes. It was written by my great-great-great grandmother, Hope."

She smiled at him. "Are you from here?"

He looked at her, obviously curious. She slid the book into her pack so nothing could happen to it.

"Yes, I am."

"Hope was the first woman to marry interracially here in town."

"Oh! That's right; my parents organize their celebration every year."

They stared at each other for a time, and Virginia contemplated what was happening.

There was something about him that fascinated her. Was it the softness of his eyes, or the way his eyes lit up when he smiled? Or was it the way he looked at her, so fiery and compassionate.

"This might seem like an odd question, especially from a stranger, but how do you feel about interracial relationships?"

She smiled at him. "I've got no problem with that."

He smiled back.

After a few moments of awkward silence, he cleared his throat. "Would you care to join me for a late dinner?"

Her heart jumped. She nodded, and took his arm.

She didn't know what was happening as he helped her into his car, or what was to come of this instant liking, but she suddenly had every reason to completely trust it. Her nana wouldn't let anything go wrong. She and Miss Hope would care for her from where they were now, and so would Joshua, the ex-slave who was lucky enough to conquer the prejudices that normally would have stopped him from loving the woman who had been the light of his life. Love really did conquer all things.

About the Author

Amanda Marie was born in Klamath Falls, Oregon. Like any other female growing up in the '90s she is a fan of artists like Backstreet Boys, Five, Aaron Carter, Nick Carter, and AJ McLean. She started writing when she was in junior high and from there went to write many "Fan Fictions" (still online today) and some of her own original stories.

Amanda lives in Klamath Falls, Oregon with her husband and three children. She spends her free time listening to music, playing video games, and watching Ghost Adventures and Castle. She also likes to rockhunt.

Amanda has a degree in business management and received her Master's degree in Creative Writing at Full Sail University in 2012. She hopes to teach at a college or high school level in the future and also to bring her books to life on the big screen.

She had the opportunity to be an extra in the film Redwood Highway starring Shirley Knight, Tom Skerritt, and James LeGros.

Author's Website: writeramandamarie.com

www.ingramcontent.com/pod-product-compliance
Lightning Source LLC
Chambersburg PA
CBHW020251200626
46816CB00001BA/232